D1271960

TEAROOM
mysteries

Dear Reader,

I am not a fan of crossword puzzles—or puzzles in general, really. Both my mom and my brother love to do them, and they'll spend hours bent over newspapers or puzzle books, totally absorbed by filling in tiny little boxes. I have never seen the appeal. I do not have the patience or the will to figure out all those tricky clues and weird words and how they intersect. Besides, there are so many books in the world! I would rather spend my free time reading.

But writing this book, which revolves around hidden messages in a series of mysterious crossword puzzles, was fascinating for me. I read up on the history of puzzle making and the strategies puzzle makers use to design their grids today. I looked at dozens of sample puzzles and even briefly tried to work one out before I gave up and decided books really are more my thing. And I talked to my mom and my brother, trying to understand why they love puzzles. What is it that drives them? What is it that makes what seems like punishment to me fun for them?

After talking through it with them, I'm still not sure I understand the appeal, but I do understand the people I love a little better. And that's what made writing this book so fun for me. At its heart, this series is about relationships— the relationship between Jan and Elaine, between the cousins and their families, and between the wacky, endearing characters that make Lancaster come to life. The fact that I got to use my work on this book to strengthen the relationships in my own life is such an amazing gift.

I hope you enjoy reading *Crosswords and Chamomile* as much as I loved writing it!

Best,

Elizabeth Adams

Tearoom Mysteries

TEAROOM
mysteries

Crosswords and Chamomile

ELIZABETH ADAMS

Guideposts
New York

Acknowledgments

This book, or parts thereof, may not be reproduced, stored in a retrieval system, or
transmitted in any form or by any means, electronic, mechanical, photocopying,
recording, or otherwise, without the written permission of the publisher.

Every attempt has been made to credit the sources of copyrighted material used
in this book. If any such acknowledgment has been inadvertently omitted or
miscredited, receipt of such information would be appreciated.

Scripture quotations are taken from *The Holy Bible, New International Version*.
Copyright © 1973, 1978, 1984, 2011 by Biblica, Inc. Used by permission of
Zondervan. All rights reserved worldwide. www.zondervan.com

Cover and interior design by Müllerhaus
Cover illustration by Ross Jones, represented by Deborah Wolfe, Ltd.
Typeset by Aptara, Inc.

Printed and bound in the United States of America
10 9 8 7 6 5 4 3 2 1

Crosswords
and
Chamomile

CHAPTER ONE

Elaine Cook leaned against the door frame to the entryway of Tea for Two and looked around the east parlor. The smell of cinnamon and cardamom hung in the air. A fire was cracking gently in the fieldstone fireplace. Golden autumn sunlight streamed in through the windows, giving the room a warm glow. The leaves of the trees that lined Main Street were a riot of fall color.

More than a dozen guests were gathered around the clustered tables, nibbling homemade scones and sipping fragrant tea from a collection of bone china teapots. Everyone was gazing at the front of the room, engrossed in the speaker.

Everything seemed to be going smoothly. A nice crowd had gathered for Tea for Two's first ever crossword puzzle event. And so far, everyone seemed to be enjoying themselves. Of course it helped that Bill Markham, the nationally known puzzle master who was speaking, was very entertaining. Elaine had imagined that a talk on how crossword puzzles are made would be dry and boring, but so far, he had the crowd riveted.

Elaine caught the eye of her cousin Jan Blake, sitting on the window seat on the other side of the room. Jan gave her a small smile and nodded.

Jan loved puzzles and had been looking forward to this afternoon for weeks. She'd been excited to set it up ever since her new boyfriend, Bob Claybrook—although the word sounded so youthful, that's what they had been now for a couple of months, wasn't it? Boyfriend and girlfriend?—had mentioned he'd run into his old classmate Bill at their college reunion over the summer. Knowing how much Jan liked puzzles, Bob offered to introduce Bill to Jan, and Jan had asked if he would be willing to speak at an event at the tea shop. It turned out Bill loved to speak at gatherings of puzzle lovers, and so here he was, standing at the front of the room, explaining how he put together his famous puzzles. More than a dozen people had paid to come hear him talk.

And, Elaine had to admit, it really was quite interesting, even if she wasn't a fan of crossword puzzles herself. He'd started out by explaining how the puzzles had developed more than a century ago and told how they had changed over the ensuing decades. He talked about how each puzzle had a theme, and how that dictated the content of the puzzle. He also talked about how he worked out the grid to be filled in and how the advent of computers had changed the ways puzzles were made. It was unexpectedly fascinating.

Archie, the British man who had been working at the tea shop for the last month or so, came out of the kitchen with a fresh batch of scones on a silver tray. Their other employee Rose and Jan's granddaughter Avery were in the kitchen pumping out baked goods to keep up with the demand this afternoon, and the pastries came out of the kitchen fresh, warm, and moist.

Elaine directed Archie toward a table where a group of women was seated. She knew they belonged to a mothers-of-toddlers Bible study at Lancaster Community Church. She wasn't sure how the group's Mom's Day Out gathering had ended up here, but Elaine had had young children once, and she knew that those women deserved an extra helping of scones. At a table in the corner, Nathan Culver, an auctioneer Elaine had known from childhood, was watching Bill intently, and Pearl Trexler and her friend Martha Nelson were seated by the window. Archie was in his element today, smoothly delivering treats and refilling teacups without detracting from the presentation.

"Are there any questions?" Bill Markham asked from the front of the room. He was a striking figure, Elaine had to admit. Tall, with a deep booming voice and a full head of dark hair threaded with gray, he gave the impression of intelligence and gravity.

River White, a reporter at the local newspaper *The Penzance Courier*, raised his hand, and Bill nodded at him.

"Do you have any advice for using crosswords and other puzzles to increase a publication's circulation?" River asked. He was an earnest man in his midthirties, and Jan and Elaine had crossed paths with him as they'd worked to solve some local mysteries in the past few months. Though he was sometimes so intent on getting a scoop that he'd frustrated Elaine and Jan's investigations, he was a decent, though sometimes overzealous, young man, with a shock of reddish-blond hair. Elaine had been chatting with him this afternoon before the event began and discovered he was also the puzzles editor at the *Courier*, and as he ran Bill Markham's puzzles in the paper every Sunday, he was very excited to meet the legendary figure.

At the front of the room, Bill adjusted his thick-framed glasses and then started to answer River. Elaine took the opportunity to slip out of the room and peek into the west parlor, where a handful of guests not here for the crosswords were enjoying afternoon tea. She looked around the room and saw that all was well. Multilayered tea servers piled with scones and homemade tarts and delicate finger sandwiches graced the tables, along with delightfully mismatched pots of fine leaf teas. Emmaline Cribbs, one of their regulars, was here with her sister Evie, who was visiting from Portsmouth, and Diane Blanchett was at the corner table with a few friends. There was a couple she recognized as weekenders from Bangor; she imagined they wouldn't visit too many more times this year. Labor Day had passed a few weeks back, and while they would still have several good weeks of sun-kissed autumn weather, there would be fewer and fewer visitors to this part of Maine as autumn stretched out.

Seeing all was well, Elaine walked down the hallway and poked her head into the kitchen. The kitchen was Jan's domain, and usually her cousin kept an eye on things in there when she wasn't doing the baking herself. But she seemed so fascinated by the speaker that she hadn't been in to check in a while. When Elaine stepped into the newly remodeled kitchen, Rose was taking a fresh tray of scones from the oven, and Jan's eleven-year-old granddaughter, Avery, was carefully arranging tarts on a tea server. Avery seemed to have inherited her grandmother's love of baking and had been helping out in the kitchen more the past few weeks, and she had been recently learning how to make her great-grandmother's famous pumpkin-cheesecake tarts.

"How's it going in here?" Elaine asked.

"Just fine." Rose set the baking sheet down on a wooden trivet to protect the granite countertops. Her long wheat-colored hair was pulled back into a braid, and she wore a flowing topaz blouse and fitted slacks. "I think Avery is going to put me out of a job though. She's got this recipe down."

Avery smiled. "I do work cheap."

"I think we'll keep you around for a while longer," Elaine said, nodding at Rose. Rose had been the first employee Jan and Elaine had hired when they opened the tearoom, and she had been a huge asset. She had moved home to Lancaster shortly before the death of her mother, and she was in something of a period of reinvention, searching for what she wanted to do. Elaine counted herself lucky that she and Jan got to work with such a talented young woman.

"How's it going out there?" Rose asked, using a spatula to slide a scone off the hot baking sheet.

"Better than I expected," Elaine admitted. "I had no idea crossword puzzles could be so interesting."

Avery blew out and her blonde bangs flew up. "A lecture about crosswords? Sounds like a snooze to me." She gave Elaine a grin, and Elaine had to laugh. The girl had spunk. She liked that.

5

"Well, let me know if you need anything," Elaine said, and headed back out toward the gathering. She poked her head back into the room just as Katelyn Grande, seated to the right of Bill Markham, finished asking a question about where he came up with his ideas. Elaine knew that Katelyn worked part time at the Bookworm, the bookstore next door to the tearoom, and Jan had told her that she also wrote puzzles for the *Courier*. Elaine guessed she was in her early thirties. She didn't know much about the girl beyond that, but she had been pleased to see her name on the sign-up list for today's event.

Bill answered her question, and then answered one from the table of young moms, and then Robert Claybrook, seated next to Jan, asked a question about another famous puzzle maker.

When there were no more questions and his presentation was concluded, Bill started to hand out a stack of crossword puzzles he'd brought for the group. They would work on the puzzles and chat and enjoy more treats and tea. Elaine took a paper from the stack as it passed by, and then she passed it to Martha Nelson.

A noisy hum descended over the room as their guests began chatting and working on their puzzles. Bill walked around the room, greeting each guest and thanking him or her for coming. He was a total pro, Elaine saw. River White seemed especially excited to talk to him, she noted, watching as he leaned in and talked animatedly. Bill Markham was a big name in the newspaper world. Even if she wasn't a big crossword fan, Elaine could acknowledge that they'd been lucky to host this event. She would need to thank Bob for arranging it.

Elaine looked down at the puzzle in front of her. These things did not appeal to her, but she might as well bite the bullet and start at the top, she decided. The clue for 1 across was *malicious computer programs.* She could see the answer was seven letters long. She had no idea.

Number 6 across. The clue was *battery part.* This one was seven letters too, and all she could think of was *cell,* which didn't fit. Well, maybe the third time would be the charm. The clue for 3 across was *besprinkle, say.* What in the world?

Oh, this was ridiculous, Elaine decided, pushing herself up from her seat. There were enough things to do around here that she didn't need to be messing around with these silly little boxes. The moms from church had started pulling on their sweaters, and Elaine collected their dishes and carried them to the kitchen. Soon the other guests were starting to clear out, and Elaine said good-bye to each and thanked all of them for coming. She especially thanked Bill Markham, who was headed out for a dinner with his old friend Bob, and soon there were only a handful of stragglers left.

Pearl Trexler and Martha Nelson were chatting over cups of tea, crossword puzzles forgotten. Jan was sitting with Katelyn Grande, looking down at the puzzle Katelyn had been working on.

Elaine started stacking plates, but Jan motioned for her to come over. "Come look at this!" she called.

Elaine set the plates down and walked over to the table where Jan and Katelyn were seated.

"This is really weird," Jan said, indicating that Elaine should sit. Elaine didn't really want to sit down and look at another crossword puzzle when the room still had to be cleaned, but she obediently sat and looked at the paper between them. "This is the crossword puzzle Katelyn got at the end of the talk," Jan said, pointing to the series of squares on the paper. "But look at this. Some of these answers are really odd."

"Like what?" As far as Elaine was concerned, all crossword answers were odd. Katelyn had filled in about half of her puzzle.

"Take this, for example," Katelyn said, pointing at a square with a small number 8 in the corner. Elaine saw that the boxes for 8 down were filled in with the name *Katelyn*.

"That's pretty crazy that you got a crossword with your name in it," Elaine said, nodding. She looked at the clue for 8 down: *A name that means "pure."* "I didn't realize that's what your name meant."

"Well, it's a variation of the name Katherine, which means 'pure,'" Katelyn said. "So any number of variations for the name Katelyn or Katherine could have worked here, but I know the *t* and the *y* and the *n* have to be where they are"—she pointed to the words that horizontally intersected the name in the puzzle—"so *Katelyn*, the way I spell it, is the only thing that works."

"That's a pretty amazing coincidence," Elaine said, nodding. "I wonder what the odds are of that?"

She'd never really noticed that Katelyn's hair was a stylish shoulder-length cut, with angled bangs. Coupled with those dark-framed glasses everyone seemed to wear these days, it gave her heart-shaped face an intelligent, thoughtful look.

"But that's not the only weird bit," Jan said, pointing at the puzzle. "Check this out." Elaine saw that her cousin was pointing at 23 across, where the word *Grande* was spelled out. The clue, Elaine saw, was *big, in Spanish*.

"Well, that's really crazy." Elaine had to admit that finding both Katelyn's first *and* last name in the puzzle was strange.

"But there's more," Jan said. "This is where it gets really odd. Check this out." She pointed to the word *bookworm* at 17 across, *brunette* at 5 down, and, at 42 down, *spectacles. Tufts* was 33 down, as in the name, Katelyn explained, of the college she graduated from.

"It's like this puzzle was made just for you," Elaine said, trying to make sense of it. Could these clues possibly be a series of coincidences? Were these terms universal enough to apply to anyone?

"That's kind of what it seems like," Katelyn said, scrunching up her face. "It's really weird."

"You're sure this is the puzzle you got from the event today?" Elaine asked, although she couldn't imagine how a switch could happen.

"Yep. When Bill started handing out the pages, I took the top one, and this was it."

"Did anyone else get the same puzzle?" Elaine looked over at Pearl and Martha. She took a few steps toward them and scanned the papers they'd abandoned. She could see they were different, even at a glance. The one she'd been given was different as well. She grabbed the small pile of leftover puzzles on the sideboard and took a look. Yes, all the other puzzles were more structured, with regular, neatly spaced black squares, while Katelyn's was a bit more freeform.

"If they did, no one else thought it was odd."

"Could it just be a coincidence?" Elaine asked, but she felt silly even saying it. It would be an incredible fluke.

Katelyn shrugged her shoulders. "I guess so. Nothing else makes sense."

"Did someone put this puzzle together for you and want you to get it for a reason?" Jan asked.

Katelyn hesitated. "Why would anyone go the trouble of putting together a crossword puzzle like this?"

"Maybe there's a hidden message," Jan said, rubbing her hands together. "Maybe you're supposed to figure out what it's trying to tell you."

"Okay, if that's the case, it isn't really working." Katelyn tapped her pen on the table.

They were all silent for a moment, thinking that through. "We just have to keep solving the puzzle, I guess," Jan finally said.

Elaine could see that her cousin was already switching into mystery mode. The two had solved a few small mysteries since they'd opened the tearoom, and both of them had enjoyed tracking down puzzles and sleuthing out secrets. Often Elaine found herself swept up in a mystery before more rational, reluctant Jan got interested, but she could see that this puzzle had already caught Jan's attention.

"Maybe," Elaine said, picking up the scent. "But who would hide a message in a crossword puzzle?"

"If someone wanted to tell me something, there are more direct ways to do that," Katelyn said, shaking her head. She filled in the word *requiem* in 3 across and tapped her pen on the table. That one didn't seem to have a connection to Katelyn, as far as Elaine could tell.

Jan waved her comment aside. "Look at this," she said, pointing at the clue for 13 across: *One who loves from afar.* Katelyn hadn't filled in the answer yet.

"The answer is thirteen letters," Elaine said, narrowing her eyes to count the small squares.

"And the second and second-to-last letters are *e*," Jan said. "The answer is *secret admirer.*" She looked up at Katelyn triumphantly. "That's it! You have a secret admirer!" She picked up the ballpoint pen lying between them and filled in the words.

Katelyn laughed and shook her head. "I think that's a bit of a leap."

"But look, 14 down," Jan said. "Juliet." She looked back at the clue, which read, *Romeo and* _____.

"Remember how Bill said every puzzle has a theme?" Jan asked, nodding. "Maybe this puzzle's theme is love." Jan was practically bouncing up and down in her seat as she said it.

"I'm not sure we should jump to that conclusion yet," Elaine said. "I mean, yes, this puzzle does seem to be written for you, Katelyn. But some of these clues have nothing to do with love. What about this one?" She pointed to 17 down; Katelyn had filled in the answer *Beethoven*. The clue was *Moonlight* Sonata.

"Actually," Katelyn hesitated, "I don't know a lot about classical music, but I do remember reading that Beethoven composed the *Moonlight* Sonata because he was in love with one of his students."

"Really?" Elaine could hear the iconic notes in her mind, but she hadn't known that. Still, it didn't prove anything.

"Well, what about this one?" She pointed to the word *harvest* in 10 across. "Or this?" *Toadstool* is the answer in 21 down, *pastoral* is 38 across, and *Four Seasons* is 22 across. "It could just as easily be a nature theme."

Jan shrugged. "Some answers don't fit the theme. That's natural in any puzzle. Remember how Bill said it's often only the longer answers that relate to the theme?" She looked down at the puzzle and made a face. "Though that doesn't really seem to be entirely the case here, I guess. But I don't think we should be surprised that not all the clues are about secret love."

"Or we could be misreading the theme."

"Possibly." Jan shrugged. "But in my mind, the question is, who is your secret admirer?" Jan asked.

Katelyn's cheeks were pink. "I don't know. Something is definitely weird about this puzzle," she said, "but I don't know about this secret admirer thing." But even as she said it, her mouth turned up in the hint of a smile, betraying her pleasure at the idea. Elaine also was not convinced, but she was growing more and more certain that the puzzle contained a mystery.

"Well, in any case, it's pretty clear this puzzle was intended for you," Jan said, nodding. "Right?"

Katelyn hesitated again, but then she nodded. "It seems that way."

"Which means that someone intended for you to figure out the message in the crossword." Elaine was getting excited about a potential mystery, and she could see the same excitement reflected in her cousin's face.

"I guess it does seem that way," Katelyn said.

"And the message, I think, is that you have a secret admirer," Jan said.

"And if that's true, we need to figure out who your secret admirer is," Elaine said.

There was a short pause, and then Katelyn answered, "I guess so." But though her words were dubious, her face showed she was pleased at the thought.

"Well then," Elaine said, turning to Jan. "It seems that we have a mystery on our hands."

CHAPTER TWO

Jan looked at Elaine and nodded. "Definitely a mystery. And clearly the first thing we need to do is talk to Bill Markham. With any luck he'll be able to explain how Katelyn ended up with a crossword puzzle written just for her."

"And he may even be able to tell us who the secret admirer is," Elaine said.

"You don't think it could be him, do you?" Jan asked.

"Isn't he married?" Elaine asked.

"He couldn't be my secret admirer; I've never met him before today," Katelyn said.

"*Hmm.*" Jan hadn't thought about that. That did throw a wrench into her theory. "Well, we need to talk to him in any case. He might be able to explain how you ended up getting this puzzle today. It might turn out that there's a very simple solution to this mystery."

Still, she stood up. "Bill was going out to dinner with Bob. I'll give Bob a call and see what he can tell us." Jan pulled her cell phone from the pocket of her sweater and wandered over to the window to place the call. The room had emptied out, and now it was just the three of them in here, but habit dictated that she not jabber on the phone right next to the others. Plus, from here she got to take in the streetlamps twinkling in the darkening evening and illuminating the nearby shops. Jan clung to the last days of summer, but the days were already getting shorter. The line rang and rang, and just as she was about to give up, Bob answered his phone.

"Hello?" he said. He sounded far away, but his deep voice still made her melt. They were both in their fifties, but sometimes she felt like a silly schoolgirl around him.

"Hi, Bob," she said.

"Hi there. Hang on a second. I'm driving and I'm trying to"—there was a noise, and then suddenly he sounded normal again—"I was trying to get my headset on. Sorry about that."

"No problem. Why are you driving? Aren't you at the Pine Tree Grill with Bill Markham?"

"No, actually, it turns out Bill had to run. There was some sort of emergency at work, and he had to get back to Boston right away."

"Oh dear. Is everything all right?"

"I don't know. I guess so. I just know he couldn't stay for dinner and had to leave town right away."

"I'm sorry to hear that." Jan was disappointed for many reasons, but mostly she hoped everything was all right. She thought quickly. She had spoken directly with Bill a couple times before the event to work out details, and she had his number stored in her cell phone. "Do you think it would be out of line for me to call him now? I had a quick question for him."

"I'm sure that would be okay. He's probably on the road now, though he had to check out of his cottage, so you might catch him before he gets in his car."

"All right, I'll try to catch him," Jan said. "Thank you so much. And thanks for helping us arrange the event today. I really appreciate it."

"Of course. Anytime." There was a hint of flirtatiousness in his voice that made Jan forget for a moment what she'd even called about. She needed to focus.

"Thanks, Bob. I'll talk to you soon," Jan said and ended the call. She glanced back at Elaine and Katelyn, who were chatting quietly at the table, and quickly dialed Bill's phone number. The line rang once, twice, and then her call was dumped into voicemail. She tried it one more time, but this time her call went directly to voicemail, so she left a message asking him to return her call.

Was he avoiding her? Possibly, but it was also possible he was in a pocket with bad reception or didn't answer calls while driving. You never knew for sure around here. In either case, she wasn't getting through to him this way.

She slipped her phone back into her pocket, and then headed over to the table. Elaine and Katelyn both looked up at her hopefully.

"It seems Bill has been called away unexpectedly," Jan said. "And I tried his cell, but I can't get him."

"Oh." Katelyn looked down, but not before Jan saw the disappointment on her face. "Well, I guess that's fine. In any case, I need to get back to…"

"Now, wait a minute," Jan said, shaking her head. "We're not giving up that easily. Just because he didn't pick up doesn't mean we can't talk to him."

"But how can we get him?"

"I happen to know that he was staying at the Green Glade Cottages," Jan said. She'd recommended the small cluster of rental cottages when they arranged the event.

"Ah." Elaine's eyes lit up. "Now you're thinking." But then she hesitated. "But if he had an emergency and couldn't have dinner with Bob, maybe we shouldn't interrupt him right now."

Elaine was right. She'd been so excited she hadn't thought of that.

"Good point." Jan felt the excitement drain out of her.

It was quiet for a moment before Elaine said, "Then again, our question will be super-quick. Even if he's in a hurry, he can probably stop for thirty seconds to answer us."

Jan felt a smile creep across her face. She felt the same way. "Bob thought he might have already checked out, but it's worth at least trying to see if we can catch him."

Elaine was already getting out of her chair.

"I'll tell them we're popping out for a bit," Elaine said, gesturing toward the kitchen.

"I'll go get my coat." Jan had started toward the door when she noticed that Katelyn was still sitting there. "Are you coming?"

"I want to," Katelyn said, "but I don't think I should. My dad is expecting me home soon. He'll be getting hungry for dinner."

"Oh." Jan hesitated. Elaine paused too, and gave Jan a questioning look. Jan realized Elaine probably didn't know about Katelyn's family situation, so she nodded at her cousin, conveying that she would explain why a grown woman had to check in with her father.

"Well, all right then. You wouldn't mind if we went without you?" Jan tried to mask the hope in her voice. She was totally intrigued now, and when she was on the trail of a mystery, she liked to keep digging.

"No, I'd love it if you could. I'm dying to know the story about this puzzle," Katelyn said. "Please go and try to talk with him, and let me know what you find out. I would consider it a favor to me."

Jan and Elaine looked at each other, and Elaine nodded. "In that case, we'll go now and try to catch him before he leaves. And we'll let you know what he says."

They photocopied the puzzle in Elaine's office, keeping the original for themselves, and a few minutes later, Jan and Elaine were in Jan's blue Toyota, headed down Main Street toward the Green Glade Cottages. It was a quick drive; they probably could have walked it, but they were anxious to try to catch Bill before he left.

"What is that noise?" Elaine asked as a loud squeal erupted from the car's engine.

"Oh yeah. It's been doing that lately. I need to get it checked out."

"You certainly do." Elaine covered her ears with her fingers.

"It stops as soon as the car warms up."

Elaine reached toward the dashboard and cranked up the heat on the vents.

"That's not what I meant."

"I'll try anything to make that noise stop." They drove past Sylvia's Closet, and after a moment of quiet, Elaine turned to Jan. "That's better. Now, explain to me why Katelyn couldn't come with us."

"Bob gave me the story on her when I mentioned she was coming to the crossword event," Jan said. "Do you remember Marcia Morris from high school? She was a few years older than we were."

Elaine and Jan had both only recently moved back to Lancaster, but they'd both grown up here and attended the high school in nearby Penzance, so Jan knew she might remember Marcia.

Elaine thought for a minute, and then nodded. "Curly brown hair? Baton twirler? Unfortunate headgear?"

"That's her. Apparently she got rid of the headgear and grew up to be quite beautiful. Anyway, that's Katelyn's mother. She passed away from ovarian cancer about a decade ago, and then just a few years ago, her father—a guy Marcia met in college, I believe—was in a car accident and ended up in a wheelchair."

"Goodness. You're full of cheerful news, aren't you?"

Jan made a slight right at the fork in the road at the I Scream Ice Cream stand—recently shuttered for the season—and turned on to Cottage Road.

"Katelyn went away for college and had some fancy job in Boston, but after the accident, she moved home to care for her father. She cooks and cleans for him and makes sure he gets to his doctor appointments. Anyway, this evening she had to get home to take care of him. That's why she couldn't come with us."

"Ah. That's a pretty good excuse. But awful news about her parents."

Jan slowed and turned on to the gravel camp road that led to Green Glade Cottages. The group of tiny, trim buildings was perched on the shore of the lake. The rustic cabins were in high demand in the summer, but things were quiet this time of year.

"Yes, it was really tragic when her mother passed away, and then when her dad..." Jan shook her head. The accident had happened out on a stretch of rural road between here and Augusta. A man on his way home from work had called the ambulance when he'd seen the car nose-deep in the woods. It had been icy out, and the car had skidded clean across the road and hit a tree head-on. "Well, of course Katelyn came home after that, but she had a fiancé back in Boston. He didn't want to leave his life there and move to small-town Maine with her, so he broke it off."

"A broken heart on top of everything else," Elaine said. What an awful string of bad luck. That poor girl.

Jan nodded as she pulled the car to a stop in front the office of Green Glade Cottages. Macy Atherton owned the cottages and ran the business with her son, Shane, and his wife, Zale. "Which is why I'd love it if we could bring a little light to her life by finding this secret admirer."

"Or whatever the message in the puzzle really is," Elaine said.

"In any case, if we catch Bill, he might be able to straighten it all out for us." Jan opened her car door. "Let's go see what we can find out."

They stepped out into the parking area and walked toward the front door of the clubhouse. The check-in desk was empty, and there was no one in the lounge area.

Jan rang the little bell on the counter, and they waited while footsteps advanced from the back room. Macy Atherton opened the door and gave a faint half smile when she saw Jan and Elaine. Macy was a regular at Tea for Two, and though she usually found something to complain about, she kept coming back. Jan knew that though she was difficult to please, Macy's involvement with various civic groups had brought enormous benefit to Lancaster's businesses and schools.

"Hi, Macy," Elaine said brightly. Jan knew that Macy got under Elaine's skin—she got under Jan's skin too, truth be told—but Elaine always had been especially good at not letting it show. "How are you today?"

"Oh, you know. These old joints can't take the cold like they used to, but I can't complain."

That would be a first. Jan glanced at Elaine, who refused to meet her eye. Probably for the best.

"We were hoping to talk to a guest of yours, Bill Markham," Elaine said. "If he's still around."

"You mean that Bill from Boston?" Macy asked. She took a peppermint from the bowl on the desk and unwrapped it, then popped it in her mouth. "Help yourself."

Neither of them took a candy, but Jan spoke. "Exactly. We were..."

"He's gone. Checked out a night early and left without so much as a by-your-leave. Sarah's already finished for the day, so Zale had to go down and clean the cottage out herself."

"So he's already left?" Jan asked.

Macy looked at her like she was slow. "That's what I just said, isn't it? And now Zale has to..."

"Can you tell us how long ago he left?" Elaine asked.

"It was about fifteen minutes ago. Right as I was putting a pot roast in, naturally, and he was in this big hurry to get out, so I had to drop what I was doing and come check him out. You know how these city people are."

Both cousins nodded sympathetically, though Jan was distracted. They'd missed him, and now he wasn't picking up the phone. How would they get in touch with him?

"He said he had to get back because of an emergency at work," Macy continued. "Doesn't he make crossword puzzles? I've never heard of a crossword puzzle emergency." She sucked on the candy in her mouth, making a slurping sound.

"Did he say anything else?" Elaine asked hopefully.

"Just asked about getting a refund for tonight, which obviously I didn't give with such short notice." She pointed to the sign that displayed the cancellation policy on the wall behind the desk. The candy clicked against her teeth. "Why are you so interested in him?"

Jan and Elaine looked at each other, and then Jan said, "We wanted to talk to him about a crossword puzzle he passed out at our crossword event today."

"Oh, that's right. How did that go?"

Jan was momentarily startled to hear Macy ask what seemed like a genuinely interested question, but she smiled and answered, "It went very well. Bill is an excellent speaker, and our guests learned a lot and seemed to enjoy it."

"But one of the puzzles he made was no good?" The sickly-sweet smell of peppermint wafted from her mouth when she spoke.

"It's not that it wasn't good," Elaine said carefully.

"Then what was wrong with it?"

"We're wondering if there might have been a message in the puzzle," Jan said.

"Like a secret message? Like a cry for help?"

"Not exactly," Elaine said.

"Well, what then?" Macy sucked on the peppermint and tapped her foot. "*Ooh*, is it a love note?"

Elaine started to answer that they couldn't be sure, but before she could speak, Jan's face was already turning red.

"So it is!" Macy said. "A love note from Bill Markham? For who?"

"We don't think it's from Bill," Jan clarified. "He doesn't even know Katelyn, but..."

"Katelyn?" The candy knocked against Macy's teeth. "Katelyn Grande?"

Jan's cheeks flushed again as she realized her mistake.

"Katelyn Grande got a puzzle that seemed to contain a message," Jan said.

"A declaration of love."

"Not exactly..."

"This is so strange." Macy sucked on her candy for a moment and seemed to be thinking. "Who in the world would have a crush on Katelyn Grande?"

Jan tried to stifle her reaction to this, and it came out sounding like a snort. Elaine, who had always been better at handling tricky situations, simply tilted her head and asked, "What do you mean?"

"Oh, she's nice and all. Don't get me wrong. And she's very helpful in the bookstore. I'm there all the time for my book club, and she's always given me good book recommendations. I always read the little signs they put under some of the books, and her pick of the month is always good. It's just—I don't know. Isn't she a bit—well, snooty?"

"I think she's lovely," Jan said. "She's a smart girl, and I'm sure it must be hard for her to adjust to living in a small town again after college and the big city."

"I guess." Macy bit into the candy and chewed for a moment. "And I guess there are probably men who are into that kind of thing. But I've never seen anything wrong with living in a small town." She sniffed.

Jan had loved living in Lancaster and had always been proud to have grown up here. Still, there had been a time when she too dreamed of getting out of here, and she would have given anything to stay at the university and study engineering, which was her passion. But funds had been short, and she was needed at home, so she'd come back, much like Katelyn had had to. Maybe that was another reason Jan felt so drawn to helping her with this mystery.

"Well, if you're looking for men who might be interested in Katelyn, you should talk to Tag King," Macy finally said.

"Tag King?" Jan asked. Jan knew Tag was a mechanic and an active leader in the local snowmobile club, the Blizzard Riders. He was a nice guy and about Katelyn's age, but he didn't seem like the most obvious fit for studious, book-loving, crossword-writing Katelyn.

"Yes, Tag. Like I said, I spend a lot of time at the bookstore organizing my book club meetings, and I've noticed him in the store a lot."

No one said anything for a moment, so Macy added, "Well, if you're looking for a secret admirer, doesn't it seem like the logical place to start to think about the men who hang around her work a lot?"

Once she said it like that, it suddenly seemed astonishingly obvious.

"Of course," Jan said quickly. She dug a pen and a small pad of paper out of her purse and recorded the name.

"And opposites attract, after all," Macy added, grinding up the last bit of her candy with her teeth.

"Have you noticed any other men around the bookstore?" Elaine asked.

Macy smiled, pleased that they were now taking her seriously. "Well, let's see. There's what's-his-name. Frank something? A teacher at the middle school. I've seen him there a few times. And there's Dutch Bigelow. He's there a lot."

"Dutch Bigelow?" Jan's pen stilled. Dutch was a retired state police detective, and though he was widowed, he was nearly sixty.

"Opposites attract, remember?" Macy said. "Besides, I didn't say it *was* him, I just said it *could* have been him."

Jan shot Elaine a look, asking what she thought, and Elaine nodded and looked down at the paper, so Jan carefully wrote the names *Dutch Bigelow* and *Frank, middle school teacher* on her paper.

"We'll see what we can find out about these people," Jan promised, slipping the paper and the pen back into her purse. "Thanks so much for your help."

Just as they were turning to leave, the door blew open, and Macy's daughter-in-law, Zale, or Azalea, as she was properly called, stepped in.

"Number eight left this behind," she said, tossing a worn notebook on the counter. "Hello, Elaine, Jan." She nodded at each of them in turn. Her long brown hair was pulled back into a low ponytail and she wore a black-and-red flannel shirt and rubber gloves. Azalea may have been named for a flower, but she was a star at the annual lumberjack competition and could logroll with the best of them.

"So now we'll have to mail this back to him, after all that," Macy said, shaking her head. "Everything else look okay in the cabin?"

"He left it in good shape," Zale said, opening a closet door and stowing a bucket of cleaning supplies on a shelf. "But we'll have to track down an address for him. He's probably halfway back to Boston now. How long do you think it will be before he calls about it?"

"You never can tell," Macy said. "Thank you for doing that."

"No problem. I think that's it for now," Zale said, straightening up. "I'm going to head out."

"That's fine." Macy turned to the computer screen on the desk. "Now let's see. Let me find the phone number he gave…"

A phone rang in the back, and Macy held up a finger and stepped away, Zale just a step behind her. Once they were both gone, Jan surreptitiously reached out and opened the notebook cover. She would just take a quick peek—she knew it was snooping, but she'd look away if she saw anything too personal. Inside were grids of squares he'd marked up, as well as notes Jan couldn't make heads or tails of. Random words were jotted here and there, such as *openness, dahlia,* and *four-letter word for chili pepper.* This appeared to be a notebook Bill used for constructing crosswords.

"Jan," Elaine said, elbowing her. Jan blocked her out. She only had a few moments. Jan flipped the pages of the notebook, looking for...she wasn't sure what, exactly. Something that would explain how that crossword had ended up given to Katelyn, and who her secret admirer was. But all she could make sense of were notes like *War and Peace* and *Upton Sinclair.* But then, as she was about to close the notebook, her eye caught on something: Vivaldi's *Four Seasons.*

Another elbow to the ribs only heightened her excitement. Was this just a coincidence, or was there more to it than that?

Jan pulled the notebook closer. But it couldn't be...?

"Are you done?" Macy asked, her eyebrows hiked. Jan looked up. When had she come back into the room? She was clearly trying to figure out why Jan was rooting through her guest's things.

"Of course." Jan let go of the notebook and stepped back.

"I'd love to take a peek," Elaine said a bit too brightly. "I am just so curious about what a crossword expert's notebook would look like." She gave Jan a look, reached for the notebook, and opened it before Macy could say a word. She was covering for her. Thank goodness for socially adept Elaine. "Jan is such a big fan of crosswords, I can't even imagine how fascinating it must be for someone like her. You wouldn't let us hold on to it for a while, would you?" Elaine continued as if nothing was strange.

"I'm afraid not," Macy said, scooting the notebook closer to herself. "I think we should take this and put it somewhere safe for our guest."

"Of course," Jan said, flashing her sweetest smile. "Thank you so much for your help."

Macy nodded, and Jan and Elaine turned to go. Macy watched them walk away, her lips pressed in a tight seam.

"Nice cover. But did you really think she'd let us take the notebook home with us?" Jan asked, plopping down into the driver's seat of her car.

"No. But I thought it was worth asking," Elaine said. "I was hoping to get a fingerprint."

Jan smiled. Elaine had recently gotten a fingerprint kit from the Internet, just like the pros used—or so she claimed— and she'd been itching to use it.

Elaine pulled her seat belt across her chest. "It's too bad we couldn't get into the cabin he rented, but I wasn't sure how to casually ask about that without sounding nuts."

"Probably just as well." Jan turned the key and the engine squealed. "It had just been cleaned anyway. Not much chance you would have found anything." Jan craned her neck to look behind her.

"Good point." Elaine looked over her shoulder. "You're clear on this side." She turned back around. "But it looked like you saw something in the notebook."

"Well, I may have. On one of the pages, I saw scribbled 'Vivaldi's *Four Seasons.' Four Seasons* was mentioned in Katelyn's puzzle."

Elaine nodded as they began backing up. It had been among dozens of other things. "It's a very famous piece of music. It wouldn't be that unusual for it to show up in crosswords sometimes, I'd guess."

Jan nodded. Her cousin had traveled more and knew more about culture than she did, but Jan knew crosswords, and she had to agree that she had seen Vivaldi as an answer more than once. Jan knew she couldn't make any judgment about Bill's involvement based on that. "But I also saw the word *requiem* in the notebook," she said.

"That is not a particularly common word," Elaine said. "And it does seem odd, given that both of those phrases were in Katelyn's puzzle and in the notebook."

"Exactly." Jan nodded and slowed as she got to the gravel drive.

"It doesn't prove that Bill had anything to do with creating the puzzle though," Elaine said.

"It doesn't eliminate him," Jan said. "And really, the fact that he made a sudden break for it and isn't answering his phone aren't exactly points in favor of his innocence."

"But they don't prove that he *was* involved. Besides, if your secret admirer theory is correct, why would he go out of his way to get a girl's attention and then split?"

Jan thought for a moment. "I'm not sure," she finally admitted. "But there could be some logic to it that we don't see."

"We need to find out more," Elaine said.

"Of course." Jan put on her blinker and turned smoothly back on to Main Street. "And in the meantime, we should look into those names Macy gave us. One of them might be the secret admirer."

"We don't know what was intended by the puzzle."

"What else could the message be?"

Elaine had to think for a moment. Jan didn't let her wait too long.

"See? There's no other explanation that makes sense," Jan said. "It's so romantic."

"Someone's feeling romantic in this car, that's for sure."

"Fair enough," Jan said with a giddy grin. "There's only one way to settle this." She pulled into the driveway and hummed a little bit as she turned off the car engine. "We'll just have to figure out the puzzle. Then we'll know who's right."

Elaine unbuckled her seat belt and smiled at her cousin. "At least we can agree on that."

CHAPTER THREE

After the cousins had eaten dinner and cleaned up, Jan went up to her bedroom to call Bob—theoretically to see if he'd heard any more from Bill, though Elaine suspected their conversation would be longer than that—and Elaine settled down at Jan's small rosewood desk in the sitting room on the second floor of Tea for Two and spread the crossword Katelyn had gotten in front of her. She was wearing white cotton gloves and had spread the components of her new fingerprint kit in front of her. There was a small jar of black magnetic power, as well as a magnetic applicator and a roll of clear cellophane tape to lift the prints, and a handful of small white cards to save the prints she found.

After she and Jan had solved a few mysteries around town, Elaine had been quite excited to try to integrate a few more professional tools into their investigations, and she had read up on the process of collecting fingerprints and using them to identify culprits. She had ordered this kit online, and she was excited about her first chance to try it out.

Elaine had read that paper wasn't the ideal material to lift prints from, because its uneven and porous surface made it difficult for oils from fingers and powder from fingerprint kits to distribute evenly, but paper was all she had to work with here, so she decided to give it a try. Elaine held the crossword up to light, looking for any visual clues about where prints would be found on this paper, but she couldn't see anything with her naked eye. She decided the top right corner of the page, where she herself had picked the paper up, was the most likely place to start, so she dipped her brush into the magnetic powder, tapped off the excess, and gently ran it over a small section in the top right corner of the page. To her delight, a series of swirls and whorls began to appear.

This wasn't so hard. She felt a bit giddy, watching the ridges of fingerprints emerge. This was a tool real detectives used; Elaine could use it too. Maybe it really would help her catch the "culprit."

She brushed the powder as gently as she could, and saw that more than one fingerprint emerged. In fact, there appeared to be many prints, facing different directions and layered on top of each other. It wasn't really all that surprising, since half a dozen people had touched the paper just this afternoon. Still, even if it required some work to narrow down whose print was whose, it would be worth it if it led them to the puzzle maker.

After a few minutes' work, Elaine had several partial prints, as well as one pretty well-developed print. She would do her best to capture each of the prints and try to match them to people she knew had touched the paper.

She reached for the clear cellophane tape and unrolled a small section. She pressed it down over the clearest print, picking up the magnetic powder, and then moved the tape to a clean white card and pressed down. The black powder transferred cleanly to the white card. There. She had collected her first fingerprint. Sure, it wasn't very pretty, and it hadn't gone quite as smoothly as it did on the crime shows on TV, but it was a fingerprint nonetheless.

She transferred the other partial prints to separate cards, and then she studied her handiwork. She had five partials and one near-complete print. Now all she needed to do was to collect prints from herself, Jan, and Katelyn so she could eliminate their prints, and then she would try to match the prints that remained to...well, she wasn't sure exactly. To whatever suspects they came up with, she supposed. She wished she'd been able to get a print from Bill Markham.

For now, Elaine had done as much as she could, so she put the lid back on the powder and had started to set her tools back inside the fingerprint kit when she noticed something. It was a small line of type running across the bottom of the page on the crossword puzzle. She wasn't sure how she hadn't noticed it before, except that the type was small enough that it looked like just a line. But she now held the paper up so she could take a closer look, and she saw that it said, in very fine print, "MakeYourPuzzle.com."

Well, that was interesting. Elaine immediately went into her bedroom and retrieved her laptop. She pulled up a Web browser and typed the URL MakeYourPuzzle.com into the address line. She was taken to a Web site that appeared to allow users to, well, make their own puzzles. You could choose from a variety of crossword puzzle grids and input your own clues and answers, and the program would assemble a crossword that you could solve online or print out.

Elaine tried it out. She had to create a username, which she did—TeaGal82, for the year she and Ben got married—and selected a small grid. Then she typed in the word *Elaine* as the answer to clue 1 down. The word appeared in the grid, and she typed *my name* in as the clue, which appeared to the left of the grid. This was pretty easy to use, she thought. Though if she were to fill out the grid and try to make all the letters fit, it would be quite a challenge.

This had to be how Katelyn's puzzle was made, she realized. Whoever had made it had used this Web site. That must be why it looked different from the other puzzles. Those had been made by a professional, and anyone could have used this site to create Katelyn's puzzle.

Elaine moved away from her own puzzle and looked around the site. There were tens of thousands of puzzles other users had created, all available for anyone to solve. Was Katelyn's puzzle one of them? She noticed it was possible to sort the puzzles by skill level or by username of the creator. She had no idea how to use those parameters to find the puzzle, so she decided to start by simply flipping through the puzzles on the site to see if she could find it.

Twenty minutes later, her eyes were bleary, and she decided to set the computer aside for the night. It was late, and they'd had a big day. But she was on the right track, she was sure of it.

After church the next day, Jan's son, Brian, and his family came over for lunch, and while Jan chatted with her daughter-in-law, Paula, and watched a video from their daughter Kelly's karate exhibition, Elaine set out the plates and silverware. She was glad for Jan that her kids lived so nearby, but she wished her own kids lived closer. They were scattered across the country and couldn't just pop over for a meal like Jan's could. She supposed that's what came of spending a lifetime moving around the world every few years. She wouldn't trade the life she and Ben had lived for anything, but she did wish that she saw her family more. She missed the chaos and excitement and even the occasional squabble of family gatherings. At least her mother Virginia lived in Augusta, and Elaine got to see her sometimes, though she was busy with her own life. Still, they had lunch planned for next Saturday, so she had that to look forward to.

She finished setting cloth napkins next to each plate and headed into the kitchen for the silverware. The smell of ham and potatoes filled the kitchen. Avery was there, her elbows on the counter, flipping through one of Jan's old family cookbooks.

"Hello there," Elaine said.

"Hey." Avery looked up through her blonde bangs.

"Finding anything good in that cookbook?"

Avery shrugged. "There are some recipes that look cool."

"I'm sure your grandmother would be happy to make them with you sometime." Elaine pulled open the silverware drawer and took out six forks. She glanced at Avery, who had turned back to the cookbook. Her face was glum.

A small mewl sounded from the back door, and Elaine turned to see Earl Gray, the stray cat they'd been feeding. Elaine smiled, set down the silverware, and reached for a can of the wet food they'd started leaving out for him. She opened the screen door, and then scooped the food into the dish. She patted him on the head and ran her fingers through his soft fur, and he purred and then nosed his way toward the food dish. She laughed, closed the door, set the empty can on the counter, and turned back to Avery, who seemed to not even have noticed the interruption.

"Is everything okay?" Elaine washed her hands before counting out six knives and set them next to the forks on the granite countertop.

"I guess." Avery turned the page of the cookbook and sighed.

Elaine was no expert on adolescents, but even she knew enough to understand that this meant things weren't okay. Elaine counted out six spoons and set them down.

"Is there a reason you're hiding out here away from everybody?"

"Because my family is annoying," Avery said.

"Ah. I see." Elaine used her hip to push the drawer closed. Elaine knew that many people couldn't stand preteen attitudes, but Elaine had always had a soft spot for girls this age. When her own daughter, Sasha, had been in junior high, or middle school as they called it now, she had relished seeing her grow, instead of pulling her hair out like so many other parents seemed to. Eleven- and twelve-year-olds could be overly dramatic and frustratingly self-centered, but they were just discovering who they were and testing the limits, and she had always felt a kind of sympathy for them. She remembered how awkward and challenging those years could be.

"Families often are. Did something specific happen, or is this just regular old everyday annoyingness?"

Avery looked up at her through the fringe of bangs again, watching Elaine—no doubt trying to decide whether Elaine was making fun of her or was genuinely interested. Finally, she seemed to make a decision.

"Mom wouldn't let me practice my cello this morning."

"Oh." Obviously this was a crime of the highest order. "I'm sorry to hear that."

"And I really had to. I have a challenge next week, and I really have to make first chair."

"I see." Elaine's son, Jared, had played the violin, and she remembered that challenges were when members of the orchestra would compete to see who got to be first chair, second chair, all the way down the line. It was a big deal to be chosen as first chair, as she recalled—at least, a big deal for junior high. "That seems like a good thing for you to be doing. Why didn't your mother want you practicing this morning?"

"Because she says the noise bothers her."

Ah. Well. Elaine had to admit, she could see how hearing an eleven-year-old practice her cello might not be everyone's idea of a peaceful Sunday morning. But if the girl needed to practice, how else was she going to do it?

"She doesn't care about whether I make first chair," Avery continued. "She doesn't get it. She says any position in the orchestra is fine. But I really have to get first chair, and I need to practice to do that."

Elaine studied Avery. She had big blue eyes and dirty blonde hair. She had just entered that awkward phase in which preteens lose the little-kid cuteness and start to look uncomfortable in their own bodies. But she was attractive, and it was clear she'd grow up to be a beautiful woman someday. And she was a bright girl, and a hard worker. Not every kid chose to play the cello, but Elaine loved the fact that Avery had chosen a somewhat complicated instrument. Nothing beat the deep, rich tones of a moody cello, played by the right hands. You had to love a girl who was so into her cello. A few years back, she'd only been interested in gymnastics, and Elaine saw this new passion for the cello as a sign of growth.

Elaine thought for a minute. "I see your point."

Was she meddling? But Jan wouldn't mind, surely. Avery was already here at the tearoom several days out of the week helping out in the kitchen. What could it hurt if she brought her cello?

"Well, how about this? Why don't you bring your cello here when you need to practice? I can't imagine you'll disturb anyone here."

"Really?" For the first time, Avery's face didn't look like she'd just eaten something sour.

"Sure. We'd love to have you practice here. We could help you take your cello back and forth."

Avery studied Elaine again, no doubt trying to decide what to make of the offer. But then she nodded.

"Okay. Thanks."

And just like that, her face relaxed into a slight smile.

"Now, how about you help me set the table, and you can tell me more about how this challenge works."

Avery hesitated again, and then she pushed herself up from the counter and closed the cookbook. Elaine held out the spoons, and Avery reached for them and gave her another smile. Elaine suddenly missed her own granddaughter just a tiny bit less.

AN HOUR LATER, Jan had finished clearing the last of the dishes from the dining room table and was just settling down into the couch in the upstairs sitting room with a cup of chamomile. Paula and the girls were washing up the dishes, and they had insisted she relax while Elaine was catching up on paperwork in her office. Well, Jan wasn't going to argue with that. She was putting her feet up on the low coffee table and reaching for a book as her son, Brian, walked into the room.

"I took a look at that whining noise your car was making," he said, wiping his hands on his good dress pants. Oh dear. Paula would have his head for that. Jan bit her tongue and smiled, indicating she was listening.

"I think your cam shaft belt is slipping," Brian continued. "If you take it in to a mechanic, I'm sure he'll be able to replace it easily enough."

"Thank you, Brian." Brian had always been a good son, but he'd really stepped up to take care of his mother and sisters when his father had passed away. He could have gotten a high-paying job in some big city, but instead he'd stayed nearby to be closer to his mother, and Jan would always be grateful. He now worked as a manager at an auto parts store in Augusta, which was steady work, but was not the sort of glamorous career he could have had. Still, there were some definite advantages to having someone who knew a lot about cars in the family. "I'll take it in tomorrow."

"Awesome. Anything else you need me to take a look at while we're here?"

"Not that I can think of. Why don't you sit down and talk to your old mom?"

"You don't have to ask me twice." Brian flopped down in an overstuffed armchair. "I'm exhausted. Avery started practicing her cello at 5:30 a.m. this morning, so needless to say none of us got as much sleep as we intended."

"Oh dear." Jan laughed. "But you have to admire her dedication."

"I would admire it more at a more reasonable hour." Brian relaxed back into the chair and turned his head. He spotted a piece of paper on the writing desk and reached for it. "What's this?"

From here Jan could see that it was the list of names she'd recorded the day before while talking to Macy Atherton.

"Oh, just some people I want to talk to." She didn't really want to elaborate. She got the impression Brian thought the sleuthing she and Elaine had done was a cute hobby, but he didn't take it seriously.

"Are you working on another mystery?" Brian asked.

Jan hesitated. And why would he take it seriously? Sometimes Jan didn't take it seriously herself. She was just a home-schooling mom turned tearoom owner; what did she know about solving mysteries?

"It's just a small thing," she said. "One of the guests at our crossword event yesterday got a strange crossword puzzle that seems like it came from a secret admirer. We're trying to help her figure out who it was."

"A secret admirer, huh?" Brian's eyes twinkled. "And you think it might be Dutch Bigelow?"

"Those are just some possibilities," Jan said.

"I can tell you that Tag King does crossword puzzles." He tapped Tag's name on the list.

"Oh yeah?"

"Yeah. Sometimes we deliver parts to his shop, and more than once I've walked in to find him huddled over a book of puzzles."

"Really?" Jan didn't know why this surprised her. Lots of different people enjoyed puzzles. She'd just never seen Tag as the puzzling type.

"I think he does them to pass the time between customers. But yeah, he definitely does them." Brian reached behind him to fluff up one of Elaine's throw pillows. "I can't say whether he's your secret admirer, but he's probably worth looking into. And hey, you need to get your car fixed anyway, so you've got the perfect excuse."

Well, he did have a point there. And if what he'd just told her was true—and she had no reason to assume it wasn't—then it seemed that they might be on the right track after all. Tag was in his late twenties, single, and not bad-looking. And he was different enough from Katelyn that he might be shy about approaching her directly.

"Thank you, Brian. I think I'll take my car in to Tag's shop tomorrow."

"Anytime. Maybe this one will be an easy solve for you." He winked. Well, maybe he didn't think her hobby was ridiculous after all. That was reassuring, at the very least.

Maybe he was right. Maybe this mystery would be their simplest yet.

CHAPTER FOUR

Sunday evening, after Jan and Elaine had eaten a simple sup-
per, Jan sat down in the sitting room to relax for a few minutes. She rested against the blue couch and took in the braided
rug, and the family photos. This room felt light and airy, and she
always enjoyed being here. Elaine sat across the room, absorbed
in some mystery novel. She had already gathered fingerprints
from both of them and had compared them to the prints she'd
gathered from the puzzle, finding partial prints from each of
them on the paper. Now she was enjoying the quiet evening.

Jan sat still for a few minutes, and then decided now would
be a good time to try to solve the remainder of Katelyn's puzzle.
There were several sections where she had gaping holes in the
grid, and she couldn't help but think solving those would give her
more clues about the person who made it. Unfortunately she was
stuck. What was a seven-letter word for *pedagogue?* She needed
a six-letter word for 14 down, and the clue was *Polish writer.* She
couldn't think of any Polish writers; certainly not one with only
six letters in their name. She shook her head. She was too tired
to think straight. She set the puzzle aside and started to get up.

"Giving up for now?" Elaine asked, looking up from her book.

Jan nodded. She hadn't realized Elaine had been paying attention. "This puzzle is impossible."

"You'll be fresher in the morning," Elaine said, giving her cousin a smile.

"I sure hope so."

Jan stood and started off toward her bedroom, but as she crossed the room, her eye caught on something.

Over on the top of the bookshelf sat a small rosewood box. She changed direction and crossed the room, reaching for the box. She opened it carefully. Inside a beautiful sapphire ring was nestled, the cerulean stone gleaming even in the low light. She turned the box to catch the light so she could see it sparkle. They'd found this ring buried in a wall when they'd renovated the kitchen shortly after they moved into their new home. They had been trying to find out who it had belonged to and how it ended up there ever since, with little luck.

"Another mystery we're no closer to solving," Elaine said from across the room.

"That's not entirely true," Jan said. She held up the box. They'd recently discovered that the markings on the edge of it were actually crudely scribbled Latin words, and they spelled out the phrase "For love and blood." The words matched a phrase etched into the silver of the ring "We know what this means."

"True, but we have no idea why it is written there. Or how the ring ended up in our wall."

"But we'll get there," Jan said, setting the box down gently on the shelf. She picked up the flue cover that had hidden the ring for so many years. A complicated design was etched on the flat metal face. It looked as though it had been carved with some primitive tool; it certainly hadn't been original to the piece. They thought it might be a crudely rendered version of an old family crest, but they hadn't been able to make heads or tails of it yet.

"I think if we figure out what this design is, that will help a lot."

"I'm sure you're right. But that's a mystery for another day, I'm afraid." Jan sighed. "I just wanted to look at it again."

"It is a beautiful ring," Elaine conceded. She gave Jan a sly smile. "Don't go getting any ideas about rings, you hear me?"

Jan felt her cheeks flame. "Bob and I have not even been dating two months," she said, though she suspected she didn't sound convincing. She had, actually, been wondering what sort of ring she'd choose if she and Bob got married. Peter had given her a small speck of a diamond when they got engaged, and she'd loved it and all that it represented. But if she were to get married again, she might like something different this time around.

Elaine nodded, trying to look stern.

"I'm headed to bed," Jan said, shaking her head.

"I'll be doing the same shortly," Elaine said. "As soon as I finish this chapter. And don't worry." She glanced back at the puzzle Jan had left behind on the desk. "We'll get to the bottom of this mystery. That's why they call us the Clever Cousins."

Jan laughed. "No one calls us that."

"They don't yet," Elaine said. "But if we get to the bottom of this, maybe they will soon."

Jan playfully shook her head and headed for bed.

CHAPTER FIVE

After the cousins had had breakfast on Monday morning and Jan had finished her baking for the tearoom for the day, they both pulled on sweatshirts, exited their house, and walked the short distance across the yard to the Bookworm. They wanted to run their list of names past Katelyn and see if she had any other ideas, and Elaine planned to get a fingerprint from her to eliminate the prints on the puzzle that were hers. The morning was clear and cool, and the ground was wet from the light rain that had fallen overnight.

The bookstore was housed in a quaint shingled Cape Cod–style house. Bristol Payson, the shop's owner, had set out lounge chairs in the small front yard, and she served lemonade to customers out here all summer. The chairs would soon be packed up and put away for the season, no doubt. The leaves of the stately oak at the front of the yard were already beginning to fall.

The wide-plank floors creaked as they stepped inside the cozy bookshop and let the door fall closed behind them. The store had blond wood shelves stacked with colorful books.

Tables at the front of the shop were piled high with staff recommendations and best sellers, and handwritten signs gave short blurbs about why staff loved different books. Elaine could spend hours reading those descriptions alone. To the left, a display of new fiction caught her eye, and she could already see that Jan, two steps ahead of her, was distracted by a new cookbook on the front table. Soft classical music played on the store's sound system. Elaine took a deep breath, pulling the smell of ink and paper deep into her lungs.

"Hello there, neighbors. Welcome." Bristol Payson was seated behind the high counter near the front, going through a stack of receipts. Her blonde hair was pulled into a low ponytail, and she wore a light sweater over a pressed button-down. "Can I help you find something?"

Bristol had been one of the first to welcome the cousins to their new home, and Elaine had always found her warm and gracious. Bristol was married to Mark Payson, the town clerk, and she had finally fulfilled her long-held dream and opened the shop when her son Greg went off to college a few years back.

"Actually, we were hoping to talk to Katelyn," Jan said. "Is she here?"

"Sure thing. She's over in the children's section." She gestured toward the rear of the store.

"Thank you," Elaine said, but as Jan started toward the back of the store, Elaine got distracted by a new hardcover book by one of her favorite mystery writers. The author's books were always set in a manor house in the English countryside, and the sleuth was a middle-aged woman no one took seriously but who always came up with the solution to the mystery.

"That's her best one yet," Bristol said.

Elaine picked up the book and read the flap copy. *Ooh,* this one centered on a mystery in the house's garden. It looked intriguing, and the blurbs on the cover, coupled with Bristol's recommendation, were too much for her to resist.

"Coming into this store is dangerous," Elaine said. "I already have a stack of books on my bedside."

"You can never have too many books," Bristol said. "Besides, if you liked her last book, you'll love this one, I promise."

Elaine smiled at Bristol, looked down at the cover again, and then tucked the book under her arm as she scurried to keep up with Jan. Jan was already walking into the children's section, which was warm and welcoming, with throw rugs and beanbags that invited children to curl up and get lost in a story.

"Hey there," Katelyn said, looking up from a box of books she was unpacking. She lifted two copies of *Charlotte's Web* and slid them onto the shelf. Elaine's heart lurched. She had so many fond memories of reading that book to her kids, one chapter at a time, every night before bed. "I was going to come see you guys on my break. Thanks for coming by. I haven't made much more progress on the puzzle, I'm afraid. Have you had any luck?"

"None at all," Jan said, "despite several hours wasted trying."

"Time spent solving puzzles is never wasted," Katelyn said. "But, yeah, I haven't gotten very far either. The clues are . . . well, it doesn't seem like a professionally made the puzzle." She reached back into the box and pulled out a picture book with a funny illustrated bunny on the cover. Elaine's granddaughter, Lucy, had loved that book. Katelyn slid the book onto the shelf.

"That's probably true," Jan said. She cracked a smile. "It's from someone who came up with this puzzle as a message to you, not someone who made a puzzle because they're particularly good at it."

Elaine considered this. That probably suggested that Bill Markham hadn't made the puzzle, actually. But they still needed to talk to him.

"On the plus side," Elaine said, "we have some names we wanted to run by you."

Katelyn brightened. "Who did you come up with?"

Elaine couldn't be sure, but she saw something like hope on the girl's face. Well, and why not? It sounded like she'd been through a lot; who could blame her if the idea of a secret admirer was flattering? But Elaine couldn't ignore the nagging feeling that something about the secret admirer idea didn't totally add up. If someone had a crush on Katelyn, why tell her with a crossword puzzle? Or, if he had to tell her with a puzzle, shouldn't he have made it easier to figure out who he was? Were they getting too caught up in the secret crush idea and not seeing something else in the puzzle?

Elaine was shaken from her thinking when Jan pulled the list of names out of the pocket of her coat and started reading them: "The first name we came up with was Tag King."

Katelyn looked up for a moment, confusion on her face. Then, she shook her head and said, "The snowmobile guy?"

"We're told he's a puzzler," Jan said. "And that he spends a fair amount of time here. Possibly to see you?"

Katelyn hesitated for a minute. "He does come in here sometimes. That's how I know who he is, I guess. But I don't know. We've chatted a few times, but we seem pretty different."

She bent down and picked up a paperback copy of *The Voyage of the Dawn Treader*, one of the books in C.S. Lewis's classic Chronicles of Narnia series. Oh, Jared had loved those books when he was a boy. Elaine longed to reach for the book and page through it, as if reading those familiar words would bring back the boy he had been. But she knew she needed to focus.

"Opposites attract," Jan said with a shrug. "Maybe those differences are why he felt the need to tell you his feelings this way."

"Maybe," Katelyn said, but she didn't look convinced. "Who else is on your list?"

"Frank somebody," Jan said, consulting her list.

"Who?"

"He's a teacher, apparently. You don't know him? We're told he comes here a lot."

"Who told you all this?" Katelyn asked, narrowing her eyes.

Elaine looked at Jan, who met her eye. She didn't want Katelyn to think they were spreading news about her all over town. "Macy Atherton," Jan said reluctantly.

"She naturally wanted to know why we were so anxious to find Bill Markham on Saturday," Elaine said. "And when we told her, she volunteered some people she'd seen come in here regularly."

"Ah." Katelyn nodded. "Yeah. I can see that. She is a faithful member of the Bookworm Book Club, and she comes in here all the time between meetings. She likes to sit in the reading area and observe," she said, indicating a small area with comfortable couches and chairs by the fireplace at the back of the store. A beverage station was on a small table near the couch, and customers were free to help themselves to coffee, tea, and hot chocolate and relax.

"She certainly seemed to know a lot about who shopped here," Elaine said. None of them were going to come out and say that Macy was nosy, but she did like to know what was going on in Lancaster.

"Which is really odd," Katelyn said. "But yes, I know who the teacher is. Frank Conrad. He teaches at Truman Middle School in Augusta. He's a nice guy. Quiet, kind of nerdy, but he seems nice. He lives nearby, I think, and I've talked with him a few times when he's come in here."

She didn't seem too excited about the idea of Frank, but they would talk to him anyway.

"She also suggested Dutch Bigelow," Jan said. Elaine could see she was trying to hold back a smile.

Katelyn didn't even try to hold it back. She laughed out loud. "That would indeed be a surprise," she said. "He does shop here every couple of weeks, but he usually just heads directly to the thrillers, picks a new book, and gets out as quickly as he can."

"Well, since his name came up, we were planning to talk to him. Is it all right if we talk to all the people on this list? Hopefully we'll be able to tell if one of them knows something about the puzzle."

"Sure." Katelyn shrugged. "It's fine with me. Are those the only names you have?"

"We were also planning to talk to River White," Elaine said. "Since he was at the event, and he knows crosswords."

Katelyn nodded. "That makes sense." She looked off thoughtfully for a minute. "We've always only had a professional relationship. But he seems like a nice guy."

"And he's not bad-looking," Jan added.

Elaine could see that Katelyn wasn't displeased by the idea of River White being her secret admirer. And she could see why—he was about her age, and with his reddish-blond hair, he could be considered good-looking if he would trim that hair and use an iron a bit more regularly. He was also smart and had a good job. He wouldn't be a bad match for Katelyn, actually, now that Elaine thought about it. But that didn't necessarily mean that he was responsible for the puzzle.

"And of course we still need to talk to Bill Markham, though we don't think he's the secret admirer," Jan said.

"Right." Katelyn reached down and pulled out a few books with yellow spines that Elaine recognized as Nancy Drew books, as well as more chapter books from a newer series that seemed to involve cupcakes, and she shelved them quickly. "That's quite a list."

"Is there anyone else you think we should look into?" Elaine asked.

Katelyn didn't say anything for a minute. She straightened the books on the shelves, lining up the spines evenly. "Not that I can think of," she said reluctantly. "The dating pool is pretty shallow around these parts."

Elaine tried to think of all the young unmarried men she knew of.

"What about Jack Weston?" she asked. Jack was in his early thirties, and he was the game warden, which meant that he spent most of his time outdoors and had the tan to prove it. He was tall and athletic and with his light brown hair and blue eyes, Elaine thought of him as very handsome.

"Nah." Katelyn shook her head. "I went out with him once a couple years back. It was like talking to a brick wall. We had nothing in common."

"So it wasn't a love connection?"

"I'm afraid not," Katelyn said. "It's too bad, because he's cute, but I've had more fun conversing with Siri."

Elaine recognized the name of the mechanical voice that spoke out of iPhones. Not exactly a nice comparison for poor Jack.

"We won't look into him yet in that case," Jan said. "Anyone else?"

"Not that I can think of," Katelyn said.

"Well, this list is a good start," Jan said. "There are some real possibilities here. We can get started talking to these people today."

"Are you sure you don't mind spending so much time looking into this?" Katelyn asked. "It seems like a lot of trouble, and I know you've got plenty going on already."

"Are you kidding? We're curious about this," Jan said. "We want you to find that secret admirer."

"Seriously, we love solving mysteries," Elaine said. "And this one's a doozy. We want to find out who made this puzzle and why." She was careful not to mention a secret admirer, but neither Jan nor Katelyn seemed to notice. "Speaking of which, can I get your fingerprint?" She pulled the fingerprint kit out of her purse.

"You two really are professionals!" Katelyn said admiringly as she let Elaine dip her fingertips in ink and press them on to a white card.

"We're definitely not pros, but we will do our best to find the answer for you," Elaine said.

After they'd taken Katelyn's prints, Elaine headed toward the register, but her eye caught on a book she hadn't seen before. A book about life in Queen Elizabeth I's court. Elaine had always been fascinated by the Tudors, and especially by the Virgin Queen who had ruled England for more than four decades. She picked up the hardcover and flipped through it. Elaine loved reading about the ways this woman—a woman who never married, no less—had brought peace and prosperity to her land, and about all the ways she had affected culture and religion, even today. But Elaine also enjoyed reading about all the intrigue that happened in the royal court. She studied the table of contents and saw that there was a section about the history and symbolism of the queen's coat of arms.

Well. It was pretty unlikely that the design etched into their flue cover was a royal coat of arms, but it couldn't hurt to learn a bit more about that topic, Elaine decided. She added the book to her stack and headed to the register.

"I'll take this one too."

Bristol Payson smiled. "That's a great book. Totally fascinating."

"I'm looking forward to reading it."

Elaine looked down at the books as Bristol started to ring them up. She knew she had her work cut out for her. And she couldn't wait to get started.

CHAPTER SIX

An hour later, Jan pulled into Tag King's mechanic shop, with Elaine following just behind in her own Chevy Malibu. Tag specialized in snowmobiles and motorcycles, but he knew his way around a car engine as well, and his services were often cheaper than other shops in town. Half-built snowmobiles and pieces from motorcycles were scattered around the edges of the cement parking lot, and Jan could see a station wagon on the hydraulic lift inside the garage.

She stepped out of her car and closed the door and walked toward Elaine, whose bright-red car looked ridiculously out of place among these dreary shells of vehicles.

"Ready?" Elaine asked brightly. She was loving this, Jan could tell.

"Naturally," Jan said. She followed behind her cousin as she pulled open the door and stepped inside the small office. There was a small waiting area with padded chairs, a hand-ful of anemic plants, and snowmobile magazines with head-lines like "Getting the Most Out of Your Treads" and "Trail Turbo Challenge!" The walls were covered with a pale wood paneling, but the room was bright and clean. They stepped up to the counter, and a voice called from the garage, "I'll be right there!"

Jan looked around the small office. There was a computer on the other side of the counter, along with a half-filled mug of black coffee. And next to the keyboard was...

Jan felt a shot of excitement course through her. Next to the keyboard was a book of puzzles.

Just then, Tag King stepped through the doorway and into the waiting area, wiping his hands on a rag. He was in his late twenties, and his brown hair was cropped close, which set off his big blue eyes. He wasn't bad-looking, Jan realized, and he owned his own business to boot. He wouldn't be a bad match for Katelyn.

"Hi, Mrs. Blake," Tag said, nodding. "Mrs. Cook."

"Hi, Tag."

Tag started to hold out his hand, but then realized it was covered in grease and shrugged awkwardly. Elaine laughed.

"How are your parents?" Jan asked. "How much longer will they be open?" Tag's parents, Burk and Abby King, ran the Hearthside restaurant, which was only open in the summer. In the winter they decamped to Florida. Jan and Elaine had quickly come to know and love the Kings since they'd moved to the area.

"They're doing great. And they'll be open another few weeks yet. They typically head down to Florida in mid-October." Tag set the rag down on the counter.

"Ah. Just in time for the first snow," Jan said. It was a joke, mostly. Snow was rare but not unheard of in the early autumn.

"Pretty much." Tag laughed. "And you? How's Brian?"

"He's doing very well, thank you. In fact, he's the one who suggested I come see you today. My car is making a squeaking noise, and he thinks I need a new cam shaft belt."

"Ah. Well, that should be easy enough to check out. I can take a look at it now if you like."

"Really? That would be wonderful."

"Which one is it?" He nodded to the two cars in the parking lot.

"The blue Toyota," she said, and handed him the keys.

"I'll be right back."

Jan watched through the big front window as he jogged across the lot, slid in behind the wheel, and started the engine. He pulled the car closer to the garage, and the moment he stepped his foot on to the gas pedal, the engine let out a loud squeal. He parked in front of the garage, popped the lid, and hopped out.

Jan turned back around and saw that Elaine was behind the counter.

"What are you doing?"

"I'm going to test for fingerprints," Elaine said, pulling the kit she'd ordered online out of her purse. Jan glanced out the window at Tag and then back at her cousin, who was smoothly unpacking her kit like it was the most natural thing in the world. The desk area was scattered with various papers and receipts, and also had a cup that held pencils and pens and a ball of rubber bands. She noticed the book of puzzles and stopped unpacking to flip through it, and then she gave Jan a thumbs-up.

"Right now?"

"Can you imagine a better time?" Elaine was already dipping her brush into the fine black powder and dusting it across the handle of the mug that sat on the counter. "The coffee is cold." She made a face.

"He's going to notice that his mug is covered in dust," Jan said.

"I'll wipe it off." Elaine leaned over and studied the handle of the mug, scrunched up her face, and then moved on to coat the side of the mug with the powder. Tag was stepping into the garage. If he looked through the open doorway, he'd see Elaine hunched over his desk. Fortunately he didn't look in, and Elaine continued to dust his mug with fine powder, looking for a usable print.

Finally, she seemed to find one that satisfied her. She pulled a roll of cellophane tape out of her kit and pulled off a small section, pressing it against the mug. Jan looked back, and Tag was now back outside and was bending over the open hood of her car again. Elaine pressed the tape against a white card. There was only a small part of a print, and it was blurry. She could see that already Elaine was looking around, trying to find another source for picking up a print, but Tag had already straightened up and was pushing the hood of her car closed.

"Hurry. He's coming back," she hissed. Elaine quickly started tossing the pieces of her kit back into the box.

Tag opened the car door and sat down behind the wheel of the car and turned the engine on again, gently nudging the car forward a bit. There was no shriek from the engine. He turned the car off and started to step out.

Jan dug through her purse and pulled out a small package of wet wipes—some habits never died, even when your kids were grown—and fished one out, and Elaine took it and wiped down the mug quickly.

A moment later, Tag stepped back in through the door to the garage, just a few seconds after Elaine had slipped around the edge of the counter and rejoined Jan in the waiting area. Jan gave her cousin a look, but Elaine smiled blithely.

"It *was* the cam shaft belt," he said, placing her keys on the counter, "and I took care of it."

"So quickly?" Jan said, turning to glare at her cousin one more time. "That's wonderful."

"Everything else looks good, so that should fix the problem." Tag turned to his computer and started pecking away at the keys.

"Thank you so much. I really appreciate it."

"Of course." He tapped again on the keys, while Jan wracked her brain, trying to think of a natural way to bring up the topic of Katelyn.

"Do you know Katelyn Grande?" Elaine asked, a sweet smile on her face.

Well, so much for introducing that topic naturally.

Tag looked up at Elaine, confusion on his face. "Katelyn?" he repeated. He thought for a minute, and then shook his head. "I don't think so. Why? Did I fix her car?"

"She works over at the Bookworm. She's single," Elaine said, winking in a comical way.

"Oh." Tag seemed to not know what to say. Jan could understand the feeling.

"I wondered if you might have met her," Elaine continued.

"I don't know. Maybe?" He thought for another moment. "Does she have brown hair? Like this?" He used his hand to indicate the angled way her hair was cut.

"Exactly," Elaine said brightly.

"I guess I've talked to her. I go there sometimes to buy presents for my niece. She's obsessed with this one series of books, which makes it easy to buy presents. Last time I was there the girl at the counter recommended another series she thought Kelsey would like." He shrugged. "That's about the extent of it though."

Elaine nodded. "Well, keep it in mind. She's single and smart to boot."

Tag ran a hand along the back of his neck. His cheeks were flushed.

"I'll keep it in mind," he said unconvincingly.

An awkward silence hung in the room.

"Are those your puzzle books?" Jan asked quickly, gesturing down at the books on the desk. "I love puzzles."

"Oh yeah." He seemed relieved by the change of topic. "Yeah, I like to do them when there's downtime."

"Do you do crosswords?" Jan asked.

"Nah. Mostly sudoku." He opened the cover of one. "There are some other word games, like word searches and stuff, but mostly I stick to numbers. They work better for my brain."

"So no crosswords? At all?" Elaine asked. Tag narrowed his eyes and tilted his head. He must think they were quite daft.

"No, just sudoku mostly."

"Well, it's been lovely chatting with you. Thanks so much for your help," Jan said. "How much for the new belt?"

Jan quickly handed over her credit card, and a few minutes later they were out in the parking lot.

"Well, he pretty clearly is not our man," Jan said. "Who's next?"

"Dutch Bigelow," Elaine said, looking down at the list Jan had made. "But I'm not so sure we should cross Tag off just yet."

"No? He doesn't do crosswords, and he seemed to not even know who Katelyn is."

"He could be a very good actor. Besides, I looked through that book of puzzles, and there were crosswords in there, and they had been filled out. So he wasn't telling the truth about that."

"Really?" Jan had been so sure he'd been truthful. Was she so off on reading people?

"Really." Elaine nodded. "And let's see whether his finger-prints turn up anything before we write him off."

"Fine," Jan reluctantly agreed. "So what's our strategy for talking to Dutch?"

"You don't really think it's Dutch, do you?" Elaine asked. "If we go with your theory about a secret admirer, he seems pretty unlikely. There's got to be at least twenty years between him and Katelyn."

Jan shrugged. "All the more reason he might hide behind the crossword puzzle. So let's go see."

A few minutes later, they'd dropped Elaine's car off at the tearoom and driven in Jan's newly quiet Toyota to the two-story colonial where Dutch lived. The house was large and well main-tained, though the grass was greenish-brown and the flower beds overgrown. An extended-cab pickup was parked in the driveway. They walked up the cracked stone path to the door and rang the doorbell, but there was no sound from inside.

"He's got to be here," Jan said, looking back at the truck in the driveway. Elaine nodded and knocked on the door loudly.

Still there was no movement. Was he avoiding them? Could he...?

Jan realized she was being ridiculous. She listened at the door, and she did hear a noise, but it wasn't coming from inside the house. She leaned back and looked around, then stepped off the porch and on to the grass. "I hear something this way," she said.

Elaine looked dubious, but she followed Jan off the porch and through the grass, crunchy with the cold, to the dirt path that led under a handful of fir trees and around the side of the house. Behind the house, across a small grassy yard, was a wooden shed of sorts tucked away under a stand of more fir trees. A small tapping noise was coming from inside the open door.

"How did you hear that?" Elaine whispered as they walked toward the noise.

Jan shrugged. "I guess I still have eyes *and* ears at the back of my head, even now that my kids are grown."

They walked toward the doorway and peeked inside. Dutch Bigelow sat on a stool in the middle of the room, using a chisel to carve a chunk out of a block of wood. Other pieces of wood in various stages of carving were scattered around him on a wooden table, and the shelves built against the back wall were lined with tools of all kinds. A space heater and a fluorescent lamp were plugged into a power strip on the wall, and soft classical music played from a radio on a worktable pushed against the side wall.

Dutch looked up. "Oh. Hello."

"Hello, Dutch," Elaine said smoothly. "How are you?"

"Oh, can't complain." Dutch set down the piece of wood and the chisel. Jan remembered now that Dutch carved exquisitely detailed birds out of wood and sold them at Gift Me., the souvenir shop down the road. Tourists went wild for them.

"I'm glad to hear it. What are you working on?" Elaine asked, stepping toward the worktable. Jan admired her cousin's confidence. She was so used to people being happy to see her it didn't occur to her to hang back and wait to be invited in. And she had to admit, Dutch didn't seem to mind. He was already reaching for the wood he'd just put down and held it up to show her.

"This one's a tanager," he said, "though you can't tell that yet. Hopefully it will look something like this one." He indicated a bird that was mostly done with his elbow, and Jan could see that it was a very good representation of the small bird.

"These are lovely," Elaine said, picking up a sparrow. "You carve these just with those hand tools?" She turned the bird over in her hands, admiring the way the wings seemed to indicate movement even though the wood was static.

Dutch shrugged. "It keeps me busy."

Jan knew that Dutch was a retired state police detective. Though he wasn't yet sixty, the work had been physically demanding, especially his last stint in the governor's Executive Protection Unit, and he'd taken early retirement after he'd suffered a heart attack a few years back.

"You're very talented." Elaine set the bird back down on the table. "And this is quite a nice setup you have here."

Jan watched the way Dutch's face lit up as Elaine talked. Was he just glad to show his work to someone who seemed interested, or was he taking a liking to Jan's outgoing cousin? Jan knew his wife had passed away a few years back. He was in good shape, his face lined but affable, and though his hair was mostly silver, it looked distinguished. Now that she thought about it, he and Elaine wouldn't make a bad match.

Then again, Jan was pretty sure someone else had his eye on Elaine. And—oh, right, they were here to see if Dutch was a secret admirer of Katelyn's.

"So what can I help you ladies with? I assume you didn't come here to admire my birds."

"Well, no, we didn't, but I'm glad to see them nonetheless," Elaine said. She set the tanager down gently and turned to look at Dutch. "We actually came to ask if you do crosswords."

His brow wrinkled. "Crosswords?"

"Yes." Elaine smiled brightly, like this was the most natural question in the world.

"I'm afraid not." Dutch shook his head. "I've never enjoyed them. I'd rather be outside hunting or fishing or working on one of my birds."

"You know, I feel the same way," Elaine said, shaking her head. "Jan loves them, and I've never quite understood why." She gave him a broad smile. "She just loves going to the Bookworm and buying those little puzzle books. They even started stocking *Cryptograms* magazine just for her, can you believe it?"

Poor Dutch seemed confused, but not altogether unhappy about the way this impromptu visit was going.

"Katelyn Grande, who works there, is also really into crossword puzzles. She writes them and everything. Do you know Katelyn?"

Both of the cousins carefully watched for his response.

"I think so." Dutch nodded. "She's the young one, right?"

Elaine nodded, and he continued. "She's rung me up a couple times, I think."

"She's really interesting. Have you ever talked to her?"

He wrinkled his brow again. "Not aside from hello and thank you."

"But you do go into the Bookworm pretty regularly, don't you?"

Dutch shifted in his seat. "I guess I do go in there every few weeks, whenever the library doesn't have any thrillers I haven't read," he said warily.

He was uncomfortable. Jan tried to decide if it was because he was confused by the questions or whether he had something to hide.

"Mind if I ask why…"

"*Ooh*, is this a robin?" Elaine asked brightly, indicating a completed bird on one of his shelves. The birds weren't painted, they were simply covered in a coat of clear shellac, but even without colors Jan could see it wasn't a robin—the body was much too large, the head too small. She assumed her cousin had simply guessed the name of a bird to distract him.

"No, actually, that's a wren," Dutch said, standing up. He started moving toward the shelf to show her. Elaine set her purse down on the table, turned back to Jan and pantomimed dusting for fingerprints, and then followed Dutch toward the shelf. Their backs were to the table.

Jan hesitated. This fingerprint business was Elaine's thing. She didn't know the first thing about taking fingerprints, and she was dubious that it would get them any closer to finding the puzzle maker.

But while Dutch talked to Elaine about the differences between the two birds, Elaine turned back and gestured for Jan to hurry up, so Jan reluctantly reached into Elaine's purse and pulled out the kit. She'd watched Elaine do this a few times now, so she knew the drill. She opened it and quickly reached for the small brush and the jar of black powder, and then she searched for a surface to dust.

She checked and saw that Elaine was now asking Dutch about a carving of a gull or some other seabird. She had to work quickly, before they ran out of birds.

Jan turned back to the table and pulled her sleeve over her fingertips, and then she reached for the chisel. She'd just seen him holding this; would he have left a print behind? She dusted black powder over the handle quickly and saw that it was crowded with fingerprints. She kept dusting until she found one that looked nearly complete, and then she quickly ripped off a piece of the tape and lifted the powder. Then she dug out a card and transferred the print. Elaine was now asking Dutch about how he decided which bird to carve. As quickly as she could, Jan tossed the pieces back in the kit and dug out a wet wipe from her purse to wipe down the chisel.

A minute later, when Elaine and Dutch turned back around, Jan was standing innocently in front of the table, pretending she'd simply been listening while Dutch talked.

"Thank you so much for the chance to see your birds," Elaine said, a touch too friendly. "It really was wonderful to see an artist at work."

"Yes, thank you," Jan added.

Dutch smiled and nodded, but he mostly looked confused. Jan could imagine why, and so she took her cousin's arm, threw up a jaunty wave with the other arm, and steered Elaine toward the doorway.

"Did you get it?" Elaine asked as soon as they were out of earshot.

"I think so," Jan said. "I'll show you when we get to the car. What did you think of Dutch?"

"I don't think he's our puzzle maker," Elaine said. They walked back around to the front of the house, dodging low-hanging pine tree branches. "He didn't seem to know Katelyn or much about puzzles."

"Plus, again, he's much too old for Katelyn." Jan wasn't positive, but it seemed very likely that her cousin was right. Still, one thing nagged her. "But he did have classical music playing."

Jan didn't know enough about music to recognize the piece, but it had sounded like some concert music performed by a full orchestra. Elaine looked at her like she was speaking a foreign language.

"What does that have to do with anything?"

"The crossword puzzle Katelyn got had several references to music in it," Jan said.

Elaine thought for a moment. "There was the reference to the *Moonlight* Sonata. What else?"

"Isn't *Romeo and Juliet* a piece of music, not just a play?" Jan asked.

"I guess so." Elaine seemed dubious.

Jan pulled her phone out of her purse and quickly did a search for Romeo and Juliet music. "Aha. It's by Tchaikovsky," she said. She scrolled through the results. "Here's a recording of it as played by the London Symphony."

The music was difficult to make out coming from her phone's little speaker.

"It sounds lovely," Elaine said. "And maybe there is a connection." But she didn't sound convinced.

Well, Jan wasn't sure about this herself, but it seemed worth noting at least. "Maybe the fingerprint I got will give us a more definitive answer."

"I hope so." They got back to the car and Jan dug the print she'd taken out of the kit, and Elaine smiled.

"Nice work. Not bad for your first attempt."

Jan shook her head and sat down behind the steering wheel. "Where to next?"

Elaine examined the fingerprint a moment longer, and then she tucked it back into the kit and slid the whole thing into her purse. "The last name on Macy's list was the junior high teacher."

"Right. He taught at Truman over in Augusta, right? That's where Avery goes."

"Well. Maybe we'll get to see her."

Jan nodded and started to drive toward the highway. While she drove, Elaine looked down at her phone.

"Oh my goodness," Elaine said suddenly.

"What?" Jan's foot hovered over the brake, ready to stop suddenly.

"He's a *music* teacher."

"What?"

"I'm looking at the school's Web site right now, and it lists a page for the staff. Frank Conrad is listed as the band and orchestra teacher."

Jan's eyes lit up. "As in, someone who would be very familiar with classical music?"

"Exactly," Elaine said, her eyes wide. "And if he teaches orchestra, there's a good chance he's one of Avery's teachers."

"Let's go see what he has to say."

Jan pressed the accelerator down a bit, and a few minutes later, they pulled up in front of the middle school in a quiet residential neighborhood in Augusta. Jan knew it well, as Brian and his family lived here and Jan had only lived a couple miles away before she'd moved to Lancaster.

The building was a typical three-story brick affair, with athletic fields and a large yard behind. Jan had accompanied Paula and Avery when they'd done a tour of the school over summer, before Avery started as a sixth grader, and she'd been impressed by the facilities and by the caring staff. The school building was nearly a century old, but it had been carefully updated and remodeled in the last decade, and now boasted some of the best equipment and facilities in the area.

As they made their way across the parking lot toward the front door, Jan tried to figure out what they would say to the music teacher. They couldn't just go around demanding to know if people liked crossword puzzles. They sounded nuts.

As soon as they stepped inside the school building, Jan was hit with the scent of floor wax and hamburger meat, along with a hint of some cheap, too-sweet perfume. It smelled like every school Jan had ever been inside.

Jan had homeschooled her own children, but she loved the smell nonetheless—it smelled like learning. A few students were scurrying through the hallways, and even through the thick safety glass windows they could hear a low roar from a set of doors that Jan knew led to the cafeteria.

"We'll have to check in first," Jan said, directing Elaine toward the office's big double doors.

"Well, hello there, Jan Blake!" called out one of the secretaries behind the high counter, after she had unlocked the doors remotely. Sally Binney, who had lived next to Jan and Peter and their family for many years, stood to greet them. "And you're her cousin, Elaine, right? Are you doing all right over there in Lancaster? How are the plans going for that tearoom you were hoping to start up? Are you here to see Avery?"

"Hi, Sally." Jan smiled at the vivacious blonde. "Yes, I'm doing fine. The tearoom is a success and you should come on over to try it. But, no, we'd love to see Avery, but we're actually here to see if we might be able to talk to Frank Conrad."

"*Hmm.* Mr. Conrad has advanced band right now, and you can imagine how loud that gets. He can never hear me when I buzz through to his room. I'll tell you what. If you two can sign in right here on this clipboard, I'll let you zip over to peep in at Avery in the cafeteria—she has lunch right now. I'll check on Mr. Conrad and be right back."

"That was almost too easy," Elaine said as the two of them exited the office and headed to the doors to the cafeteria.

"It brings back memories, doesn't it?" Elaine said as Jan looked in, nodding at the scores of preteens sitting around tables, laughing, chatting, and eating.

Jan had to admit that she'd had some good times with her friends—and her cousin—around similar tables when she'd been younger. Junior high was a time when you really needed your friends, especially as an awkward young girl, and she could see that dynamic playing out in this room. Groups of girls were clumped together, all braces and sharp angles, while the boys were mostly on the far side of the room, talking and pretending not to notice the girls. The one exception was a long table in the corner that even Jan could tell held the popular crowd. This group was mixed genders, and the students sitting around that table all had the same wardrobe and a more relaxed manner about them. They were more confident, more certain about their place in the pecking order.

Wait a minute. Wasn't that...?

Jan narrowed her eyes and looked carefully. Yes, she was pretty sure that was Avery's best friend Alicia sitting there at the popular table. The two girls had grown up together, spending full weekends at one another's houses and imagining entire worlds together. Jan's computer was full of photos of the two of them dressed up for Halloween, for school concerts, all packed and ready to go to summer camp.

Only now, Alicia looked different. Her hair had been combed stick-straight, just like the hair of every other girl at that table, and she wore a tight-fitting top and had a slash of red lipstick across her mouth. She looked like a different, heavily made-up version of the Alicia Avery had played dolls with just last year. But if Alicia was at that table, where was Avery?

Jan scanned the table, looking for the familiar face of her sweet granddaughter, but she didn't see her.

"Oh, look. There's Avery," Elaine said, pointing to a table at the far side of the room. Jan looked to see where she was pointing and spotted her with a few other awkward-looking girls. One girl had a frizzy brown mane, and several of them had acne and braces; all of them had that ill-at-ease look of girls who hadn't grown into their bodies. Jan didn't recognize any of them, but she did recognize the uncomfortable way they held themselves. Still, the sight of her granddaughter made her heart swell.

"Hi, Avery!" Jan called, waving.

Her voice carried, but at first Avery didn't turn. Several dozen faces were now looking at her, trying to figure out who she was. But Jan only saw her granddaughter. "Hi, sweetie!" she called, waving.

"I don't know if...," Elaine began.

"Avery!"

Finally, Avery turned and saw her grandmother and Elaine in the doorway, and also saw half the school watching them. Avery's face froze, and then she started to sink down in her seat.

"Maybe we should go," Elaine said. Jan gave one last big wave, and then she followed Jan back toward the office.

"Well, it was nice to see her," Jan said, feeling much more cheerful than she had been when they had arrived.

Elaine nodded, but her lips were pursed. Oh dear. She wasn't happy about something. Well, Jan would find out what it was later. Right now, they were back at the school office, and she followed Elaine inside.

"Did you get to see Avery? She's such a sweetie. We really love having her." Sally beamed at them through her cat's-eye glasses.

"Thank you," Jan said, pride filling her. "We did see her. She's a wonderful girl, isn't she?"

"She is very sweet," Elaine said, nodding. "Did you find out if Frank Conrad is available?"

"I'm sorry, but his class is still in session and I can't disturb him," Sally told them. "But I'll be happy to take a message and ask him to contact you."

Jan was about to ask if they could wait until he was free when Elaine said, "That would be wonderful."

A few minutes later, they were heading back toward the house. Jan was ready for lunch, and though they both wanted to keep investigating, they agreed that they needed sustenance first.

But when they got back to the tearoom, they discovered that Rose had called in sick, and customers kept coming in. Archie had done an admirable job on his own, but Jan and Elaine jumped into their work.

Pearl Trexler came in with a woman she introduced as her old friend Ruth, visiting from Boston, and Jan led them to a table by the bay in the east parlor, with a nice view of Lake Chickadee Main Street.

"Have you been to Lancaster before?" Jan asked Ruth as the older woman settled into her chair. Her white hair was brushed into a neat bob.

"Oh yes, many times." The woman wore a tweed skirt suit and pearls, but she gave Jan a wicked smile. "I used to come up and see Pearl all the time. We used to get into all kinds of trouble when I'd come visit."

"Now, Ruth. I have a reputation to uphold, you know."

Ruth slid the napkin out from under the silverware and settled it onto her lap.

"Well. I'd best not tell the specifics then, I guess." She gave Jan an exaggerated wink.

Jan laughed. She'd liked Pearl before, but she liked her even more now. The Trexlers were very wealthy, but you would never know it, and it made her happy to think of Pearl having a few skeletons in the closet.

"We'll take two afternoon teas," Pearl said demurely.

"What type of tea would you like?" Jan asked.

"English Breakfast for me please," Pearl said.

"And I'd like something a little more adventurous. Maybe a Darjeeling?"

"Coming right up," Jan said. She passed Archie in the hallway as he was coming out of the kitchen.

"Oh, Jan, I'm glad I caught you," Archie said. He carried one of the delicate bone china teapots Jan and Elaine had collected before they opened the tearoom.

Archie's credentials had been impeccable for the job at the tearoom—born and bred in London, degrees from Oxford and Cambridge, experience living all over the world—but Jan wondered sometimes if perhaps it was really his posh accent that had won Elaine over when she hired him. It certainly had won her over. Talking with Archie sounded like talking with someone from one of those British dramas. "Macy Atherton would like to lodge a complaint about the Lapsang souchong."

Jan had seen Macy in the west parlor, seated with several of her friends. Archie was good at dealing with her, and Jan was glad he had taken her table today.

"What's wrong with it?" Jan asked. Lapsang souchong was a peaty, smoky blend of black tea from China. The flavor was intense and distinct, and it appealed to some tea drinkers and put off others. It wasn't Jan's favorite blend, but she appreciated the rich earthiness of it. You couldn't disguise it with milk and sugar.

"What was wrong with it?"

"She says it tastes like dirt."

Jan could see that Archie was barely holding back a smile.

"I promised I would pass along her feedback."

"Noted." Jan smiled. "For now, maybe it would be best to offer to give her another kind of tea."

He held up the teapot in his hands. "Earl Grey, on its way."

"Thank you, Archie."

Jan, Elaine, and Archie managed to keep things running, and before Jan knew it, the afternoon was half gone. They would need to wait until tomorrow to do any more sleuthing.

Jan tried to contain her frustration. They were hot on the trail! They needed to be out investigating.

But then she remembered that a full house of paying customers was exactly what she and Elaine had been praying for. So, with a reluctant heart, she thanked the Lord. The crossword puzzle mystery would be there tomorrow.

Still, that night, after they'd cleaned up from dinner, Jan and Elaine both sat in the sitting room trying their best to find answers. Following Elaine's earlier lead, Jan was searching through the puzzles on MakeYourPuzzle.com, but not getting any closer to finding Katelyn's crossword, and Elaine was working with the fingerprints they'd collected that day, trying to match them to the prints she'd collected from the puzzle itself. She was using tweezers to count whorls and lines or something. Jan wasn't sure what all she was doing, but from the way Elaine kept shaking her head, she could tell it wasn't getting her the results she was looking for. Jan's eyes were glazing over from staring at the computer screen. She adjusted her glasses, but it didn't help.

Finally, Jan gave up on the Web site. She'd have another look tomorrow. She closed the laptop lid and set it aside.

"Did you find anything useful in that book you bought?" Jan asked. The book about Queen Elizabeth I was on the low coffee table, and Elaine had explained that there was a section about coats of arms.

"I haven't had a chance to look yet," Elaine said, looking up from her paper.

"Would you mind if I took a peek?" Jan asked.

"Of course not. Have at it."

Jan reached over and picked up the book. It was a thick hardcover with creamy paper, and it was hefty. She flipped to the section about Queen Elizabeth's coat of arms and began to read.

Heraldry was an ancient practice, she read, though it really took off in the high Middle Ages, when coats of arms allowed differing armies to distinguish themselves. A coat of arms was typically made up of a central shield, as well as supporters on each side, an elaborate crown above it, and a motto written on a ribbon or scroll beneath it. She set the book down and went over to pick up the flue cover and studied it for a moment. Elaine looked up from her work but didn't say anything.

If they were right, and this flue cover depicted a coat of arms, it mostly focused on the shield in the center. The crude design was divided into four quadrants, with a shape made of a vertical line and a curved line in the upper right and lower left, and some unidentifiable shape in the other sections. It looked like a stick with clouds on it.

There were vague squiggles on the sides, and the suggestion of a ribbon at the bottom, but it was just a curved line, with no words carved into it.

She carried the flue cover back to the couch and sat down again, setting the cover down next to her before picking up the book again.

Each of the Tudor rulers had their own coat of arms, she read. Well, Henry VIII, who famously went through six wives in his quest for a male heir, actually used a couple variations throughout his reign, but each featured the same central blue and red shield and what looked like a red dragon on one side. His daughter Mary I, also known as Bloody Mary for her ceaseless and merciless execution of Protestants in her quest to make England a Catholic nation, used a variation that incorporated elements of the coat of arms of her husband, Philip II of Spain. Elizabeth I's coat of arms returned to the blue and red shield of her father, supported by a lion and a dragon, with an elaborate crown on top. Underneath was her motto: *Semper Eadem.* "Always the same."

It wasn't exactly an inspiring motto, she thought. It was probably the sort of message England needed after decades of turmoil in its rulers, but she tried to imagine a modern-day politician using that tag line in their campaign and laughed out loud at the thought.

"I'm glad to see the book is entertaining at least," Elaine said. "Anything useful?"

"I'm not sure," Jan said. "I'm more certain that this design on the flue cover is a coat of arms. And I'm pretty sure the coat of arms didn't belong to any of the Tudors."

"Well, that's good. It would be hard to figure out what Henry VIII had been doing in our house, considering he died a couple hundred years before it was built."

"Indeed." Jan looked back down at the flue cover. They knew what the design was not.

But what was it? How could they find out what their coat of arms meant?

"Do you think it's the coat of arms for the Gardners?" Jan asked.

"I don't know. Though that would make sense." The Gardners had owned this house for decades. If there was a coat of arms in this house, it made the most sense that it belonged to them. "But I don't have the slightest idea how to find that out."

"We'll just have to keep searching," Elaine said.

Jan couldn't do anything but nod. They would keep searching. They were on the right track, she was sure of it.

CHAPTER SEVEN

The next morning, as soon as Jan was done with the baking, the cousins set off again, headed this time to Penzance, the town on the far side of Chickadee Lake. They knew that River White was likely to be at his desk, and they hoped to catch him off guard and get a genuine reaction from him, since he seemed, in some ways, the most likely suspect they had.

As Elaine drove, she noticed that the trees along the lake had turned, and they reflected across the still water in stunning shades of orange and gold.

Soon they were approaching the outskirts of Penzance. The houses here were smaller and closer together, but the town was charming, with old stone fences and crumbling brick homes mixed in with newer clapboard and vinyl cottages. Elaine navigated to the small commercial strip that served as downtown Penzance. There were small shops and cafes housed in the brick storefronts, and at the far end of the picturesque block was the office of *The Penzance Courier*. Elaine smoothly parallel parked in front of the bakery next door.

The Penzance Courier's office had large plate glass windows etched with the paper's name, and inside was an open room with high ceilings and exposed brick. Desks were lined up along the walls, topped with sleek computers and high-tech phones. The space retained so much old-fashioned charm that Elaine loved to imagine what it must have been like back when these desks were topped with typewriters and manned by gentlemen in fedoras. Today, however, a young woman at the front desk looked up from her silver laptop computer as they stepped in.

"Hi there," she said, a bright smile crossing her face. She had strawberry-blonde hair pulled back into a ponytail and skin so pale it was almost translucent. She couldn't have been out of college yet, Elaine thought. "Classifieds?" She pushed a clipboard with a paper on it across the desk toward them.

"Excuse me?" Elaine said. She glanced at Jan, who looked bewildered.

"Are you here to place a classified ad?" the young woman asked again. "We've got a special going. Half price, and we'll throw in a cool tote bag for free." She pointed to a small canvas tote bag with the paper's logo on it.

"Oh. No." Elaine laughed. "We're actually here to talk to River White."

"Oh." The girl's shoulders fell and she took the clipboard back. "He's back there." She jerked her thumb toward the back of the office. "River's desk is at the rear. You can go on back."

"Thank you," Jan said and gave the girl an encouraging smile, and then followed Elaine down the aisle between the two sets of desks. A few people looked up from their computers, but most just continued typing or chatting on their phones. Elaine saw Candace Huang, a reporter they'd worked with in the past, but Candace was concentrating on some notes she was reading, so Elaine focused instead on finding River. There he was, at a desk in the far back corner. He was facing toward them but was wearing big headphones and was intent on something on his screen and didn't look up as they approached. A diploma from Cornell was displayed prominently on the wall behind his desk.

"Hi, River," Elaine said. He looked up and his eyes widened.

"Oh, wow. I didn't hear you coming," he said. He took off the headphones and set them gently on the keyboard in front of him. "Hi. What can I help you with?"

Elaine didn't think she was imagining the hesitation in his voice. They were both on good terms with River, but they'd had some, well, encounters with him in the process of investigating mysteries in the past. He was an aggressive reporter, sometimes crossing boundaries to get a good story. Was that why he wasn't totally pleased to see them, or was there more to it?

"First of all, we wanted to thank you for coming to the crossword event at Tea for Two this weekend. It was really great to see you there."

"Thanks for hosting." He ducked his head, nodding without really nodding.

"You edit the puzzles section here at the paper, is that right?" Jan asked. After skimming the headlines and reading the weekly food feature, Jan always turned to the puzzles section, which was nestled in with the comics.

"Among other things, yes. That's why I was so interested to meet Bill Markham," River said. "That's really the main reason I came, to network."

"And were you able to? To network?" Elaine asked, trying to ignore the note of derision she detected in his words.

River shrugged. "I gave him my card and followed up with an e-mail. We'll see if anything happens from there."

"Am I right in thinking that you buy puzzles from local puzzle makers as well as from the big names?" Jan asked. "I think I've noticed some local names when I do the puzzle section."

Of course they both knew that Katelyn Grande wrote puzzles for him, but they wanted to see how he responded.

"That's right. Of course, the puzzles I pick up on the wires are often stronger, but there are a few locals who do a good job." He shrugged. "Plus, you don't have to pay them as much."

Once again, Elaine tried to overlook what she'd just heard and asked innocently, "Then you must know Katelyn Grande."

"Yes, I've bought puzzles from her. She's one of the better ones around here." If the name meant anything beyond that to him, he hid it well.

"How well do you know her?"

He shrugged. "I've spoken with her on the phone a few times, but most of our correspondence is over e-mail. We're friendly, but our relationship is professional." His eyes narrowed. "Why?"

"She's pretty, isn't she?" Jan asked. River's brow furrowed. Elaine looked at her cousin, torn between shaking her head is dismay and laughing out loud. She would need to work with Jan on subtlety.

He hesitated. "I guess. I haven't really noticed."

Elaine wasn't sure she believed that. In her experience, men always noticed pretty girls, whether they admitted it or not.

He cleared his throat. "Again, our relationship is purely professional." The tone of his voice made it clear he was done with that topic of conversation.

Elaine thought fast, searching for some way to change the direction of this conversation, stat.

"What are you working on?" she asked, trying to sound as innocent as possible. She leaned in and tried to get a good look at his screen. And—wait a minute. Was that…?

"Um…" He looked up at her, seemingly confused. "A story about a car crash over on Route 105 outside Augusta," he said. "Why?"

"Oh, I'm just fascinated by the world of journalism," Elaine said quickly. She risked another long glance at his screen and then, certain she'd seen it correctly, pulled back.

"Oh. Well, it is an interesting career," River said, though his reservations were still apparent on his face.

"In fact, I'd love to chat with you about it more some time," Elaine said. "Do you happen to have a card I could take with me?"

He watched her for a moment. Obviously they knew how to contact him, and he knew that. But that wasn't the point. Finally, he slowly reached into his desk and pulled out a business card. She tried to not be offended that he didn't seem certain he wanted her to contact him. She wasn't really planning on calling him anyway. She took it by the edges, careful not to touch the front or back.

"Well, thanks so much for your time," Elaine said, and she gave a small wave and started back toward the front of the office.

"We really appreciate it," Jan added.

Elaine glanced back and saw that River appeared to be thoroughly confused by the interaction. She was sorry about that, but from her perspective, the visit had been successful.

As soon as they were back in the car, Elaine turned to Jan. "He was listening to Vivaldi."

"What?" Jan buckled her seat belt and pulled the door closed. In the cold, a small puff of steam came from her mouth with the words. Elaine turned on the engine, and within seconds, warm air was shooting out of the vents.

"When I asked what he was working on, I looked at his screen, and I saw his iTunes window was up. You know how it displays the name and cover of what you're listening to?"

Jan nodded uncertainly.

"He was listening to *Vivaldi*!" Elaine felt triumphant. "And what was a clue in Katelyn's puzzle?"

"*Four Seasons* was," Jan admitted. "But I'm not sure..."

"It has to be him! He knows Katelyn, he knows puzzles, he knows *she* knows puzzles, he was there at the event, *and* he listens to Vivaldi, which just so happens to show up in the crossword puzzle he gave Katelyn. Maybe he's our guy."

"I don't think..."

"Now we just need to figure out a way to prove it," Elaine said, talking right over her cousin. "I suppose once I prove that his fingerprint was on the puzzle, it will be easy, but..."

"Elaine. I don't think he made the puzzle."

"What?" Elaine turned her head, hearing her cousin for the first time. "What do you mean?"

"I don't think River is secretly in love with Katelyn."

"Why not?" They were still sitting at the curb in front of the bakery, and a woman walked out trailed by a toddler, balancing a pink cake box in her arms.

"There was a picture of him and a girl at Bass Harbor Head Light on his desk," Jan said. She'd immediately recognized the iconic lighthouse perched on the rocky coast. Located within Acadia National Park, it was a perennial favorite among tourists, and a romantic spot for picnicking and hiking.

"Maybe it was his sister," Elaine said.

"I don't think so. For one thing, she was Asian, so that's unlikely. But more importantly, if the way he was looking at the girl in the photo is the way he looks at his sister, there's something wrong in that family."

"Huh." Elaine thought about that for a moment. That certainly took the wind out of her sails. "Well, maybe that's why he needed to be so secretive. He has a girlfriend, so he wanted to let Katelyn know about his interest in a roundabout way. See if she's interested before he breaks up with his girlfriend."

"Charming."

"But possible."

Jan shrugged, refusing to acknowledge that. Elaine knew she didn't like to say bad things about other people.

"Or maybe, like we considered before, the puzzle isn't meant to be about love anyway. Maybe it's something else altogether."

"Like what?"

"I'm not sure yet," Elaine said.

"I guess we can't say for sure whether it was River based on what we learned today. But we can't discount him either," Elaine said.

"I think that's a fair assessment. We'll just have to see whether his fingerprints are on the paper."

Elaine nodded, and she put the car in gear, checked her mirrors, and pulled out on to First Street.

CHAPTER EIGHT

The cousins were just finishing up lunch back at the house when Jan's cell phone rang. She dug it out of her purse and looked at the screen.

"Bill Markham!" she mouthed to Elaine as she pressed the button to answer the call.

Elaine gave her a thumbs-up sign, and froze in the middle of loading their plates into the dishwasher.

"Hello, Bill," Jan said.

"Jan. I'm so sorry it has taken me this long to get back to you."

"That's all right," Jan said. "We heard there was an emergency at work and you had to rush back to Boston."

"Yes, it was really quite awful. One of my colleagues had a stroke."

"Goodness."

"Yes, it was scary. He's resting in the hospital now and the doctors are hopeful he'll recover fully. But I had to rush back and finish up the puzzles for the week since he wasn't going to be able to do it."

"I hope it went all right."

"Yes, thank you. I made it back just fine, and I was happy to take over for him while he's recovering. As long as he's okay, that's all that matters. In the meantime, though, I'm really sorry to have missed dinner with Bob, and I'm also sorry that I didn't get the chance to thank you properly for hosting the event. I always enjoy meeting fellow puzzle enthusiasts."

"Thank you so much for coming." Jan tried to focus on what she needed to ask, and not get caught up in the fact that she was once again talking to the biggest star in the crossword puzzle world. "The thing is, something strange happened at the event, and I wondered if I could ask you about it."

"Oh?"

Jan could hear him typing on a keyboard.

"When you passed out puzzles at the end of the talk, the first one went to a girl named Katelyn Grande. When she started solving the puzzle, though, she discovered that the puzzle seemed to have been made just for her."

"How so?"

"It had both her first and last name in it, for one thing," Jan said. "As well as the name of where she works and her hair color and where she went to college."

"Whoa. That is very strange."

"And I wondered if you might have any idea how that happened."

"No. None at all. None of the puzzles I brought had any of those words in them."

"It didn't seem like a puzzle that had been made by a professional. In fact, it seems to have been made on a site called MakeYourPuzzle.com."

"Oh yes, that's a popular site. But you're right, if it was made there, there's not much chance a professional had anything to do with it. We use much more advanced software at the paper. But I can tell you for certain that I didn't have anything to do with making that puzzle. I am flabbergasted, truth be told. You're sure she was given the puzzle from the pile I passed out?"

"Yes," Jan said, though a flash of doubt crossed her mind. She supposed she didn't have proof that that was where the puzzle had come from. All they had was Katelyn's word. Was there any chance she had...?

But why would Katelyn make something like this up? What could she possibly have to gain from sending Jan and Elaine on a wild goose chase to find the maker of a puzzle she'd created herself? Jan shook her head. It didn't make sense. "I'm positive that's where it came from."

But still, now that it had been introduced, a flicker of doubt remained.

"Oh my, I have no idea. Let's see. I put the stack of puzzles down on the sideboard when I was unpacking before the guests started arriving."

Jan nodded. The sideboard was by the door to the east parlor, while Bill stood by the fireplace when he gave his talk.

"I didn't really pay much attention to them after I put them down," Bill said. "I suppose that someone could have slipped a puzzle onto the stack at any point after that, and I wouldn't have noticed."

"You didn't see anybody put anything there?"

"I'm afraid not," he said. "And I can promise you that I had nothing to do with Katelyn's crossword at all. Though I have to admit, I'm intrigued. What a fun mystery."

"Yes, it is interesting," Jan said. "We're trying to figure out where it came from and how it got there."

"I'm sure you'll figure it out, though I'm sorry I've been no help."

"Thank you for calling me back." She was getting ready to hang up when she saw Elaine making strange hand motions on the other side of the kitchen. "What?" Jan mouthed at her cousin.

Elaine put her hands together like a book. "Notebook," she whispered.

"Oh, that's right, I have one more question," Jan said. "Macy Atherton said you left a notebook behind. I hope that wasn't important."

"Thankfully, no. I always carry a notebook around with me so I can jot down ideas wherever they hit," Bill said. "In my rush to get out, I neglected to pack it. But thankfully, Macy is sending it back to me."

"Oh well, that's good." Jan thought quickly. She couldn't think of a way to ask about what was inside his notebook without sounding like a terrible snoop. How could she ask this?

"Well, if there's anything I can do to help you solve this one, I want to, so please let me know," Bill said. She realized the conversation was over.

Unsure of what else to do, Jan promised she would, thanked him, and hung up.

"So? Nothing?" Elaine asked. She set the remaining dishes into the dishwasher and closed the door.

Jan shook her head. "I don't think he knows anything."

Elaine sighed. "It does mean that we can cross him off our list, I suppose."

"Hey, that's not nothing." Jan set her phone down on the counter.

"But it's not really something either."

CHAPTER NINE

Later that afternoon, Jan went upstairs to spend some more time looking through the puzzles on MakeYourPuzzle.com, hoping to come across anything that might point to the identity of the creator, while Elaine stayed downstairs to work in her office. She was going through a pile of receipts when she heard a knock at the office door.

"Come in," she called.

The door cracked open, and Avery stood in the doorway, her cello strapped to her back in a black nylon case. "Mom dropped me off so I could practice here. Is that okay?"

"Of course." Elaine stood and set down the receipts. "I'm glad you're here. Come on. Let's get you set up. I was thinking maybe in the dining room?"

"Okay." Avery hiked the cello up on her shoulder. "That sounds good."

Elaine led her into the dining room and closed the doors that led to the hallway and to the west parlor, where a handful of guests were enjoying afternoon tea. She checked to make sure that everything looked all right. Rue Maxwell was here with a woman who had to be her sister. Delicate china teapots sat in front of them, and Archie was chatting with them, clearly charming them both. Archie was such an asset to the tearoom. He caught Elaine peeking in and winked without missing a beat in the conversation.

Elaine turned back to the dining room. "Maybe you could sit here," Elaine said, pulling out one of the heavy padded dining chairs. "And you could use this as a music stand?" She pointed at the chair rail that ran along the wall. Avery nodded and sat down and started unzipping the nylon case.

"Why were you guys at my school?" Avery asked as she pulled out a bow and set it on the dining table.

"We were hoping to speak with one of the teachers," Elaine said. Which reminded her—they needed to follow up with Frank Conrad. He hadn't yet contacted them.

"In the cafeteria?" Avery screwed up her face.

"Yeah. Sorry about that," Elaine said. "We didn't mean to embarrass you. Your grandma just got really excited when she saw you. I hope we didn't cause any problems for you."

Elaine remembered how middle school could be. It was dog-eat-dog back when she'd gone, and couldn't imagine it had gotten any easier. One wrong move could get you branded for life.

"Only from the kids who hate me anyway." She mumbled this under her breath, and at first Elaine wasn't sure she'd heard right, but she ran the words back through her mind.

"The kids who hate you? Who could possibly hate you?"

Avery just shook her head and pulled the cello out of the case.

"Are there kids who are giving you a hard time?" Elaine asked.

"Never mind," Avery said. "I need to practice."

Elaine hesitated. Avery seemed like she didn't want to talk. But was that just an act? Elaine knew that kids this age could be tricky. Sometimes what sounded like an offhand comment could actually be a cry for help.

"I will leave you alone if you want me to," Elaine said. She hovered just inside the doorway, uncertain of what exactly she was trying to say. "But if there's anything you want to talk about, I'm happy to do that as well."

Avery set the music along the chair rail, carefully resting it against the wall.

Elaine waited a moment longer, but Avery didn't even look at her. Laughter and quiet conversation from the west parlor filled the silence. Finally, Elaine turned to go.

"Did you ever have a friend turn on you?" Avery asked quietly.

Elaine turned back and regarded Avery. She was looking down at her cello, running her fingers along the strings. Her blonde hair fell in her face.

"I have," Elaine answered, and slowly lowered herself down into one of the chairs. "And it hurts."

Avery nodded, still keeping her eyes on her instrument.

"Did something happen with one of your friends?" Elaine asked.

Avery didn't say anything for a moment, then nodded again. "Alicia was my best friend up until this year. We did everything together. And then, ever since we got to middle school, it's like she hates me. She started hanging out with the popular crowd, dressing differently, and talking differently, and she doesn't want to hang out with me anymore."

Elaine could hear the pain cloaked in those words. She knew that it wasn't uncommon for friends to grow apart as they got older—and there were so many changes and pressures in the middle school years—but that didn't make it any easier. Starting junior high was hard enough; losing your best friend in the process would be excruciating.

"I'm sorry," was all she could think to say.

"And I don't know why. I mean, the kids she hangs out with now are always getting in trouble and don't seem to care about anyone but themselves. And Alicia's not like that." Avery sighed. "At least, she wasn't. Now I guess she is."

"And you feel left out."

"Yeah. But also now whenever she sees me, she makes little comments, like about how dumb my hair looks or how bad my clothes are. She only does it when Bella is around, so I know she's just doing it to impress her new friend, but it still stinks."

"Oh, honey, I'm so sorry."

"I don't want to hang out with the kids she hangs out with, but..."

"But you don't like losing your best friend. That's only natural." Elaine ran her fingers along the smooth top of the antique cherry table. Frankly, if this Alicia was that easily swayed to turn on her old friend, Elaine didn't think she was good enough for Avery anyway. But she knew that was not what Avery wanted to hear right now. "You have made other friends, right? You were sitting with some girls who looked nice when we saw you yesterday."

"Yeah." Avery blew out and her bangs flew up. "They're nice enough."

"But it still hurts when you lose a friend," Elaine said. "I know. It's happened to me too. When we were stationed in Hawaii, we lived on base and I got to know one of the other wives pretty well. Our kids played together, we had barbecues together, and it was such a comfort to have a friend so close. And then, just like that, she was gone. A new family had moved to post, and suddenly I saw her all over with this other woman, who was younger and I guess more fun than I was. I didn't know why what happened, and I still don't to this day. It was just like I'd been replaced by a better model."

Avery laughed, a sad, bitter laugh. "I feel like that too. Like I'm just not cool enough, so she found better friends that fit her new image better."

"Alicia 2.0."

"Huh?"

"Oh. Do people not say that anymore?"

"I don't think they ever said that."

"Yes, they did—2.0 was a thing!"

"Well, it's not a thing anymore. What does that even mean?"

"It's a computer thing! Like, a better version of software or something. An update. I think. Oh, I don't know."

By this time, both of them were laughing, which Elaine saw as progress.

"Anyway, that's why I have to practice really hard," Avery said. Elaine was glad she still had a tinge of laughter in her voice.

"To take your mind off Alicia?" Elaine asked, nodding.

"No. To beat Bella. She's first chair right now, and I really want to take it from her."

"Oh." Suddenly Avery's intense dedication to her instrument seemed less noble. But, she had to admit, a tiny bit more understandable. "I see."

"Now you think I'm a horrible person," Avery said, her eyes downcast again.

"On the contrary," Elaine said, "I think you are a very human person." She reached out and brushed a hair away from Avery's face. "And there are certainly worse ways to try to best your old friend than by playing the cello well."

"But?" Avery looked up expectantly. "I can tell you want to say more."

Elaine smiled. Her face often did give her away. "But I guess I wonder if that will get you what you really want."

"What do you mean? Can you think of a better way to show her I'm fine without her?"

"Possibly," Elaine said. "But I don't think that's what you really want."

"Yes it is."

"I think what you really want is to be on good terms with both Alicia and Bella."

"I don't want to be in with the popular girls, if that's what you're trying to get at. I don't need..."

"I know that. That's not what I'm saying," Elaine said gently. "But I do think that you want both Alicia and Bella to see that you're not what they think you are. To be on friendly terms with them. Not that you want to hang out with them at lunch every day, but to be able to say hello and not be laughed at."

Avery thought for a moment and then slowly she nodded.

"But how am I supposed to do that?"

"I don't know. Maybe start by praying about it."

Avery nodded but didn't say anything.

"And then, maybe try just being nice to her."

Again she didn't answer.

"I'll be praying for you."

"Thanks, Elaine." Avery reached for the bow on the table and gave Elaine a shy smile.

Elaine pushed herself up out of the chair. "Any time. You just let me know if you need anything."

"I will."

With that Elaine stepped out into the hallway and closed the door to the dining room to give Avery privacy, and she headed back to the office. She had just settled down at her desk and picked up the stack of receipts when she heard the first notes sound. They were...

She cringed. She didn't think that was the note Avery had meant to play.

Avery started over, playing each deep note carefully. They resonated all through the first floor. And then...

Elaine cringed as she hit a sour note.

Avery dutifully started the piece over. She wasn't bad—not at all. It was just that she was evidently learning this piece, and it was tough. The cello was a beautiful, moody instrument, and when played in skilled hands could bring tears to grown men's eyes. And, well, Avery was not quite there yet.

Elaine tried to ignore the music and focus on her receipts. She had just finished entering them into her spreadsheet when Jan appeared in the door of her office.

"What is that noise?" she asked.

"That's Avery, practicing her cello."

"Oh dear."

"She's doing all right."

"She's trying her best, I know that. It's just… it's not quiet, is it?"

"No, it's not." Elaine laughed.

"I think the guests in the tearoom might be finding it hard to hold a conversation right now."

Elaine nodded. What had she been thinking? "I know," she said. "But I hate to disturb her. She just got settled."

"Maybe we could move her up to our sitting room?"

Just then, Rose appeared in the doorway. "I'm sorry to disturb you both, but Macy Atherton just arrived with some of her friends, and she's asking for someone to, as she says, 'put that cat out of its misery.'"

"All right. We'll move her upstairs," Elaine said, standing. "Please tell Macy we're working on it."

Rose nodded and turned back down the hallway.

"I love that you told her she could practice here," Jan said, shaking her head. "But I'm not sure we should have her do it during business hours."

Elaine nodded, realizing her mistake. "Let's just be thankful she doesn't play the drums."

Jan laughed, and together they went to talk to Avery.

CHAPTER TEN

Wednesday morning, just as they were finishing up the breakfast dishes, Jan's phone rang.

"Hello?" Jan said, after she'd dug it out of her purse.

"Jan? It's Katelyn."

"Hello, Katelyn." Jan turned and looked at Elaine.

"I was coming out to my car to go to work, and I found the weirdest thing. There's another crossword puzzle here in the front seat, along with a bouquet of flowers."

"What?" Jan couldn't help saying. Elaine looked as if she was dying to hear the other half of the conversation.

"They're just sitting there on the front seat. Somebody must have left them sometime in the night."

Jan looked at Elaine, who had overheard enough that she was already pulling on her coat.

"Hang on," Jan said. "We'll be right there."

A few minutes later, they pulled up in front of the address Katelyn had given them. It was a ranch-style house with a mobility ramp leading up to the front door. In addition to a garage, there was a carport at the side of the house, sheltering a two-door Ford Focus.

As they pulled up into the driveway, Katelyn pushed open the screen and came out the front door.

"Thank you for coming," she said, stepping on to the small cement porch.

"Are you kidding? Of course we came," Elaine said, rubbing her hands together. "So let's see this puzzle."

Katelyn led them over to carport and toward the driver-side door.

"Don't touch it," Elaine said, gesturing toward the handle. Jan knew that Elaine had been up late examining the fingerprints she'd collected the past few days, but so far she hadn't found any clear matches. The prints from River White's business card hadn't been complete enough to tell if they made a good match with the ones from the puzzle, and she hadn't had much luck matching the others. Jan was beginning to doubt the merits of collecting these prints, but Elaine was still hopeful they would lead them to the puzzle maker.

Katelyn pulled her hand back. "I touched the handle this morning before I saw the flowers."

"Hopefully that didn't obscure any prints the puzzle maker left behind." Elaine nodded and set her purse down on the hood of the car and dug her fingerprint kit out of it. While she was dusting the door handle for prints, Jan peered inside the car.

There, on the driver's seat, was a crossword puzzle that looked just like the first one, partially covered by a bunch of lilies wrapped in plastic.

"They were just sitting there?" Jan asked.

Katelyn nodded. "I was heading out for work, and just as I started to open the door, I saw them, sitting right there." She looked at Elaine. "I didn't touch them. I called you first."

"Thank you." When Elaine was finished dusting the handle for prints, she opened the car door and Katelyn pulled blue latex gloves out of her pocket, slid them on, and then reached inside and carefully picked up the paper with one hand and the bunch of flowers with the other.

"Let's bring them inside to examine them," Jan said. It wasn't unusual for nights to be cold this time of year, but the chilly air this morning was a sure sign that fall was on the way.

"Good call," Katelyn said, and they all moved toward the front door and then inside the house.

"Can I take your jackets?" She set the crossword and flowers down on the counter and reached for the light coats they gladly held out for her. While Katelyn was hanging them up on hooks by the door, Jan looked around. It was a modest, comfortable house, with worn hardwood floors and furniture that had seen better days. The kitchen was new, however, and had clearly been modified with low counters so someone in a wheelchair could access them. The hallways were also wide— again, Jan thought, to accommodate a wheelchair.

"Can I get you something to drink? Coffee? Tea?"

"Some tea would be lovely," Jan said, and Elaine nodded. They'd already had a cup each this morning, but she rarely turned down tea.

Elaine was huddled over the counter and had already started dusting the puzzle for prints. Jan noted that there was the same small line of text at the bottom of the paper. She couldn't read it from here, but she was sure it must reference MakeYourPuzzle.com again. When Katelyn returned, Jan asked, "Your car was parked in the carport all night?"

Katelyn nodded. "Dad's van is parked in the garage, and he needs the other side of the garage clear so he can get his wheelchair inside, so I always park out here."

"It must be miserable in winter," Elaine said, looking up from the paper. Jan agreed. Most people around these parts parked in a garage if they could. When the air was in negative temperatures and snow and ice were piled up, getting cars to even turn over the ignition outdoors could be tricky.

"It's not ideal, but not a lot about our situation is," Katelyn said with a shrug. She reached for the teakettle and pulled off the lid. "Dad needs the garage, so I just go out and turn the car on ten minutes before I want to leave. It usually takes at least that long to shovel the driveway anyway."

"I'm sorry," Jan said. "It must have been hard for you since your dad's accident."

"It's okay. This very definitely wasn't in my ten-year plan, but it's not a bad life." She moved to the sink, and then she held the kettle under the faucet and filled it.

"You were living in Boston before the accident, right?" Jan asked.

Katelyn put the lid back on the kettle and set it on to the stovetop on the low counter.

"Yep. I had a job in marketing, a great apartment, and a man I thought I was going to marry. I thought my life was set."

"It must have been hard to give that all up," Jan said gently. She'd had to give up her dream once too. She sometimes still wondered what her life would have been like if she'd been able to afford to stay in college.

"Yeah." Katelyn opened a cabinet door and pulled down a basket of assorted tea bags. "I'll be honest. It was. I tried to figure out ways to not have to come home. Could I hire a nurse to care for Dad? Could he live on his own? But in the end, it just became clear that he needed me. How could I say no after all he's done for me?" She set the basket on the counter. "Help yourself," she said.

"Do you like it now that you've settled in?"

"I like working at the bookstore. And I like writing cross-word puzzles." She shrugged. "There's not much of a singles scene around here though."

"And that's precisely why we need to find your secret admirer," Jan said.

Katelyn's cheeks turned a little pink, and she tried to stifle a smile. "Do you think this puzzle is from the same person, then?"

"I think it seems likely. But we won't know for sure until we start to solve it." Jan looked over the selection of teas and chose a rooibos. She unwrapped the tea bag.

"Or when we match the fingerprints," Elaine said.

"How's that coming?"

"Just about done." She had covered most of the edge of the paper in black powder and had coated the plastic wrapper on the flowers as well. "I'm not finding much on the paper. I got some partials on the plastic, but they were mostly obscured. Whoever left these must have been wearing gloves."

"That's possible. It was chilly last night," Jan said.

"Speaking of which, tell us more about this situation. Was your car parked outside all night?" Elaine asked. She set the brush down and shook her head.

"Ever since I got home from running from errands about six o'clock," Katelyn said. She pulled three mugs down from a cabinet and set them on the counter. "I parked in the carport and came inside and made dinner. I didn't go back out until this morning." She saw that Elaine was finished dusting and indicated the bouquet. "Can I put these in some water now?"

Elaine looked surprised for a moment, and then nodded. "Right. Of course." She watched as Katelyn scooped up the flowers, leaned over, and took a long sniff. They were stargazer lilies, a perfect blushing peach color, and very fragrant. A shy smile filled her face, and she pulled down a vase and filled it with water, then set the flowers inside. Jan glanced at Elaine. Her brow was crinkled, and her eyes were narrowed just the teensiest bit.

"So the flowers and the puzzle could have been left any time between six o'clock last night and a half hour ago?" Elaine asked, bringing them back to the topic at hand.

"I guess so."

"You didn't hear anything?" Elaine asked, starting to pack up her kit.

"No. I didn't, and neither did Dad," she said. "He's back in the den, and I asked him before you got here. He didn't hear a thing."

"And your car was unlocked?"

Katelyn nodded. "I never lock it."

Jan didn't lock her car either. Few people around here did.

"We should probably ask to see if your neighbors saw anyone," Elaine said, more to Jan than to Katelyn. Jan realized she was probably right, but personally she couldn't wait to get going trying to solve the crossword puzzle.

"Yes, we should, but I'm hopeful that when we fill in the crossword, it will be clear who left them," she said.

The kettle whistled, and Katelyn turned the stove off and poured hot water into the mugs.

"Let's hope so," Elaine said. She hesitated for just a second too long.

"What?" Jan asked. "What is it?"

"I don't know." Elaine hesitated again, which was how Jan became sure Elaine was thinking something she didn't want to say.

"What are you thinking, Elaine?"

Elaine looked from Jan to Katelyn, lovingly arranging the stems in the glass vase, and back at Jan.

"Doesn't it seem a bit...invasive? I mean, it's one thing to slip you a crossword at a party, but to go into your car and leave it?" She shrugged. "That's your personal space. And someone obviously knows where you live. Isn't that...a little creepy?"

"I guess, but I thought it was sweet," Katelyn said. "Sure, maybe it's a little odd that they opened my car door, but it's not like it was my bedroom door or something. And whoever it is knows that I love crosswords, and flowers..."

"Well, most people love flowers," Elaine said.

"True. But I've gotten really into gardening the past few summers. You can't see it now, but in the summer,

the yard is blooming with all kinds of flowers." She indicated the backyard, visible beyond the sliding glass doors.
It was brown and dead right now, but Jan could see that
it had been carefully tended. "Whoever it was could have
known that."

"Yeah...though, if they knew your backyard had flowers in
it, that's actually helping my case for this being invasive."

"Stargazers are my favorite flower," Katelyn said, leaning in
for another sniff. She set the vase of flowers on the table, gazed
at them for a moment, and then reached into a kitchen drawer
and pulled out a few ballpoint pens. "Do you want to help me
get started on this puzzle?" She looked at each of them in turn,
holding out the pens.

"Do you have time right now?" Elaine asked. "Weren't you
on your way to work?"

"I called Bristol, and she said it's no problem and to take
my time. It's usually quiet this time of day anyway."

Jan looked at Elaine, who shrugged. "We don't need to
rush back. I'd love to help."

Elaine clutched her mug of tea. "I think I'll skip the puzzle-
solving," she said. "You said your dad was here. Would it
be possible for me to talk to him?"

That sounded like a great idea to Jan. It would keep Elaine
from getting bored while they worked on the puzzle, and
maybe she'd be able to glean more about any men who might
have expressed an interest in Katelyn.

"Oh, sure," Katelyn set the pens down on the counter. "Let
me introduce you." Elaine turned and followed Katelyn down
the hall. Good. Elaine was great at reading people, and she

would no doubt be able to find out more from him than Jan would. And in the meantime, she would dive into...

But just then, her eye caught on something on the plastic wrapper from the flowers, which was still sitting out on the counter. Well, that was interesting. She leaned in and took another look. How had she missed this?

CHAPTER ELEVEN

Elaine followed Katelyn out of the kitchen, past the living room, and down the hallway. Photos of Katelyn as a girl hung on the walls, and Elaine smiled at the big toothy grin and the oversized round glasses.

"This is my room." Katelyn indicated a bedroom on the left side of the hallway. Elaine stopped in the doorway and looked in. It had been painted a soft robin's-egg blue and had a wooden platform bed, a duvet cover with a contemporary blue-and-white pattern, and a midcentury modern desk with matching bookshelves. A sleek silver laptop sat on the desk.

"This is the room you grew up in?" Elaine asked.

Katelyn nodded. "But I redid it when I moved back home. I had bought some grown-up furniture by then, and I decided that even if I had to move back home, I wasn't going to live like a little kid anymore."

"That's wise." Elaine scanned the bookshelves and saw quite a collection, from Dante and Chaucer to Steinbeck and Hemingway to Plath and Eliot. There was also a sizeable shelf stuffed with contemporary fiction, as well as—she squinted. Could she be seeing that right?

"I like romances." Katelyn saw where Elaine was looking and smiled. "It's my guilty pleasure."

There, on the bottom shelf, was a row of paperback historical and Amish Christian romances.

"Dad spends most of his time in the den these days," Katelyn said as she started walking again. Elaine followed just a step behind, mulling this over. She couldn't help but wonder if Katelyn's enjoyment of romances might have a little something to do with how excited she seemed to be about the idea of a secret admirer. Was she so ready to find her own happily ever after that she was ready to believe anything?

She shook her head. Of course the girl was excited about the messages, and the flowers. What girl—romance reader or not—wouldn't be a bit thrilled that a man had taken notice of her?

"Dad?" Katelyn knocked on the door frame of a room at the end of the hall. Elaine saw that he was a large man with broad shoulders. He was probably just a few years older than she was, with graying brown hair and a wide forehead. She could see Katelyn in his high cheekbones and bright-blue eyes. A plaid wool throw covered his legs. "This is Elaine. She runs the tearoom with Jan Blake. She's one of the people helping me with the puzzles."

"Oh. Hello there," he said, picking up the remote control that sat on the arm of his recliner. He pointed it at the screen and the TV at the far side of the room went silent. "I'm Ken. Excuse me for not getting up," he said with a wry smile.

"Elaine," she said, stepping into the room. It was a small room, and though the blinds were open, it was dim in the morning light. At one end of the room was a wooden entertainment center, and a small side table with a brass lamp sat between the two chairs. The walls were covered with posters of the New England Patriots. Elaine noticed that next to his recliner was a folded wheelchair. "And that's quite all right."

"Please have a seat." He gestured toward the matching brown leather recliner next to his own. The TV was tuned to some news program with several blonde women sitting on a couch, and there were a lot of flashing graphics.

"Thank you," Elaine said, stepping in.

"I'm going to go back out and work on that puzzle," Katelyn said, gesturing toward the kitchen. "Dad, do you need anything?"

"I'm all right. Thank you."

Katelyn waited just a moment longer to make sure, and then she turned and headed back down the hallway.

"So," Ken said, turning toward Elaine, "you bought that old Gardner house on the water?"

"I did, along with my cousin Jan," Elaine said. "And we turned it into a tearoom."

"That's great," he said. "Tea's not really my thing, but it's good for the town to have things like that."

"We like it," Elaine said, nodding at the posters on the walls. "You're a Pats fan?"

"Diehard." He nodded. "You a football fan?"

"I'm afraid not."

"There's no accounting for taste," he said, a smile on his face. "Katelyn says you've been helping her with these crosswords?"

"We are. She called us this morning after she found the one in her car."

He grunted and bobbed his head.

"We're trying to narrow down the window when it could have been left. Did you hear anything out of the ordinary last night or this morning?"

"Nope. I didn't hear a thing."

"Have you seen anything unusual around here in the past few days? Any people you don't recognize hanging around? Or unusual phone calls?"

He laughed. "What is this, a murder investigation? Why would someone be hanging around the neighborhood scoping it out if they only wanted to leave a crossword puzzle in a car?"

Elaine laughed. "Good point. I suppose you're right."

He grunted again. "That said, I guess I have seen someone poking around next door. I don't see how it could be related to the crosswords though."

"Really?" Elaine looked toward the window. "Which house?"

He pointed toward the window. "The white one next door. It's a summer place, and the people don't come up much during the rest of the year. But this man was over there in the yard looking at something on the ground yesterday, and I saw him there once last week."

From here Elaine could see the house he was talking about. It was a small cottage, covered in white clapboard, with a cheerful red door. The lawn was brown and the flowers dead, but the bushes were cut back and Elaine could tell it was cared for even when the owners weren't there. A lot of people who owned second homes around these parts hired gardeners or real estate–management companies to manage their properties when they weren't around. Could this man Ken saw have been one of these?

"What did the man look like?" Elaine asked.

He blew out a breath. "Hard to say. He was wearing a big heavy black jacket and a black hat. I couldn't really see much more than that."

"And where exactly did you see him?"

"He was crouched down by the corner of the house, right there at the back. I almost called the cops, but he left."

Elaine nodded. She didn't know if it would be relevant, as he'd already pointed out, but it was worth investigating. If a strange man hanging around the empty neighbor's house had any connection to the crossword, that might point to the idea that the puzzles weren't as innocuous as they seemed.

She looked back at Katelyn's father. He looked like he wanted to say something. She waited, but he didn't open his mouth.

"What do you think about the crossword puzzles Katelyn has gotten?" Elaine asked, hoping to draw him out.

He sighed, his eyes focused on the silent TV screen in front of him. Then he looked away and turned to Elaine.

"Katelyn is a good girl," he finally said. Elaine nodded and waited for him to go on. "I know it's been hard for her, with her mom, and then having to move back here for me. It's..." He took a deep breath. "She is so smart. So clever. She never really fit in around here, you know? Even as a kid, she was reading all the time, and she would say these things that would just blow me away. It was like everything she read she remembered. And you could tell she knew it. This town was too small for her. She couldn't wait to get out of here and be around people more like her."

"She went to Tufts, right?"

"On scholarship," he said, and the pride in his eyes was completely endearing. This man, however gruff he came across, was incredibly proud of his daughter. "And then she got this big job in Boston, and we all thought, *Okay, now she's got what she always wanted.* And then—just like that. One skid on the ice, and both of our lives were changed forever. I know she didn't want to move back home, but she did it for me. And that bozo fiancé left her. Well, she's better off without him, honestly, but it was still hard to see how sad she was for so long about him. I'll never forget what kind of sacrifice she made for me. So all I want for her is to find some happiness."

"But...?" Elaine could sense there was a qualification coming.

"But I find it hard to believe that a man is declaring his love to her through crossword puzzles."

Elaine felt a smile creep across her face.

"And even if by some miracle these puzzles are from a secret admirer, it's hard to imagine that I'll like him. In my day, if a man was interested in a woman, he worked up his courage and he asked her out on a date. He picked her up at her house and talked to her parents. He didn't send cryptic messages through some kind of game."

Elaine again felt herself smiling, agreeing with his words. Even if these puzzles did come from a man who was interested in Katelyn, was it the kind of man who would be right for her?

"And here she is, getting all moony and swanning around, thinking some man is in love with her. Yesterday at dinner she told me it's like something from one of those romantic comedies she loves to watch. You know what I told her? I said, 'Katie, those movies *aren't real*.' Well, she didn't like that, and then here she finds another one in her car along with a bunch of flowers this morning." He shook his head. "She's all excited about it, but I don't know. Something is strange about this, and I hate to see her get her hopes up for something that probably isn't going to pan out like some romantic comedy."

Elaine was nodding along. Jan was caught up in the romance of this, but Elaine felt herself agreeing more and more with Ken as he talked.

"What do you think the crosswords are about, then?" she asked.

He hesitated again. "I don't really know." His eyes glanced back at the television. "I worry that it's some kind of scam."

"Scam?"

"Yeah. You see stuff like this all the time on the news. I saw this one where you get an e-mail saying you have a secret admirer. It takes you to some Web site, and you have to go in and enter your credit card information to find out who the secret admirer is. Well, of course there's no real secret admirer, it's just some robot sending you an e-mail, but thousands of people have fallen for it, and then the Web site has your credit card information."

"Huh." Elaine thought this through. She knew that scams like this existed. She couldn't figure out how someone would be getting useful information out of Katelyn with these puzzles though. Her eyes drifted to the flickering graphics on the TV screen. Was Katelyn's father falling prey to the conspiracy theories the networks all seemed to love to dish out these days, or was there some merit in what he said?

Elaine would see what she could find out. In the meantime, she should check on Jan and Katelyn's progress with that puzzle. She stood up.

"I should probably get going," she said. "It was great to meet you."

"Thank you for your help with all this. I know Katelyn appreciates it," he said.

"It's our pleasure," Elaine said. She walked back out into the kitchen, where Katelyn and Jan were huddled over the puzzle.

"Guess what? This one has a flower theme!" Jan's eyes were shining, and a smile filled her face.

"Really?" Elaine leaned over and looked. Sure enough, some of the answers they'd filled in so far were *soil*, *petal*, and *St. Rose*.

"Any clues as to who made the puzzle?" Elaine asked.

"Not so far," Katelyn said, shaking her head. "But I'll keep working on it." She gestured toward a piece of paper next to her. "Here, I used the home office to make you a copy."

Jan was clearly pleased at this development and snatched the copy of the puzzle.

"We should let you get to work," Elaine said, and Jan pouted but stood up.

"Let us know when you finish filling it out," Jan said.

"I will. And in the meantime, you'll keep looking for the secret admirer?"

She looked so hopeful it almost broke Elaine's heart. If this whole thing turned out to be a scam and this sweet girl's hopes were crushed, Elaine was going to...

"Right, Elaine?"

Elaine looked over and realized that Jan had said something to her.

"I'm sorry. What?"

"I said that you would check the fingerprints and see if any of them matched the suspects we've printed so far."

"Exactly." Elaine gave them a smile, and together, they went outside. "I think we should check with the neighbors. See if any of them saw or heard anything."

"Yeah, you're probably right," Jan agreed.

They knocked on the doors of the houses around Katelyn's, and while people were home in two different houses, only one had heard anything out of the ordinary. The neighbor to the east side of the house, just on the other side of the wooden fence by the carport, reported that her dog had started barking at around 6 a.m., which he sometimes did when he heard strange noises, but none of them had seen anything. Elaine also led Jan over to the empty house on the other side of Katelyn's house, the one where her dad had seen the man in black, but there was nothing out of the ordinary aside from a stack of mail piling up in the mailbox.

Elaine buckled up and Jan started to back the car out of the driveway. "I want to make a stop before we go home," Jan said.

"Where?"

Jan gave her an enigmatic grin. "I know how we can find out who gave Katelyn the flowers."

CHAPTER TWELVE

A few minutes later, Jan pulled up in front of Blooms Flower Shop. The store was housed in a small wooden building off Lincoln Street in Penzance, and there was a narrow parking area in front. The weathered wood siding was faded to a dusty gray, and the shingled roof was the same shade. In summer, climbing roses and hydrangeas in beautiful, deep blues and pinks adorned the entrance. But those were past now, and half-barrels filled with mums and decorative gourds made the shop feel welcoming and inviting.

"Ah. You think the flowers Katelyn got came from here," Elaine said, nodding.

"I know they did," Jan said, pulling out the key from the ignition. The cousins bought everyday flowers from Blooms regularly for the tearoom, and when they had catered larger events, Maya Rudy, who owned the shop, had done a wonderful job creating special centerpieces. It was also the nicest flower shop in the area, though not the only one. Including shops in Augusta, there were easily half a dozen that could have sold those stargazer lilies. But that wasn't why she had come here.

"While you were focused on dusting the plastic wrap on the flowers for fingerprints, I noticed this."

She pulled a small round sticker out of her purse. It said Blooms, using the same scripty font that graced the wooden sign by the street.

"This was on the edge of the plastic around the flowers. It must have been used to seal the plastic, but I guess when Katelyn opened the bouquet it fell off without any of us noticing."

"Brilliant." Elaine unbuckled her seat belt. "Let's go see if they can tell us who bought those stargazers."

They walked up the wooden steps and in through the heavy front door. As soon as she stepped in, the heady floral-scented air hit her. It was sweet, and it smelled wonderful.

"Maybe we should have opened a flower shop instead of a tearoom," Jan said, sniffing. "Can you imagine smelling this every day?"

"It would certainly be better for my waistline than sniffing those pastries you make every morning," Elaine teased.

Jan smiled and followed her cousin to the long wooden counter at the back of the shop. Along one wall, a refrigerated case held premade bouquets, and bins of gorgeous stems in water filled the other side of the room. In the front of the shop, baskets and vases and centerpieces were displayed, and behind the counter were rolls of ribbon and colored paper. The warm wooden floors and soft lighting made the whole place feel homey.

As they stepped up to the counter, a young woman with hair dyed black and a piercing through her lower lip came out of the back room. Dark eyeliner rimmed her eyes, and her skin looked almost ghostly white against her black baggy T-shirt.

"Oh. Hello." Elaine was rarely lost for words, but Jan could tell that her cousin was as surprised by this girl's appearance as she was. She wasn't exactly what Jan had been expecting.

"Is Maya here?" Jan asked.

"Sorry, she's not in today. She's out today for a field trip with her son's class." The girl's voice was low and throaty, but her smile seemed genuine. "What can I help you with?"

"Um, my cousin and I had a question," Jan said, stepping to the counter uncertainly. "We were wondering if we could find out who bought some flowers yesterday."

The girl raised an eyebrow and gave Jan a strange look. Elaine seemed to have recovered and quickly said, "A friend of ours received a bouquet that we believe was purchased here, but there was no note attached, and she's not sure who to thank."

"Ah." The girl nodded. "I see. Well, I'll see if I can help. You said they were purchased yesterday?"

"We believe so," Jan said. "It's possible they were bought the day before, but they seemed really fresh, so I doubt it."

"I wasn't in here yesterday, so I don't know for sure, but I can look through the receipts and see if that tells us anything. If not, I'll have to ask my aunt when she gets back."

"Your aunt?"

The girl nodded. "Aunt Maya. She hired me as a favor to my dad, I think. I come in a few mornings a week to help out, but mostly I handle deliveries. But since she was out today, here I am." She smiled and opened a drawer beneath the counter and pulled out a stack of receipts. Jan could see that they were a mix of handwritten invoices on the store's carbon paper receipt form and cash register receipts on the traditional white receipt paper.

"Let's see if there's anything useful in here. What sort of flowers were they?"

"Stargazer lilies," Elaine said.

"Nothing else? Just stargazers?"

"That's it," Elaine said.

"Well, that makes it a bit easier. If we'd been looking at all the mixed bouquets it would be a lot more difficult."

The girl squinted at the handwriting on the first paper and put it into one stack, and then matched it to the cash register receipt underneath. Her nails were painted a deep purplish black, but her hands moved quickly and efficiently.

While she sorted, Jan wandered over to the bins of cut stems. There were delicate pink peonies, lush birds of paradise, creamy calla lilies, colorful tulips, and gerbera daisies. Bins overflowed with roses in every shade of pink, as well as asters, mini chrysanthemums, and snapdragons. Jan leaned in, took a long sniff of the lilies, and touched the outer petals of one of the peonies gently. She'd always loved the delicate flowers. She didn't even want to begin to imagine how much these would cost this time of year.

"Okay, I think I found them all," the girl said from behind the counter.

Jan turned back, and Elaine returned from perusing the cooler case. They saw that two sets of receipts were on the counter, each with both a handwritten and a cash register receipt.

"It looks like we sold two bouquets of stargazers yesterday," she said, indicating the two sets. "This first one was sold at around 4:30 yesterday. They were bought with cash, so I can't see who purchased them. I'll have to ask Aunt Maya when she gets in."

She pointed to the other pile. "This bouquet was purchased just after 6:30, right before we closed for the night," she said. "The stargazers were the only thing this customer bought."

"Was this one with cash too?" Elaine asked. Jan could hear the hope leaking out of her voice; she felt the same way.

"Actually, no," the girl said brightly. "This customer used a credit card, so his name is on the receipt."

Jan looked at Elaine. She'd picked up on the word *his* as well.

"Can you tell us what his name is?" Jan asked.

"Sure." The girl picked up the receipt and squinted at it. "It looks like those stargazers were bought by a River White."

CHAPTER THIRTEEN

A few minutes later, they were stepping inside the office of *The Penzance Courier* again. The same chipper girl was at the front desk.

"Change your mind about that classified ad?" she asked brightly.

"I'm afraid not," Elaine said. "We're here to see River White again."

"Oh, I'm sorry, he's not here. But I can give him a message."

"You're sure he's not here?" Elaine craned her neck and peered toward the back of the room. She could see his desk, and the headphones he'd had the day before were plugged in and a mug of coffee was sitting on his desk. There had been a car with a Cornell bumper sticker parked out in front of the office.

They had parked directly in front of the big glass windows. And Elaine had stood there out in front of the building for a while, waiting while Jan ducked into the bakery next door to sample their blueberry scones. Could River have seen them out there and made himself scarce?

"I'm afraid he's stepped out."

Elaine admitted she was being paranoid, but she still wasn't sure she believed it. Okay, Elaine *didn't* believe it. She could see his cell phone sitting there on his desk. People these days didn't go anywhere without their cell phones. "Big story?" she asked, her eyebrows raised.

"Oh yes," the girl said. "Huge. He had to rush out of here."

"Do you know what the story is?" Elaine asked.

"Um...some big crime...thing," the girl said. Her eyes were darting around the desk. "A bank robbery, I think."

"Oh dear. A bank robbery?" Jan said, her eyes meeting Elaine's. "There aren't too many of those around here. That *is* a big story."

"Yeah, well." The girl laughed. "So now you see why he couldn't talk to you."

"Indeed." Elaine glanced back toward the back of the room one more time. Did she see steam rising from the coffee mug, or were her eyes playing tricks on her? "Well, in that case, can we leave him a message?"

"Of course." She reached for a message pad and a ballpoint pen.

"Can you ask him to call Elaine Cook?" Elaine asked. She gave the girl the number of the tearoom, and they went back out to the car.

"He was there, wasn't he?" Jan asked as she pulled away from the curb.

"I think so," Elaine said. "I guess we'll know for sure tomorrow, if we read about a bank robbery in the newspaper."

Jan laughed. "The poor girl. But really. Bank robbery was the best she could come up with?"

Elaine laughed as well. "It was a tad obvious. Which isn't a bad thing, since it makes our job easier. Now we just need to figure out *why* River is avoiding us."

"Maybe it's because we asked him some crazy questions yesterday," Jan suggested.

Elaine shook her head. "That's possible. But if he is the one behind the crosswords, why is he avoiding admitting it?"

"Maybe he's embarrassed?" Jan suggested. "Maybe he really isn't ready to confess his true feelings to Katelyn yet."

"Maybe," Elaine said. She wasn't convinced.

"What do you think the reason could be?" Jan asked.

"I'm not sure." Elaine didn't even want to entertain the idea that it was some kind of cruel joke, though she couldn't get the idea of the scam Katelyn's father had mentioned out of her head.

"You still aren't sure the puzzles are from a secret admirer, are you?" Jan asked, as she turned on to the road that hugged the lake.

"No, I'm not sure," Elaine said. "In some ways, it's the obvious answer. Especially with those flowers today. And I do hope that's what it turns out to be. But I don't know if the obvious answer is always right, and I don't want to get so certain we've got it figured out that we miss out on another answer."

"What do you think the puzzles are, then, if not messages from a secret admirer?"

"I don't know. Invasive, for one. Someone seems to know a whole lot more about her than she knows about him. That's kind of eerie if you ask me." Elaine shrugged. "Her father is worried it might be a scam."

"A scam?"

"Someone trying to get personal information from her to use for nefarious purposes."

"But how could they get her personal information?"

"I guess we don't know that yet. But maybe that's coming."

"Honestly, Elaine." Jan smiled and gave her a sidelong glance. "It wouldn't hurt you to be a bit more optimistic."

"I'm plenty optimistic. It's just that you're smitten with Bob, and I worry that you're seeing everything through rosy-colored glasses, believing love is right around the corner for everyone."

"Maybe it is," Jan said. She nudged her cousin with her elbow. "Maybe if you were willing, you'd find love again too."

Elaine shook her head. Ben had only been gone a year. That was not nearly enough time to grieve after a lifetime together. And even if she were ready, it wasn't exactly like there were men waiting in the wings, ready to step in and sweep her off her feet. Elaine was glad Jan had found love again, but for Elaine, that door was closed.

"Maybe someday," Elaine said simply.

"I'm sorry," Jan said quietly. "That was thoughtless of me. I forget sometimes how recent it was for you."

"That's okay." Elaine sighed. She knew Jan only wanted to see her happy.

"But when you are ready to think about romance again, could you make poor Nathan Culver's life easier and go out with him?"

It took Elaine a minute for the words to register. "What?"

"Oh, Elaine, you really haven't noticed? The poor guy follows you around like a lost puppy dog."

"He does not." Elaine liked Nathan a lot, but he certainly wasn't interested in her. They were good friends, but *just* friends.

"Why do you think he came to the crossword event?" Jan asked. "If you saw how quickly he gave up on his puzzle, it would be painfully obvious it wasn't because he likes crosswords."

"Nathan Culver, really?" Elaine rolled this idea around in her brain a bit. No, she decided. Jan was seeing things through those rosy glasses again, spotting romance where none existed.

"Trust me on this one," Jan said. She gave her cousin a shy smile.

Elaine thought about Nathan. He was kind. He had a strong faith. He was an old and faithful friend. He was a nice-looking man. Could Jan be right about him? But even if she was, what did it matter, since Elaine wasn't anywhere near ready to consider romance again? She decided to focus on the problem at hand.

"So what's our plan of attack for the day? Should we try again to get in touch with Frank Conrad, the music teacher?" Elaine asked as Jan slowed for a red light.

"I suppose so, though it seems pretty unnecessary," Jan replied. "My money is on River White."

They both had to agree that his behavior today was more than a little suspicious. Still, they needed more information. As Jan drove, a canopy of orange and gold leaves arching above them, Elaine pulled out her phone and opened a social media app. She opened up the site and typed River White's name into the search field.

There. That was him. She found his name easily and recognized the red hair. She scrolled through his page and stopped on the first post. It was a photo he'd posted just last night.

"On the other hand, Frank Conrad is looking better every minute," Elaine said.

"What do you mean?"

"You've been right about River from the start," she said. "He's not interested in Katelyn after all."

She held out her phone so Jan could see the picture of River and the Asian woman that had been in the photo on his desk. She was clutching a bouquet of stargazer lilies and holding up her hand to show off a sparkly diamond on her ring finger. The caption read: "She said Yes!"

Jan sighed. "Looks like we *really* need to talk to Frank Conrad."

CHAPTER FOURTEEN

That afternoon, after they'd tried calling Truman Middle School to talk to Frank Conrad and left another message, Jan settled down with a copy of the new crossword puzzle and a cup of tea, and Elaine headed for the Lancaster Public Library. She'd read through the section about heraldry in the book she'd bought at the Bookworm, and she'd realized that she needed a way to figure out what the coat of arms on the flue cover represented. She hoped they would have a book that would help her understand how to find that information.

Fallen leaves scudded across the pavement as Elaine crossed Main Street and stepped inside the small brick library. It was cozy inside, with the circulation desk front and center, the children's area to the right, and the new media and local history sections to the left. There was a small upstairs area where a good amount of fiction was housed, as well as some nonfiction, and the basement contained classrooms and a reference room, along with a spotty collection of microfiche for older newspapers and magazines.

Elaine waved hello to Priscilla Gates, the librarian, and wandered into the history section. She browsed the shelves, looking for anything about coats of arms or heraldry. She pages through books on England, on various wars, and on Maine, but wasn't finding anything like what she needed.

"Need some help?" Priscilla had appeared at her side. Elaine was surprised; Priscilla was quiet and reserved and generally stayed at the desk unless she asked for help. Now, Priscilla gave her a shy smile and indicated the piles of books that lay scattered on the table around Elaine. "You seem to be looking for something."

Elaine laughed. "I am, in fact. But I'm afraid I haven't really found it, though I seem to have taken every book off your history section shelves."

"Don't worry about that. I'll reshelf those. What are you trying to find?"

"I'm looking for information about a coat of arms."

"Hmm." Priscilla pressed her lips together as she thought. "I think you'll find that in the social science section." She indicated a section of shelves under the window on the far side of the room. "Let's check it out."

Priscilla led her over to the shelves and crouched down. Elaine squatted too and started looking, but before she even had a chance to make sense of the titles, Priscilla was sliding a heavy illustrated volume off the shelf.

"Is this the kind of thing you're looking for?" She held out the book. Elaine took it, and the plastic cover crinkled gently as she opened the cover. It was a book that showed and identified hundreds, probably thousands, of family crests. Elaine flipped through the pages gently. The book showed only the shield part of the crest. There were probably twenty crests on each page, each with the family's name underneath. And there were hundreds of pages of crests.

"This is exactly what I'm looking for," Elaine said. She saw that the shields were in alphabetical order, and she flipped to the section with G names, looking for Gardner. There it was—a single yellow rose in a green field. Not at all like their crest.

Well, she would look through the pages until she found the right one, she decided. It would take hours, if not days, to look at each crest in the book and see if it matched the crest carved into the flue cover, but if it was in this book, she would find it. "Thank you so much."

Elaine stepped out of the library, book checked out and clutched under her arm, feeling lighter. The sky seemed brighter, even as an incoming autumn storm clouded the sky. They were getting close to solving this mystery. She could feel it.

JAN HAD BEEN working on the new mystery crossword puzzle in the upstairs sitting room for the past hour, and she decided to pop downstairs to make sure all was well. She checked that everything was under control in the kitchen and in the parlors, and as she suspected, Rose and Archie had everything taken care of.

There were only two tables occupied at the moment—Sylvia Flood was here with Faith Lanier, chatting over sandwiches. Sylvia owned Sylvia's Closet, a cute boutique on Main Street that sold mostly vintage clothes—or, as Jan liked to think of them, clothes she wore when she was younger. Faith Lanier owned A Little Something, a gift shop nearby. The two women business owners were about the same age, and sometimes they got together to talk shop. And an older couple Jan didn't recognize sat at a table in the corner. Tourists, probably, she thought, and went over to say hello. She found out they were from a small town in Nova Scotia and were driving to Boston to meet their first grandchild, who was only two weeks old. They'd stopped in to have a bite to eat before they pressed on.

They were sweet, and chatting with them, Jan remembered her own drive to the hospital to meet her first grandchild, Avery. She had been filled with emotions she couldn't even begin to understand—hope, excitement, expectation, and gut-wrenching fear. And the first time she'd held hours-old Avery in her arms, she knew she'd do anything in the world to protect that child, and that she'd love her with a fierceness that shocked her, no matter what happened. She knew right away that it was a different sort of love than she'd felt for her own children—more confident, more tender, in some ways—but no less strong. Jan chatted with the couple for a few moments, and then wished them well with their new grandson.

Satisfied that all was well down here, she headed into the kitchen and steeped a fresh cup of Darjeeling tea. Then she climbed the stairs and took a seat at the desk in the sitting room once again. She looked down at the copy of the puzzle she'd spent the last hour working on. She had filled in most of the boxes, though there were still a few she hadn't managed to solve.

She scanned the notes she'd taken. Just as they'd thought at Katelyn's house, the theme seemed to be flowers, or plants in general. There were references to amaryllis, stock, coxcomb, iris, and heather in the puzzle, as well as several other kinds of plants. But she hadn't figured out what the connection to Katelyn was yet.

Jan settled back down and began working away at the puzzle again, checking references in a big gardening book she had, as well as online. She was absorbed in her work and didn't even hear Elaine come in until Elaine touched her shoulder.

Jan jumped in her chair. "Whoa. You could give a person a little warning."

"I called your name three times," Elaine said, shaking her head, but she was smiling. "What has you so absorbed?"

"I've been researching different kinds of flowers." Jan rubbed the back of her neck. She tapped the gardening book with her pen. "But all the flowers mentioned in the puzzle grow in different climates and at different times of the year. So I'm not seeing any pattern there. The only connection I've been able to make out is between ivy, cedar, and cypress, which are all mentioned in the puzzle."

Elaine wrinkled her brow. "What do they have in common?"

"They're all evergreens. Evergreens stand for constancy. So maybe the puzzle maker is trying to tell Katelyn he'll always be there for her."

Elaine thought. "It seems that instead of coming up with different kinds of evergreens and hoping she'd pick up on it, he might have simply given a clue as to who he is."

"I'm sure he has. We just haven't found it yet." Jan tapped the pen on the book again. There had to be some clue here.

Elaine leaned over and looked at the puzzle her cousin had been working on. "Rosemary," she said, pointing at the empty space for 18 down.

"What?"

"The clue is *for remembrance*. The answer is *rosemary*."

Jan couldn't believe she'd missed it. And she couldn't believe Elaine of all people, who didn't even like crosswords, had figured it out. She filled the squares in with the correct letters and saw that the *r* completed the word *fir* in 23 across.

"Another evergreen," she said.

Elaine nodded, but Jan could see in her eyes that she wasn't convinced.

Just then, they heard Avery calling.

"Grandma? Elaine?"

"Up here," Jan called. Footsteps stomped up the stairs and a moment later Avery peeked her head inside the sitting room.

"Mom dropped me off to practice. Hope that's okay. She texted you, Grandma."

"Of course that's okay," Jan said, ushering Avery into the room. The girl stepped in and took the cello in its vinyl case off her back and set it on the floor. "I can't believe I missed her text. I was so absorbed in this puzzle. But I'm so glad you came."

"Where is your phone?" Elaine asked, looking around.

"In my purse downstairs," Jan said, and then realized what her cousin was getting at. She saw Elaine and Avery exchange a look. "Okay, so maybe it's not a huge surprise I missed the text," she admitted. "But I am delighted you're here. Here, why don't you set up in this room? I need to go and check on things downstairs anyway."

"And I need to get to work looking through this book I got at the library," Elaine said. "Is it okay with you if I sit here while you practice, Avery?"

Avery nodded, and Elaine took over the spot Jan vacated at the desk.

As Jan stepped out of the room, she looked back and saw her cousin and granddaughter together. Something about it felt so right.

CHAPTER FIFTEEN

Avery had practiced for a solid two hours—during which both Elaine and Jan stayed busy downstairs. Elaine had only lasted through about five minutes of screeching on the strings before deciding that maybe she would come back to the book some other time and went to see what was going on in the tearoom. When Avery finally packed up, Elaine had to admit she was getting better. She was hitting most of the notes now, and the tune was starting to sound like music. Elaine was in the kitchen hand washing some of their delicate teapots when Avery stepped inside.

"Hi there, Avery," Rose called brightly. She was arranging shortbread cookies on a silver tea tray and gave the girl a genuine smile. Elaine turned and waved with one dish-soapy hand.

"Hey. Can I help in here? Mom has to pick up Kelly from karate, so she can't come get me for a while."

"Of course," Rose said, indicating that Avery could take over the cookies. Avery and Rose always got along well, and Elaine could see that Rose was happy to have the girl help out.

"You're welcome here, of course," Elaine added. "But if you need a ride home, I can give you one."

"Really?" Avery's face brightened. "That would be super-helpful. I've still got tons of homework to do tonight."

"Sure thing." Elaine set the teapot she'd been washing on a clean dish towel on the counter to dry, and then she rinsed her hands under warm water. "Let me just go make sure that's okay with your grandma. I'll be right back."

Jan was busy chatting with a group of women from church who'd come in for afternoon tea, and she was glad to have Elaine take Avery home and promised she'd call Paula to let her know.

A few minutes later, Elaine was heading down Main Street, Avery strapped into the passenger seat beside her.

"You seem to be making good progress," Elaine said.

"Thanks."

"When is the challenge?"

"Tuesday."

"You'll do great."

Avery nodded, but she didn't say anything. The sky was dark and moody. They were predicting a storm tonight, and Elaine fiercely hoped it wouldn't strip all the leaves from the trees. Once the autumn leaves were gone, it would be nothing but naked branches all the way till April. Elaine looked over at Avery. The lights from the dashboard gave her features a greenish glow.

Elaine didn't want to pry, but she also didn't want to sit here in uncomfortable silence.

"Are things any better with the girls from school?"

Avery didn't say anything for a minute. The hum of the engine and the low whisper of the radio were the only noise. Elaine reached over and switched the radio off. She started to wonder whether Avery had heard, but then finally, Avery spoke.

"Why don't you see your mom more?" she asked, staring straight out the windshield.

"What?"

"Your mom lives in Augusta just like me, and I'm here all the time. Why doesn't she come see you more? I think that's weird."

Elaine thought for a moment about how to answer the question. She supposed it could seem strange that her mother didn't come to visit more often. They only lived about twenty minutes apart. And Elaine didn't simply pop over to see her mom whenever she felt like it either. Elaine and her mother loved each other deeply, but that wasn't what their relationship was like. They set up times to see each other in advance. Elaine was so busy with the tearoom, and her mother was always busy with her own friends, that this was what seemed to work best for them. But how do you explain to a child that sometimes you can love someone enough to let them have their own space?

"I moved away when I was eighteen," Elaine said. "I came home for holidays most of the time after that whenever I was able. But I married Ben shortly after I graduated, and then we were stationed so many different places where we couldn't come home. So I got used to not seeing her very often, and I guess Mom got used to that as well."

"But now you're back home. And you don't have Ben."

"True," Elaine said, wrestling for words. "And of course I want to spend time with my mother. I would love nothing more. But she has her own things going on, her own habits and social life, and I want to respect that."

"Don't you miss her?"

How did Elaine answer that honestly? Elaine tried to put herself into an eleven–year-old's shoes. Avery wasn't even allowed to be left alone with her little sister yet; she certainly couldn't imagine what it would be like to move out of your parents' home and start your own life. At this age, your friends were starting to become more and more important, and you made little grabs at independence, but your identity still rested mainly in your family.

"I do miss what it was like to grow up in a tight-knit family," she said. "My brother Nick and I were close, and we loved to ride our bikes around the neighborhood and play hide-and-seek with all the neighborhood kids. We'd spend long days at the pool in summer and what seems like entire school breaks at the library. We'd have dinner as a family every night. It was such a lovely time to grow up. We were all a lot more innocent back then. I do miss those days." There was nothing like the peace and security of childhood; you never appreciated it until it was gone. "But I'm glad for my mom to have her own life now. It makes me happy that she has friends and hobbies that matter to her."

"Huh." Avery nodded, but the look on her face showed that she was still trying to make sense of this. Well, good. Elaine hoped she would hold on to her family and their traditions as long as possible. She would understand when she got older, but best to let her enjoy the innocence of childhood for now.

They were quiet for a few minutes while Elaine pulled on to the highway. The evening sky was steely gray and thick with heavy clouds, and the orange spots of light from the streetlamps were warm and welcoming, even here on this highway.

"Not really."

"What?" Elaine looked at Avery, trying to make sense of her words.

"You asked if things were better with the girls at school. The answer is not really."

"Oh dear." Elaine's mind was catching up with her mouth now. "I'm sorry to hear that."

"It's okay."

"Did something else happen?"

Avery hesitated for a minute, and then said, "Alicia said hi to me today on the way to social studies."

"Well, that sounds like good news to me," Elaine said.

"I said hi first, since you said to be nice. But she smiled and everything. It even seemed like she meant it."

"See? A victory," Elaine said. "You just had to be willing to extend the olive branch."

"But she only did it because none of her cool friends were around."

"That's not true." Well, that did take some of the shine off things, but no need to let Avery see that. This was still good as far as Elaine was concerned. "She still likes you. That's good news."

"Sure. She's willing to talk to me when no one else is around. I don't know that that's exactly the kind of friendship I'm looking for."

"No, nor should you. But I wonder if there's some way to get her to give you a chance around her other friends."

"I don't want to hang out with her stupid new friends." Avery crossed her arms over her chest.

"Of course not." Elaine tried to hold back a smile. Avery might truly have no desire to be part of the cool crowd—and frankly, Elaine was grateful for this; in her experience being part of the popular crowd led kids to do things that might not be good for them—but Elaine believed that if she had the opportunity to get to know those kids, as well as reconnect with her old friend, it would do Avery a world of good. "But I wonder. What if you invited them all to something? Some event?"

"Like what?" Avery wasn't vetoing the idea off the bat. Elaine took that as a good sign.

Elaine thought for a minute. "What if you invited the girls all over to the tearoom? You could have a little tea party."

"Oh." Avery's disappointment was clear on her face.

"I bet they would enjoy it."

"Um . . ." Avery hesitated.

"You don't think so?"

"I don't know."

There was something she wasn't saying, Elaine could tell. "What?"

Avery hesitated. "I don't know. They may think that's kind of dorky."

"Dorky?" Elaine shook her head. How could fancy sandwiches and delicious pastries be dorky?

"I mean, no offense, the tearoom is great and all. It's just that a few years ago, they might have thought tea parties were cool. But now?" She shook her head. "I think we might be too old for tea parties."

"Nonsense. You're never too old for tea parties."

"Okay."

"Okay?"

"Thanks for the idea." Avery gave her an apologetic smile.

Ah. So that was a no. "Well, maybe a tea party isn't right, but I bet if you extended an invitation for something, they would go for it."

"I'll think about it."

She'd struck out.

"But, Elaine?" Avery looked up at her, and even in the dim light in the car, Elaine could see a shy smile on her face. "Thank you. I really appreciate you trying to help."

Elaine couldn't stop the smile that spread across her face as she drove down that darkening highway.

CHAPTER SIXTEEN

Elaine hadn't even rolled out of bed yet when the phone rang Thursday morning. She'd been up late, trying desperately to find anything in the fingerprints she'd collected to link one of the suspects to the crosswords, but there was nothing. She only had partial prints from some of them, but even with the full prints she had, there wasn't much of anything to go on. Elaine knew she wasn't an expert, but she would have thought she'd at least turn up *something*. They made it look so easy on those cop shows she loved. Finally, she'd fallen into bed and dreamed of whorls and ridges and lines, and had woken just a few minutes before the phone rang.

Jan must have been downstairs baking and picked up the phone, because the ringing stopped. Elaine slipped her feet into slippers, pulled on her robe, and moved over toward the window. It was a bit later than she usually woke up, she could see by the light. Last night's storm had blown through, and the morning was bright, the sky a pale shade of blue, but she could see that the wind had knocked off some of the leaves, but most were still hanging on. She stretched, yawned, and turned toward the bathroom, but paused when she heard footsteps pounding up the stairs. She hadn't heard her cousin move this quickly in—well, ever. What in the world?

"Elaine? Oh, good, you're awake." Jan stood in the doorway, her apron askew, a smudge of flour on her cheek. "That was Ken Grande on the phone."

"Katelyn's father?"

"Exactly. He said the guy is there again."

"Who?"

"The guy in black who's been hanging around next door."

"Oh." Elaine felt a jolt of excitement go through her.

"He just pulled up in his truck. Katelyn has already left for work, but he said if we hurry we might be able to talk to him."

"I'll be right down." Elaine threw on some clothes, ran a brush through her hair, and flew down the stairs. Jan was already waiting in her car, the engine idling.

A few minutes later, they pulled up in front of the Grande house, but there was no one near the house next door, and whatever vehicle the man had driven was gone. They walked up to the Grandes' door and knocked, and they heard Ken call "Come in." Elaine pulled on the front door and found it unlocked, and they stepped inside. Ken was sitting in his wheelchair in the kitchen, looking out the sliding glass doors that looked out over the backyard. If you looked past a row of rose bushes, you could see straight to the white cottage next door.

"He was just over there," he said, pointing toward the back corner of the house. "He left maybe five minutes ago."

It had been less than ten minutes since he'd called, so the man hadn't stayed long.

"And he arrived just before you called?" Jan asked.

He nodded, keeping his eyes trained on the house. "I recognized the truck as soon as he pulled up—it was the same one parked there when he was hanging around before. I called you right away."

"What did he do while he was here?" Elaine asked.

"He walked right over to the side of the house and crouched down at that corner. He was pulling on something down at the corner on the ground over there," he said, indicating the grass by the corner of the house. "I would have run over and asked him myself, but..."

He let his voice trail off, and Elaine noticed that the back door led to a small cement step, and then a rocky field of dug-up dirt. "We were going to put in a ramp out there this summer, but didn't get it finished and we're worried that we'll run out of time before the first frost, so we're waiting until spring," he said by way of explanation. "I could have gone out the front and then around, but I figured he might be gone by the time I worked my way around that fence and across the grass. It's slow going on rough terrain."

"I'm glad you called us," Elaine said. They didn't know who this man was or what he was up to. A man in a wheelchair didn't need to be confronting him on his own. "When this man shows up, does he seem to come at the same time of day? Or does that vary?"

"Usually in the morning, I guess," he said. "It's not real regular. But I would say morning mostly."

Elaine was just wondering whether they would need to stake out the house to catch him when Jan spoke again.

"But I did get something," he said, a slow grin filling his face. "He parked his truck there in front of the house, just like he always does, and I rolled myself on over to the window and got this." He pulled his phone out of a pocket of his pants and held up a cell phone. He unlocked the phone and opened the pictures, and proudly held up a photo of the back of a Dodge Ram.

"Genius," Jan said, using two fingers to enlarge the photo. Sure enough, there it was—the license plate. "Can I send a copy of this to both of us?" Jan asked, and when he nodded, she attached the picture to an e-mail and typed in her e-mail address and Elaine's. Elaine wasn't sure yet how they would use the number to track him down, but she was sure there was some way to use the information to find the owner of the truck. She also wasn't sure if the owner of the truck was related to the crossword puzzles, but they had to follow every lead.

"One other thing was strange this morning," Ken said.

Both Elaine and Jan looked at him.

"The front door was open when I got up."

"Open?" Elaine asked. "Do you mean it was cracked?"

He shook his head. "Wide open. It was cold in here, which is why I noticed it at first. I came out of my room and felt the cold and thought something must be wrong, so I came in here and saw that it was standing wide open."

"Had anything been disturbed inside?" Jan asked.

"No, not that I noticed. But the floor was wet from the rain coming in."

"Do you have any idea how long it had been open?" Elaine asked. Elaine crossed the kitchen floor and examined the door. It was solid wood, painted a glossy white on the inside, and slightly wider than a typical door to accommodate Ken's wheelchair.

"No idea, except the floor was pretty wet, so I imagine it had been a while. Katelyn was still asleep in her room when I discovered it."

"Had this ever happened before?" Jan asked. Elaine saw what she was doing. She was trying to see if there might be something wrong with the door. The alternative—that someone had forced their way into the house—was frightening, and it shot holes all through Jan's theory that these puzzles were innocuous.

"Nope." Ken pushed away from the glass door a bit. "That's a new door—well, new when we redid the house a few years back. We've never had problems with it." Elaine pulled her sleeve over her hand and touched the doorknob. It turned smoothly, and the lock mechanism seemed to work properly. There was no deadbolt, only the traditional doorknob that locked with a key.

"Who all has the key?"

"Me and Katie, of course," he said. "And a neighbor a few houses down, Art. We've known Art for decades, and his wife, Melissa, comes in and checks on the plants when we go out of town. Well, not that I go all that many places these days. But they used to come a lot."

"Is there any reason that he or his wife might have tried to get in last night?" Jan asked.

"Not that I can think of."

Elaine's unease grew. The previous night someone had come into their carport and left a puzzle inside Katelyn's car.

Now someone had come inside the house. The two were likely to be related—and if they were, there wasn't a lot of room for belief that the puzzles were simply innocent declarations of love. Something darker was going on here.

"Do you lock the door before bed?" Elaine asked.

"Either Katelyn or I do. Last night I went to bed first, so she did."

"You asked her to make sure?" Jan asked.

"I checked with her this morning as she was getting ready for work, and she said she was 'pretty sure.'"

"Did she seem at all concerned about the door being left open?" Jan asked.

"No, she wasn't worried, but then she didn't think it was strange when that puzzle showed up in her car either. She's so caught up in this idea that someone is secretly in love with her that she probably wouldn't be concerned if the house was on fire."

Elaine used her fingerprint kit to quickly dust for prints, and then they looked around a bit more and climbed back into Jan's car.

"The door blew open in the storm," Jan announced as soon as they pulled away from the curb.

"I'm not so sure about that," Elaine said.

"It would be scary to wake up and find your door open," Jan said. "At first I thought it was creepy too. But then I realized nothing inside was disturbed. Katelyn was pretty sure she locked it but couldn't be positive. There was a big storm with strong winds. The door must not have been latched properly, and it must have blown open in the wind."

"It's a solid wood door, and extra-wide to boot. If it had been yanked open, that must have been some strong wind."

Jan slowed to steer around a four-foot branch in the middle of the road and gave her cousin a look.

"Okay, the wind was strong, but not strong enough to open a locked door," Elaine said. "Plus, it was too much of a coincidence that their house was entered the day after her car was entered."

"The front door couldn't have been locked," Jan said. "He wasn't sure it had been. It probably hadn't been closed properly. We can ask Katelyn to be sure. But"—she flipped on her blinker and navigated around another fallen tree limb—"I really don't think this has anything to do with the crossword puzzles. And I am pretty sure the mysterious man next door doesn't either."

"I don't know," Elaine said. "Maybe you're right. But I am just looking at all the evidence, trying to follow where it leads. I know you're seeing love everywhere these days..."

Just then, Elaine's phone rang, and she dug it out. Maybe it was Frank Conrad, finally calling them back. Or maybe it was Maya from the flower shop with the name of the other person who had bought stargazers Tuesday. But when she dug the phone out, she was surprised to see the name on the screen.

"Who is it?" Jan asked.

"Nathan Culver," Elaine said. She stared at the phone for a moment, remembering what Jan had said about him.

"Well, are you going to answer it?"

Elaine hesitated a moment, and then silenced the phone. She'd let him leave a message. Then she turned back to Jan, who was giving her a strange look.

"What?" Elaine asked.

"Oh, nothing at all," Jan said, a smile creeping across her face. "What was that about love not being everywhere?"

Elaine put her phone back into her purse. "We have no idea why he is calling."

"You would if you'd answer it."

"I'll pick up the message later."

"Away from prying eyes." Jan nudged her with her elbow.

"Let's just go talk to Katelyn, shall we?"

Jan took her eyes off the road to glance at Elaine briefly, and then she nodded. "All right. Let's see what Katelyn has to say about this door."

A quick trip to the Bookworm yielded little that was useful, at least in Elaine's view. Katelyn confirmed that the front door had been open this morning, but she couldn't promise she'd remembered to lock it or even to check it to make sure it had been latched; she was, she admitted, a bit distracted.

If the idea that someone out there had a crush on her made her happy, then that was good. No matter what the truth turned out to be, at least this all was making Katelyn happy. There was nothing wrong with that. At least, Elaine hoped so.

CHAPTER SEVENTEEN

After lunch, Jan was antsy. Elaine had sequestered herself back inside the office, declaring she couldn't do anything else until she got some invoices cleared out. Jan had finished her baking, and while she served tea and chatted with customers, her mind was far away. She couldn't stop thinking about the crossword puzzles. Finally, she found a free moment and escaped upstairs to think about where they were on the mystery. She pulled out her list of suspects and saw that many of them had been cleared.

River White was crossed off the list. There were still some question marks about Tag King, but Jan didn't think he was especially likely, and his fingerprints hadn't show up on the puzzle. Dutch Bigelow seemed extremely unlikely to both of them. Bill Markham had been crossed off the list. They needed to find out more about the guy who'd been hanging around outside Katelyn's neighbor's house, in case he was involved in leaving the crossword on her car.

Which left Frank Conrad. They had left him another message with Sally at the school, but he hadn't responded. Well, school would be out soon, Augusta was a quick trip from here, and she'd wanted to pick up some of those frozen burritos she loved at the grocery store near her old home anyway. And the tearoom was slow today—certainly Rose and Archie could handle it if she ducked out. She'd just go talk to this Mr. Conrad. She grabbed her coat and purse and popped into the office to tell Elaine where she was off to.

"Oh. You're sure?" Elaine asked, looking up from a pile of receipts.

"You're welcome to come along," Jan said. "But I think we should go now, since school will be out soon, and I'd like to catch him before he leaves."

Elaine hesitated. Jan could see that she was trying to decide whether to put her work aside and come along. Elaine was often better at reading people, plus she could never resist a good mystery. But finally, it seemed like practicality won out.

"Why don't you go ahead?" Elaine suggested, looking around at the mess surrounding her. "I need to get these taken care of, and I need to call my mom this afternoon, so I won't be ready to go for a while. Please go talk to him. And don't forget to get his fingerprints."

Jan smiled. "I won't." Though she was unconvinced of its usefulness, she dutifully dug the kit out of Elaine's bag and tucked into her own before she climbed into the car and headed for Augusta.

School had just let out, judging by the scores of kids streaming away from the school. Jan looked around for Avery but didn't see her, so she made her way to the office to ask for Frank Conrad. Sally, the woman who had helped them earlier, wasn't at her desk, but the other receptionist, who seemed focused on completing some task on her computer, told her that since school wasn't in session she could go right on back to the music room. Jan thanked her and stepped out into the hallway before she could change her mind. Now, all she had to do was find the music room...

She looked around, trying to decide which way to go. She stood in a long hallway, with classrooms and offices branching off. She knew that door there led to the cafeteria, since they'd gone through it a few days ago. About halfway down the hallway there seemed to be a set of stairs leading to the second floor. Let's see. She knew she'd seen it when she toured the school with Avery, but she was at a loss. If she were a music room, where would she be?

Then she noticed something. Next to the fire extinguisher on the wall, there was a map of the floor, with each room marked. She saw that the names of two teachers were listed as fire wardens, and surmised that the map was meant for helping crisis crews make sure they'd searched all the rooms in an emergency. Jan leaned in and read the labels on each classroom carefully. There...a large room at the back of the first floor. It was labeled *127, Mr. Conrad.* Jan studied the map for a moment, making sure she knew how to navigate to the classroom, and then started off. A few moments later, she was pushing open the door for room 127.

It was a large, open room, with rows of folding chairs arranged in a semicircle in the center. At the front was a large projection screen and whiteboard, and to the sides were shelves where instruments of all kinds rested, covered in black cases.

Toward the front, there was a desk that seemed dwarfed by the size of the room, and a man sat behind it looking at her, waiting for her to say something.

"Hello," Jan said, stepping inside. She let the door fall closed behind her. The floor was covered in blue industrial carpet, and it had that overly quiet sound of an empty classroom. "My name is Jan Blake." She gave him what she hoped was a charming smile. "My granddaughter Avery is in orchestra."

"Oh yes," he said, and his face relaxed. He was probably in his late thirties, Jan guessed, with brown hair and glasses. "Avery is a sweet girl, and a hard worker. She's such a delight to have in class."

Well, Jan couldn't argue with that. Avery *was* pretty special. "Thank you," she said. "She loves orchestra. She's been practicing a lot for this upcoming challenge—it's great to see her working so hard."

Mr. Conrad nodded. "It's wonderful when kids find something they love, isn't it?"

He wasn't unattractive, Jan decided. Just a bit awkward, the way he moved his hands too much. And he had something of a self-effacing demeanor.

"It really is," Jan said. She smiled and tried to change gears. She'd figured out a line of questioning that she'd hoped wouldn't be too suspicious before she'd left the house, and had printed off a couple of pages from the Internet. She pulled them out of her purse now. "Actually, I wanted to ask you about her newfound dedication to music. I want to encourage it as much as I can, and I was trying to figure out creative ways to help her learn musical terms, and I found these crossword puzzles online." She slid the pages across the desk toward him.

They were crosswords some music teacher somewhere had designed, with clues such as *the musical staff contains this many lines* and *a _____ note receives ¼ count.*

"I was wondering if you'd ever used anything like this to teach music, and how effective you thought it was."

Frank Conrad looked at her, clearly confused. And okay, back at home she'd thought it was a solid approach, but now Jan could see it was flimsy at best. Still, she smiled brightly, determined not to show that she realized what a strange question it was.

"You mean, have I ever used crossword puzzles to teach music?" he asked, his brow furrowed.

"Yes," Jan said. "It seems like such an interesting idea."

"Has Avery ever"—he cleared his throat—"has she ever mentioned me doing something like that?"

Jan puzzled through that answer. *Should* Avery have?

"Not to me," Jan said. "But then, she doesn't talk to me about homework very often anyway." She watched him for a moment. "Why?"

It took him a few seconds to answer. "I haven't ever used a crossword to teach music," he said slowly. "It never occurred to me. But it's not a bad idea. I prefer to test my students by hearing them play, but sometimes I have them do desk work, and it's an interesting idea, having them do crosswords."

"Have you ever made a crossword?" Jan asked. "It's actually not that difficult, with the software they have online these days."

He narrowed his eyes, his brow wrinkled. Then he shook his head. "No, I've never made a crossword. Online or otherwise."

The words were clear enough. But the way he said them, the way he looked just to the left of her eyes, the way his cheeks turned a light shade of pink, made Jan suspicious.

"The reason I ask is that a friend of mine, Katelyn Grande, has received two crossword puzzles that seem to be made just for her, and we're trying to figure out where they came from."

"Katelyn?" He thought for a moment. "I'm not sure I know her."

He was moving his hands too much. He was either nervous, or he was just an awkward guy. It was hard to tell.

"She works at the Bookworm," Jan said. Nothing in his expression changed with that news. "She's really sweet, and my cousin Elaine and I are trying to help her figure out where the crosswords came from."

"Well, like I said, I've never made a crossword in my life," he said. "Though I do hope you find who you're looking for. Katelyn seems like a nice person. Last time I was in the store she recommended a mystery that I really loved."

Jan watched him as he spoke. It was really hard to tell if he knew something he wasn't saying or if he was just a bit of a nervous person in general. On the one hand, someone like him might be exactly the kind of awkward person who would decide to hide behind a puzzle to try to woo Katelyn. On the other hand, if he *was* the one behind the puzzles, wouldn't he want to own up to them? Wouldn't the point of the puzzles be to have Katelyn realize who he was so she could give him a shot?

"It's just that the first puzzle she received had several musical references, and you obviously know music pretty well," she said. She hoped she didn't sound like she was babbling.

"That's true." He laughed—well, it was a cross between a laugh and a snort, actually. "That's why they pay me the big bucks." He gestured around the empty classroom endearingly. He wasn't traditionally handsome, but he seemed like a genuine, caring man. "And if I were to make a crossword, I feel certain I would make it full of musical clues. But I'm afraid I wouldn't have the first idea how to go about making a crossword puzzle." He shrugged.

"How do you feel about Vivaldi?" she asked.

He blinked. "I like Vivaldi...," he said uncertainly. "A bit overdone, but nice music."

"What's your favorite flower?" she asked.

He blinked again, and then looked at her, his head tilted, like he was trying to make sense of what she was doing. And, okay, she had to admit that she probably seemed somewhat demented. But she was trying to catch him off guard to see how he'd react. She couldn't decide if he was completely and sincerely innocent or lying through his charmingly honest-seeming teeth.

"I grew up in South Africa," he said slowly. "My parents were missionaries. I've always been partial to birds of paradise, because they grew all over our backyard when I was a kid."

Ah. That explained the hint of an accent she'd picked up in his speech.

He was looking at her like he was waiting to see what she'd do next.

Jan thought quickly. *Bird of paradise* wasn't mentioned in the flower-themed puzzle. Did that mean he had nothing to do with the puzzle? Or did he know that bird of paradise wasn't mentioned, and give that answer to throw her off? She had no idea. She was getting more confused the more they talked.

"Do you have any other questions?" he asked, a bemused smile on his face.

Did she have other questions? Well, she had promised Elaine she'd try to get a fingerprint. But she couldn't just ask him to give her one of those. How was she going to do that while he was sitting here? She looked around the room quickly. She needed a way to get him to leave for a few minutes, and then she could dust the coffee cup on his desk.

She thought quickly, but nothing came to mind.

"You look like you want to ask me something," he said.

He was right, of course. She thought that people who worked with children all had to be fingerprinted, and she was sure his fingerprints would be on file with the Maine Department of Education, but she didn't know if they would let her access those. Maybe she should have waited until Elaine could have come with her. She was sure Elaine would have smooth-talked her way into getting a fingerprint some very seamless way. But couldn't think of any more elegant way to get one.

"My cousin and I tried to get I touch with you earlier this week. Did you get that message?"

"I did, and I am really sorry about that. I am usually quite good at responding to messages, but I've been crazy busy with the new school year, and this totally slipped my mind. I'm so sorry." He gave her what seemed to be a genuinely sheepish smile. "My apologies. Was it crosswords you wanted to talk to me about, or was there something else?"

From someone else, it could have come out sounding harsh, but his tone was gentle, like he genuinely wanted to please her.

She tried to think of what to say. The only idea she had couldn't possibly work. But she had nothing better. This had worked for Elaine.

"Do you ever teach private lessons?" she asked.

He looked surprised, but he nodded. "Yes, during summers," he said. "Do you think Avery would be interested?"

"Perhaps," Jan said. It wasn't untrue. Perhaps she would be. "Do you have a business card I could pass on to her mother?"

"Of course." He smiled and reached into his desk and pulled out a glossy card. She was pleased to see that he stuck his finger square in the middle as he handed it over. "Avery has shown real improvement since the beginning of the school year. If she continues to work hard, she could be quite good."

"Thank you so much," she said, grabbing it by the edges. Frank Conrad, Private Music Lessons, it said, and it had a phone number beneath. "I will pass this along."

"Please say hello to Avery for me."

Jan thanked him again, and then she walked out of the classroom, thinking through the exchange. He *had* acted strangely when she brought up Katelyn, it seemed to her. But then, he was a little awkward. Sweet and earnest, and probably exactly the type of man who would cherish any woman he loved, but kind of awkward. Was this the kind of person who would declare his love through a crossword puzzle? Jan didn't know. He hadn't returned their message. But he had said flat-out that he hadn't made any crossword puzzles. That wasn't how a guilty man would act.

Jan didn't know. As she got back into her car, she realized she was more confused than ever.

CHAPTER EIGHTEEN

When Jan got back to the house, she was out of sorts. Elaine could tell it hadn't gone as well as she'd hoped.

"I did manage to get a business card, which will hopefully have a fingerprint," she said. "But he seemed to be telling the truth about not having made the puzzles."

"Did you believe him?" Elaine leaned back in the desk chair. Her eyes had been glazing over from staring at the computer screen for too long, so she was glad of the interruption.

"I did. I don't think he made those puzzles. But the proof is in the pudding, as they say." She indicated the card on the desk. "Speaking of pudding..."

Elaine nodded and stood up. Jan had been working with Rose on how to make a smooth custard, and there was some delicious salted toffee custard in the fridge. "I could use a break."

A few minutes later, they each had a bowl of the custard and had gathered around the small table in the kitchen. Archie had come in for a tray of sandwiches shortly after they arrived, and a teakettle was heating on the stove, but otherwise it was quiet.

"I did some research while you were gone as well," Elaine said. Truthfully, she'd spent almost the whole time Jan had been gone looking into this mystery. She'd intended to tackle the invoices, but she'd started off with a call to her mother to work out the details for their dinner Saturday. Her mother had been in good spirits, though she mentioned her car had a funny smell ever since she'd left the window cracked open and rain had come in. Mentioning the car made Elaine remember that she wanted to look into that license plate, and suddenly the whole afternoon had been gone.

"Oh?" Jan sampled a spoonful of the custard. She gave an approving smile as she tasted it.

"I found a site online where you can look up license plates and see who they're registered to."

"Really?" Jan was constantly surprised by what you could find online these days. "That's a little disturbing."

"Not unless you're doing something wrong," Elaine said, scraping her spoon against the dish to get a bite of custard. "So obviously I looked up the license plate of that truck Katelyn's father took a picture of." She put the bite into her mouth. This was *good* pudding. Salty and sweet and smoky all at once. She had to force herself to not shovel it in by the spoonful.

"And?" Jan seemed to be enjoying the pudding as well, judging by the approving look on her face.

"It's registered to a James Walden, who lives in Watertown."

"Who's that?"

"A little bit of research..."

"You mean you Googled his name?"

Elaine took another bite of the pudding and smiled, and then she continued. "I did some research and I discovered that he works for the utilities company."

"Utilities?"

"Exactly."

Jan rested her spoon against the side of her dish.

"But that would give him a perfectly valid reason for poking around at the side of the house."

"It does indeed. And when I talked to him ..."

"You talked to him?"

"It wasn't hard to find his phone number online."

"Goodness. It's enough to make you want to give up all contact with the modern world."

"To be fair, the phone number was harder. I had to use some tips from professional sleuths."

"Like yourself," Jan said.

"I get the sense you're mocking me." Elaine took another bite.

"Just a little."

"Well, you're lucky I'm in a good mood. And that's because, lo and behold, he picked up when I called, and he was very nice."

"And? Did he say why he's been hanging out by the empty house so much?"

"He did." Somehow Elaine's dish was almost empty. Would it be ridiculous to help herself to some more? She needed sustenance to make it through the rest of that stack of invoices, after all. "It turns out the panel that protects the meter is stuck, and he needs to get into it so he can read the meter. He's been getting a lot of pressure from his boss to get that information, so he's been coming back trying different tactics for getting it open."

"Oh." Jan's voice sounded deflated. "In other words, he has a perfectly logical reason for being there."

"Yes, I'm afraid so." Elaine scooped up the rest of her pudding and savored it for a moment. "That's what I told Ken Grande when I called him to tell him the news. But honestly, our man in black was a bit of a long shot anyway. I may not be totally convinced the crosswords are coming from a secret admirer, but I didn't think it was incredibly likely that the guy hanging around outside the neighbor's house was involved. Aside from opportunity to leave the puzzle in the car, there's not much linking him to anything here." She set the spoon into the empty bowl and pushed it away from her so she wasn't tempted to go back and get that refill.

"I guess you're right," Jan said.

"Don't look so disheartened." Elaine tried to make her voice seem more optimistic than she felt. Truthfully, they were running out of leads. "We'll find this person, whoever he is."

"I know we will."

Just then the teakettle started to whistle and Rose came in with an armload of dirty dishes, and Elaine and Jan spring into action. They would find out more about those puzzles by hook or by crook. But for now, they had a tearoom to run.

CHAPTER NINETEEN

Elaine rubbed sleep out of her eyes. She'd hit the hard stuff this morning—espresso—because she'd been up too late going over and over the whole collection of fingerprints they'd received so far. None of them was a match, from what she could tell. Granted, some of the prints she'd collected were blurry or smeared, and some were only partials, and she wasn't exactly a professional, but she doubted even the police could have been more thorough. And still...nothing useful.

Earl Gray was pawing at the door to the porch, and Jan went out to refill his dish and pet him for a minute while Elaine thought. One thing was clear: Frank Conrad was looking like an unlikely suspect. His prints weren't even close to the prints she'd collected from either the puzzle or the plastic wrapper on the flowers. Jan had told her that he'd acted awkwardly, but she didn't think he was involved, and forensic evidence doesn't lie. Which left them with... well, pretty much no one.

"Want another cup?" Jan asked from over by the stove. She was setting the kettle on for another cup of tea, Elaine saw. Evidence that she, too, had been up too late. She'd been dutifully searching through MakeYourPuzzle.com, looking for any puzzles that had been made by a Conrad or Mr. Conrad or a Frank of any description, but she too had come up short.

"Sure, but I'll take the hard stuff." Elaine stood up to make herself another espresso from the industrial machine. Just as she was reaching for the milk, the phone on the wall rang. "Tea for Two," Elaine said, cradling the phone between her shoulder and her ear.

"Hello. This is Maya Ruby from Blooms Flower Shop," the woman said.

"Hi, Maya. This is Elaine." She straightened up and gestured to Jan. When her cousin was looking at her, she mouthed the words, "It's Maya." Jan perked up and watched her, waiting.

"My niece Hilary told me you were in here the other day asking about stargazer lilies."

"Yes, we were. We were hoping to find out who had bought bouquets on Monday night. She told us who bought one, but we were hoping to find out who purchased the other."

"Sure thing. I actually remember exactly who it was. It was Rachel Leon."

"Rachel Leon?" Elaine repeated. She saw that Jan seemed as confused by the news as she was. Elaine vaguely knew who Rachel was. She worked in the Whisper Art Gallery, which was owned and run by her sister, Elsa. While Elsa was distinctive and bohemian and created gorgeous bronze sculptures, Rachel was quiet and studious and dressed much more, well, normally. But it didn't make any sense that she had bought the flowers. Had Rachel left the flowers for Katelyn? What connection could she possibly have to Katelyn, or to the puzzles?

Elaine started to get a sick feeling in her stomach. Someone could be playing a horrible joke on Katelyn.

"Yes, she came in here as we were about to close for the day, and asked for lilies. I suggested the stargazers, because the bunches we had in were this gorgeous peach color and smelled like heaven. She didn't seem to know or care much about the different kinds of flowers, but was just in a rush to buy them and get out."

"Do you mean she seemed furtive?" Elaine asked.

"No, not really." Maya thought for a moment. "More just that she was in a hurry."

"Hmm." Elaine tried to figure out how this information fit into what she already knew, but she couldn't make sense of it. "Did you get any idea what she was buying the flowers for?"

"She didn't say, and I didn't ask. Honestly, she didn't stick around for much small talk. She zipped in and out in probably under two minutes."

"Is it unusual for a customer to be so quick?"

"I guess it depends. But it did stand out to me."

"Huh." Elaine switched the phone to her other ear. "Did she say anything else about the flowers?"

"I'm afraid not," Maya said. "I wish I could help you more, but that's all I know."

"That's quite all right," Elaine said. "I really appreciate your help."

"Anytime."

Elaine hung up and turned to Jan.

"Rachel Leon?" Jan asked, her confusion showing on her face.

"Apparently," Elaine said.

"Why would she be buying flowers for Katelyn?" Jan asked, echoing her own questions.

"I don't know." Elaine scooped a spoonful of sugar into her cup. "I guess we need to ask her."

Jan smiled at her over the rim of her mug. "How soon can you be ready?"

A FEW MINUTES later they were walking inside the front door of the Whisper Art Gallery. The gallery was housed in an old barn on the lake that had weathered to a gorgeous light gray. The gallery was just a short distance from Tea for Two along Main Street, and they had decided to walk to enjoy the crisp fall day. The little town was quiet but beautiful, and they waved to Bianca Stadler as they passed the Pine Tree Grill and listened to the soft lapping of water against the boats in the marina. Soon those boats would all be pulled in for the season, but Elaine enjoyed the sight of them now.

In the yard next to the barn that housed the Whisper Art Gallery, Elsa Leon had set up a sculpture garden, featuring works of her own as well as pieces by other local artists. You could wander through the meticulously maintained pebble paths that meandered through hedges and between beds of flowers that bloomed with the seasons. Right now the last roses of summer were still holding on, and Elaine also recognized clematis and anemone and asters. It was beautiful.

Elaine pulled open the glass front door and stepped inside. Inside, the original wide plank floors had been polished to a high gloss, and the walls had been covered in sheetrock and painted a bright white. Works from various local artists were spaced around the walls. There were several pictures that looked like someone had thrown paint randomly at the canvas, and one that looked like someone had blown up a photograph and painted the tiny portion of it in colored dots. Elaine was drawn to the more realistic landscapes—the sweeping sea grasses bent before an impending storm; the glimmer of sunset over a wind-tossed lake; Portland Head Light, perched on an outcropping of the craggy coast. Something about the way the artist had captured the light in these pictures was stunning.

Elsa Leon was perched on a high stool behind the counter. "Hello, Elaine, Jan," she said. She was wearing a chunky sweater that went down to her knees over a loose long-sleeved blouse and a floor-skimming gauzy skirt. "Thanks for coming in. Can I help you find something, or are you just looking around?"

"Actually," Elaine said, "we were looking for Rachel. Is she around?"

"I think so. She's up in the apartment," Elsa said, gesturing up toward the ceiling. "Hang on, I'll give her a call."

"Thank you." Elaine knew that Rachel had built an apartment on the second story of the barn, and both she and her sister lived up there, above the gallery.

Elsa quickly dialed, and after a brief conversation, she hung up. "She'll be right down," she said.

"Thank you," Elaine said. She saw that Jan had wandered over to one of the splatter paintings and was staring at it. Elaine walked up beside her.

"I keep thinking there's something here I'm missing. Something that makes these pictures great that I'm not seeing. But nope, I don't think so," Jan said quietly.

Elaine laughed. "I do prefer the pictures where you can see what it's supposed to be," she said.

"Me too. That probably means I don't have very artistic taste, but it's true."

The phone on the counter rang, and Elsa picked it up. Elaine wasn't listening in exactly, but she did notice that Elsa asked, "What do you mean?" and started to talk quietly, but in an animated tone. It was almost like she didn't want Elaine and Jan to hear something. "They're here waiting," Elsa said. "Why not?" After a few moments, Elsa hung up, sighed, and looked up at the cousins.

"It seems my sister has to step out, and she won't be able to talk to you after all," she said, without much conviction.

"Oh dear. I hope everything is all right," Elaine said.

"I—I hope so too. I'm sorry about this." Elsa was shaking her head.

"Was there some reason she didn't want to talk to us?" Elaine asked.

Elsa waited just a bit too long to answer. "Of course not," she said, but her eyes wouldn't meet Elaine's.

"Well, can we leave her a message?" Elaine asked.

"Sure thing." Elsa reached for a pad of paper and a pen from the jar on the counter.

"Can you tell her we'd like to ask her about a bouquet of lilies?" Elaine asked.

Elsa tilted her head and wrinkled her brow. "A bouquet of lilies?"

"That's right," Elaine said. "Here's my number." She rattled off her cell number, as well as the number for the tearoom, and then they turned to go.

"That was weird, right?" Jan said as they walked across the parking area.

"It was." Elaine stopped and looked up at the windows on the second floor of the barn. Was Rachel up there? Why didn't she want to talk to them? "It was like she changed her mind once she realized who we were."

"Like she was hiding something."

"Exactly."

Elaine thought for a few more seconds, running through the interaction in her mind, and then shook her head and climbed into the car. Rachel had been avoiding them, she was almost sure of it.

The question was why. What was she hiding?

CHAPTER TWENTY

The whole way back from the gallery, Jan ran through possibilities with Elaine. Maybe Rachel had bought the flowers to give to someone else, but they had ended up with Katelyn for some reason. Rachel had bought them on behalf of someone to give to Katelyn. Rachel had given them to Katelyn herself. Rachel was playing a horrible joke on Katelyn. Elaine seemed to be growing more and more certain that was the case, but Jan wasn't sure. The puzzles were from a secret admirer, she was sure of it. She just couldn't figure out how Rachel was involved.

Finally, Jan grew tired of going through scenarios in her mind and pulled out her cell phone.

"What are you doing?" Elaine asked, looking over at her.

"I'm calling Katelyn."

"Ah. Good ." Elaine nodded. "That's why I keep you around, you know."

"Because I'm good at pointing out the obvious?"

"Well, it's one of the many reasons."

Jan pulled up Katelyn's number and waited as it rang.

"Hello?" Katelyn said. "Jan?"

"Hi, Katelyn. Quick question. Does the name Rachel Leon mean anything to you?"

"Rachel Leon?" Katelyn thought for a minute. "No. Wait. That name sounds familiar. Who is that?"

"She works at the Whisper Art Gallery with her sister Elsa."

"Oh, that's right. I went to school with Elsa. But Rachel was a few years older and we didn't really cross paths. Why?"

Jan tried to figure out how much to say. "Her name has come up in our investigation," she said. "We're trying to figure out how she might be involved."

"Huh." Katelyn thought for a minute. "Now that you mention it, I seem to remember Elsa is Tag King's cousin. But I thought you said he seemed unlikely?"

Well, this was an interesting connection. But Katelyn was right—Tag King seemed pretty unlikely to Jan. And even if he was involved, why would he get his cousin to buy flowers for him to give to Katelyn?

"I hadn't realized that connection," Jan said. "We can look into that. Can you think of any other reason her name would have come up?"

"How did her name come up, exactly?" Katelyn asked.

"She bought the bouquet of stargazers you found in your car," Jan said.

"What?" Katelyn's reaction was about what Jan's own had been. "How is that possible?"

"That's what we're trying to figure out," Jan said. "If you can think of any other reason she might have been involved, please do let me know."

"I will." Katelyn seemed as disoriented as she did.

"No luck?" Elaine asked when she hung up.

Jan shook her head. "She did say that Rachel and Elsa are Tag's cousins, so maybe that's an angle worth looking into?" But even as she said it, she heard how ridiculous it sounded.

"It seems pretty unlikely he would ask his cousin to buy flowers for a girl for him," Elaine said, stating what they both thought. "Especially since he didn't seem to know who Katelyn was, and his fingerprints didn't match the ones on the puzzle."

"Yep." Jan thought it all through. It sure seemed like one more dead end. "But I'll probably still call him just to ask."

"To ask if he really is secretly in love with Katelyn after all and got his cousin to buy flowers for her?"

"I might phrase it slightly differently than that."

Elaine laughed. "Well, I hope so. And if you think it's worth a phone call, be my guest. But I'm starting to doubt this whole thing."

"Starting to?" Jan shook her head. "You've been doubting this all along." They had just arrived at the front of Tea for Two. "But we're getting closer. I can feel it."

Elaine gave Jan a sidelong look. "Well, I'm glad you can, because I'm beginning to feel like this is all a big waste of time."

"Don't give up yet," Jan said. She knew that Elaine had always had her doubts. And sure, maybe there was a tinge of truth to the idea that Jan was so excited about helping

Katelyn find love because she was happy with Bob. But it was more than that. Something real was going on. Someone had put a lot of time into creating those puzzles. There had to be a reason.

And whatever that reason was, Jan wasn't going to give up until she found the truth.

CHAPTER TWENTY-ONE

When they went inside, Jan went into the kitchen to help Rose, who had arrived and was starting the day's scones in Jan's absence. Elaine went upstairs to spend some time on her devotions, and she meditated over the passage in that day's reading: "You will seek me and find me when you seek me with all your heart" (Jeremiah 29:13). Elaine read the verse slowly, savoring the words, letting herself relax into the promise. God was faithful; all she had to do was seek Him. She was grateful that that was true, no matter the circumstances. She prayed, asking God to lead her, asking Him to help her seek Him with all her heart.

When she set her devotional and Bible aside, she felt refreshed and peaceful. She may not know how to find the answers Katelyn was looking for, but God was always there, waiting for her to simply seek Him. There was an enormous amount of comfort in that.

Elaine headed downstairs to get to work on those invoices, and greeted Rose and Jan in the kitchen on her way to the office.

"Those smell heavenly," Elaine said, indicating a batch of what looked like pumpkin muffins that Rose was just taking out of the oven.

"Would you like one?" Rose gave her an eager smile. "I'm working on the brown sugar crumble topping now, but even without the topping these are pretty good."

"Even Earl Gray agrees," Jan said, pointing to the porch, where the gray cat was nibbling at a muffin from the previous batch.

"I didn't think cats liked sweets."

"It's a testament to Rose's baking."

Elaine nodded, though she wasn't sure at all the cat should be eating that muffin. It had to be bad for his teeth, if not his digestion. But she had to admit, he did seem to be enjoying it. She decided to let it be.

"As much as I want to say yes, I'm afraid I should pass." If Elaine gave in every time something delicious came out of this kitchen, she'd barely fit through the door soon. She started toward the office.

She sat down at her desk and tried to focus, but her mind wandered. She thought about Avery and the little drama that was playing out in her world. Elaine remembered how your friends could feel like your whole world at this age. Then she thought that maybe age had nothing to do with it; her mother's world had been built around her friends for so long they had become like family. She thought about what Avery had said, about how sad it must be to not see her mother more, and she realized it was true. It did seem a bit strange that she ate with Jan's kids and grandkids more than with her own mother, who lived the same distance away. But the truth was she was grateful that her mother and children had their own lives. And she thought about that phone message from Nathan. She still hadn't responded. She just wasn't sure what to say.

Elaine wasn't getting anything done here. She walked out to the east parlor and saw they had a few customers. She helped Archie bring out sandwiches to Rue Maxwell and Macy Atherton, and then Elaine delivered a child's-size afternoon tea to a grandmother and her granddaughter. The little girl couldn't have been more than four, and she was wearing a pink dress and patent leather shoes, and her beautiful blue eyes widened when she saw the tea tray stuffed with crustless peanut butter and jelly sandwiches cut into triangles.

"Here you are, sweetie," Elaine said, her heart lurching at the ecstatic look on the little girl's face.

"This must be how princesses eat," she said, wonder in her voice.

Elaine and the grandmother both chuckled. After she checked in with Jan, Rose, and Archie in the kitchen, and they insisted they had everything under control, she made herself a cup of Earl Grey and headed back to the office, this time with the book about the family crests tucked under her arm. She'd given up on real work but hoped she would find something worthwhile in this book.

Elaine started at the beginning with the A names and paged through the book slowly. She tried to look at each one carefully to see if it was a match. Some of the shields were divided into parts, while others had predominant symbols that took of most of the space on the shield. She recognized some obvious symbols, like a snail and a mermaid and a horse, but she couldn't figure out many of the others, and she couldn't figure out for the life of her why any family would choose to have a snail on its crest in the first place. Elaine looked for the ones that were divided into four parts, but was having a hard time figuring out what exactly the symbols on her shield were supposed to be.

She sipped her tea and flipped through the pages, but she grew frustrated. It would take forever to go through every one of the images in this book, and it wasn't getting her any closer to figuring out what the ring had been doing in their wall.

"Elaine?"

She looked up and saw Archie standing in the doorway of the office.

"Hello," she said. She set the book down on her desk and sat up. "How is it going out there?"

"Just fine," Archie said, smiling. "I'm sorry to disturb you. I just wanted to let you know that we're running low on raspberry tea. You'll probably want to order more."

Elaine figured he could tell her anything, and as long as he said it in that clipped, high-born accent, she wouldn't mind. *The house is on fire. Your cat is dead. I've just robbed you.* In his warm, lovely accent, she wouldn't worry about it.

"Wonderful. Thank you for letting me know." She picked up a pen and made a note to order more.

Archie stood in the doorway, and he seemed to be hesitating. She could see he was eyeing her book. And then she realized something obvious. Archie was British, and, she suspected, from the upper-crust of society. He was well studied and well traveled.

"Archie, do you know anything about family crests?"

"Actually, I do know a bit," he said. "I studied heraldry at Cambridge for a while. I don't know how useful I can be, but if you have questions I'd be happy to try to help."

"I'm trying to figure out if this is a family crest, and, if so, what family it might be for," she said. She indicated the flue cover, which sat next to the book on the desk.

"Fascinating." Archie stepped into the room and picked up the flue cover and studied it for a moment. Then he turned to the book. "May I?"

"Of course." He set the flue cover down and pulled the book close to him. Elaine indicated that he should sit down in one of the cane-backed chairs on the other side of her desk.

"Heraldry is such a fascinating subject. It's chock-full of history and tales of ambition and pride," he said. He started flipping through the pages. "In England, and in other places too, I'm sure, all matters relating to heraldry were governed by the crown."

"So a family didn't simply make up their own coat of arms? It was assigned to them?" Elaine asked.

"Exactly. And the symbols and colors and everything on it were carefully chosen." He flipped through the pages gently. "Of course it varied by country how they were assigned and what the symbols all meant. I can only speak to the British tradition." He seemed to find a page he was looking for.

"Here, take a look at this," he said. Elaine looked down and saw that he was pointing to a red-and-white shield. It was divided into four quadrants and had red flowers in two and yellow suns in two, with a white and red cross separating them.

Elaine looked it over, and then she saw the name written underneath. Bentham.

"This is your family crest?" she asked.

"Just the escutcheon," he said.

"Huh?"

"The shield part. It's called the escutcheon. But yes. This is the symbol of the Bentham family, though it's so far back and history is so convoluted it's impossible to say how I'm related to the man who first earned this coat of arms. But chances are, I am somehow."

"That's so interesting. I don't think I know anyone who has a family coat of arms."

"It's probably far more common than you realize. Though again, most of us these days are so far removed from the ancestors who gave us our names that it's hard to legitimately claim that these crests have anything to do with us."

Elaine nodded, and she looked down at the picture he'd shown her.

"You mentioned something about symbols. What do these symbols mean?"

"Ah yes. Many of the images that were used on the crests were rife with meaning. The sun, for instance"—he pointed to the upper right and lower left quadrants of the shield—"was used to symbolize glory and splendor. And the red is meant to symbolize hope and beauty. And see this cross here that separates it all?" She nodded. "That's one of the most common ways to divide up the shield, and it stands for faith and protection."

"That's really fascinating." She'd had no idea these crests were so invested with symbolism.

"Now, may I take a closer look at that design you're looking for?" Archie asked. Elaine handed over the flue cover and he studied it for a moment.

"I've been trying to make out what these squiggles are," she said, pointing to the four quadrants of the shield.

He nodded and continued to study it.

"It's such a crude etching that it's hard to say," he said slowly. "But it does indeed look like a family shield." He held the flue cover at an angle so the sunlight streaming in through the window shone on it fully. "But I have a few guesses."

"You do?"

He nodded and pointed to the top right quadrant. "This looks to me like an anchor."

"An anchor?" Elaine thought for a second. "Like, maybe the originators of this shield were mariners or something?"

"Possibly," Archie said. "Though the anchor was also a symbol for salvation and religious steadfastness."

"How lovely." Elaine felt heartened by the idea. She was familiar with the idea of Jesus as the anchor in a storm, and it gave her good feelings about whatever family this crest belonged to.

"And this one could be a couple of things," Archie said pointing to the other quadrants. "But it looks to me like a plant of some kind."

Elaine nodded. She could see that now. The straight line could be a stem or trunk, and the cloud bits could be leaves.

"It could be a trefoil, which stands for longevity," he said. "But that would likely indicate Irish roots, as the trefoil and the shamrock are sometimes conflated."

"There's nothing to say that the family behind this crest didn't come from Ireland," she said.

"True, but I don't actually think that's what it is," Archie said. "My guess is that this etching is supposed to represent a tree stump."

"A tree stump?" That wasn't exactly inspiring.

"It's not as bad as it sounds," Archie said. "This is the trunk," he said, pointing to the squiggle down the middle. "But I think these scratches here are meant to indicate buds growing from the stump."

"What does that mean?" she asked.

"It's a symbol of rebirth or regrowth," he said.

Elaine thought about that for a minute. It was a comforting thought—life coming from death.

"That's really nice."

"It is lovely," Archie said. "And this crest has the same cross that separates the quadrants, just as mine does, and again, that references faith and protection."

Elaine liked that the shield had several elements that pointed to faith. Whomever this crest belonged to, she already thought a bit better of them. But as much as she loved learning all of this, it hadn't gotten her any closer to finding out who the owner of the crest was.

"Is there any way to trace the name of the family based on these symbols?" Elaine asked.

Archie laughed. "I'm afraid that I haven't quite memorized which names go with which symbols."

Elaine nodded. That would be quite an impressive memory. She guessed she was back to flipping through the pages, looking for the right picture. But at least she had a better idea what she was now looking for.

"Elaine?" She looked up and saw Jan standing in the doorway, holding out the cordless phone to her. "Avery is on the phone for you."

"For me?" Elaine pushed back her chair and stood. "Thank you so much, Archie."

Archie excused himself and went back out into the kitchen, but Jan hovered in the doorway, no doubt curious about why her granddaughter had called to speak to Elaine. Well, Elaine was curious about that as well.

"Hello, Avery."

"Elaine? Guess what?" It sounded like Avery was outside the school, or somewhere where there were lots of people around. She heard a girl screeching in excitement and the thud of basketballs on pavement in the background.

"What?"

"They said yes!"

It took a minute for Elaine to work out what Avery was saying. She thought back on their last conversation in the car. Then she remembered—she had suggested Avery invite the girls from her class to come here for tea.

"To a tea party?" When she had suggested it, Avery seemed to think the idea was silly.

"Yes! I invited them to a tea party, and they all said yes!"

"Well, that's wonderful," Elaine said. She gestured to Jan, trying to signal that she'd explain what was going on when she got off the phone. "Now we'll just pick a date, and . . ."

"Oh, I told them Sunday. I hope that's okay."

"Sunday?" It was Friday now. "As in *this* Sunday?"

"Yeah. Does that work?"

Elaine ran through the weekend schedule in her mind. But the truth was, it didn't matter what else she had going on. She was going to make sure this party happened for Avery.

"Of course. We'll set it up in the special dining room. How many girls are we talking?"

"Eight, including me."

"All right." They'd figure out how to make that work. "That sounds fine."

"Thank you so much, Elaine!"

"We're looking forward to it."

The line went dead, and Elaine hung up and turned to Jan, who was looking at her, questions written on her face.

"It looks like we're hosting a tea party."

CHAPTER TWENTY-TWO

Jan was up before daybreak on Saturday, getting an early start on the pastries for the tearoom. Before she and Elaine had opened this business, Saturday mornings had been a time to sleep in a bit and to take it easy. But around here, Saturdays were one of their busiest days. It made things go smoother when she could get up early and get a jump on baking. And Jan didn't mind. She enjoyed the quiet mornings alone in the kitchen, watching the sun break through the trees. The lake was quiet and still, and she could hear the distinct cry of the loons that made their homes nearby. This time of day was when Jan felt closest to God, and she talked to Him while she measured and mixed.

This morning, the familiar rhythms of baking also allowed her mind to wander to the puzzles, and to Avery. She'd had no idea until Elaine told her about the tea party that Avery was having trouble with the girls at school. She was glad that Avery had confided in someone, and she was glad that she and Elaine were developing a special relationship, but if she was honest, it also stung a little. Avery was *her* granddaughter; a small part of her wished Avery had come to her first. She knew it was childish, and she knew it was good for both Avery and Elaine that they had become friends, so she would never let on. But working through it in prayer while she shaped and cut the scones helped.

Elaine was soon up, and while they both ate breakfast, Elaine read the newspaper and Jan worked the daily crossword. This was one by Bill Markham, and it was tricky, but Jan got most of it filled in before her tea went cold.

They were just finishing cleaning up the kitchen when the doorbell rang. They looked at each other. Who was coming to see them this early? Jan shrugged, and she set down her dish towel and walked down the hallway to the front door. Elaine followed just a step behind.

Jan opened the door and was surprised to see Katelyn standing on the front porch, wearing a light fall coat, holding—

"Oh my goodness. Is that another crossword?"

It looked just like the others, with the crossword grid printed in the middle of the page and, as Jan could see from where she was standing, a line of text at the bottom that she was sure said MakeYourPuzzle.com. There was a single piece of cellophane tape at the top.

Katelyn nodded. "I just got to work"—she gestured at the bookstore next door to the house, through the trees—"and this was folded and taped to the door of the Bookworm!"

Jan's first instinct was to invite her in and get started solving the puzzle, but Elaine was already grabbing her coat from the hooks by the door.

"Show us where you found it," she said.

She wanted to look for physical clues first, Jan knew, and she could see the logic in that. She ran to turn the oven off and then grabbed her jacket and followed Elaine and Katelyn out. They walked through the grass, wet with dew, out to the sidewalk, and then through the gate into the small yard in front of the Bookworm.

"I parked over there," Katelyn said, indicating her red two-door parked in the small lot at the side of the building. "And I saw something on the door, but I didn't know what it was. When I came closer, I saw that it was another crossword."

Elaine studied the door. It was old-fashioned, with a wooden frame painted deep green and a central flat glass panel where the bookstore's name and hours were painted in gold. "Where was it taped?" she asked.

"Right about here." She indicted just below the words The Bookworm.

"Bristol didn't see it when she came in?" Jan asked.

Katelyn shook her head. "I got here first today. She had some errands to run, so the plan was for me to open up the store."

"Do you open up often?" Elaine asked.

"Sometimes. It's not uncommon," Katelyn said.

While Elaine was asking questions, Jan was studying the area around the door. There was a fieldstone walkway that led from the parking area and met up with the path that ran down from the sidewalk. There was a brown sisal doormat, and junipers stood on each side of the door. Jan didn't see any sign that anything had been disturbed, and no clues either.

"What did you do when you realized what it was?" Elaine asked.

"I looked at it for a minute, and then I pulled it off the door to be sure." She glanced at Elaine. "Don't worry, I used my sleeve to pick it up, so my fingerprints shouldn't mess up whatever's on there." She turned back and looked at the door. "And then I ran over to your place. I wanted to show you right away."

"So you haven't been inside the bookstore yet this morning?"

Katelyn shook her head. "But I should probably get inside and start getting things set up. Besides, it's freezing out here."

She was right about that. Katelyn pulled her keys out of her coat pocket and inserted a small key into the brass lock. She pushed the door open, and they all stepped inside. It took Katelyn a few minutes to flip on all the lights, turn the heat up, and get the beverage station brewing. While she was working, Jan studied the puzzle and Elaine examined the door from the inside. Soft classical music started playing out over the store's loudspeakers.

This puzzle looked just like all the others. It was a square, with smaller black squares separating the answers. It was indeed another puzzle made on the same Web site. The first clue in this puzzle, 1 down, read, *War and* _____. Well, that one wasn't difficult. The five-letter answer was obviously *peace,* but she didn't want to start filling in the answers until Katelyn had a chance to make a photocopy. *Famous book by the daughter of a transcendentalist* was 3 down. That took Jan a few minutes to work through, but the answer, at eleven characters long, had to be *Little Women.*

When Katelyn had finished brewing the coffee and came back up to the counter, Jan told her, "I think this one has a literary theme."

"Really?" Jan didn't miss the note of pleasure in her voice. "Here, let me go make copies, and then we can fill this in." She saw Elaine looking hopefully at the paper. "And you can dust the original for fingerprints." Elaine smiled.

Katelyn took the paper into the small room at the back of the shop, holding it with a tissue so as not to add fingerprints, and she returned a few minutes later with a couple of photocopies. She handed the original to Elaine, and she and Jan leaned over one of the copies.

Jan quickly realized that she was right. In addition to clues about Dickens, Steinbeck, and Grisham, there were references to folios and typewriters among the answers.

"It *is* literature-themed," Katelyn said, her voice almost giddy. "That's so perfect."

"Is there anything that points to who made the puzzle?" Elaine asked, studying the paper that she'd coated in dust. "By the way, 16 down is *Eliot*. As in George Eliot."

"Nice," Jan said, quickly filling in the squares.

Elaine made a face, but Jan could tell she was excited.

"No clues to the writer that I can see so far," Jan said. She thought through the list of suspects. Would Tag King know these references to literature? It seemed unlikely to Jan. Books didn't seem to be his thing. Dutch Bigelow might, but Jan was still having a hard time believing he was behind these puzzles. Of all of the "suspects," River White seemed the most likely, given his journalism career and the link to the flowers, but if he really was newly engaged, that pretty much ruled him out as a secret admirer. Besides, his prints hadn't checked out. Could Rachel Leon know anything about literature? And music and flowers? Jan didn't know her well enough to know. The more names she went through in her mind, the more confused she got.

"A man who quotes literature to me is pretty much my dream guy," Katelyn said. Jan looked up and saw that she had that moony look on her face again.

"We'll find him," Jan said confidently, though her optimism was starting to wane.

Elaine looked thoughtful, and then she asked what seemed to Jan an odd question. "If this were a romance novel, or a romantic comedy, what would happen next?"

Katelyn laughed, and then she thought for a minute. "I suppose we'd figure out who it was and fall in love. Though, no, wait. There would probably need to be some obstacles to overcome, like it's secretly my enemy who's been in love with me the whole time or something like that. So it would look like we weren't going to get together, and then I'd finally fall for him and he'd have moved on, and then he'd stage some grand romantic gesture to show how much he cares, and we'd live happily ever after." She was smiling, but her cheeks were a bit pink.

"So who are your enemies?" Elaine asked.

Katelyn laughed. "I'm afraid I don't really have any."

Jan had a different sort of question. "What do you mean by grand romantic gesture?"

"Oh, you know, like in *Sleepless in Seattle,* where he asks her to meet at the top of the Empire State Building on Valentine's Day, or something. Or when Mark brings Bridget a new diary in the snow in *Bridget Jones's Diary.* These days it's when people do things like propose on the Jumbotron at a baseball game or ask a girl to the prom in front of the whole school or serenade her with an entire orchestra."

People did such things in real life? What an awful lot of pressure. Jan was glad she and Bob had simply done things the old-fashioned way.

"Well, I can't promise any of that will happen, but we will try to find whoever is behind them," Elaine promised.

"Any luck on the prints?" Jan asked.

"There's nothing on this one. I can't even find a partial."

"So our puzzle maker is being careful these days." Jan thought through the implications of that. Was it someone they'd already talked to, who knew they were collecting prints? Or had their puzzle maker heard that Elaine was on the look-out somehow?

Just then the front door opened, and they all looked up as Bristol Payson stepped inside the shop. "Oh, hello," she said, smiling at Jan and Elaine. She was bundled up in a heavy parka and a cheerful red knit hat. "Nice to see you. Thanks for opening up, Katelyn." She unwound a scarf from her neck and looked down at the papers on the counter. "What's going on?"

"Katelyn got another crossword," Elaine said.

"It was taped to the front door of the shop when I got here," Katelyn said.

"Wow, that's crazy." Bristol turned and looked back at the door, which had fallen closed gently behind her, and then back at Katelyn. She hung her coat up on a hook by the door, set her purse down, and sat down on one of the stools behind the counter. Katelyn scooted one of the photocopies toward her. "This is so crazy," she repeated, shaking her head. "This is, what, the third one you've gotten?"

"Yep." Katelyn nodded. "This one has a literature theme, as far as we can tell."

"Well. That's handy. Your secret admirer is quite cultured, isn't he?"

Katelyn's cheeks turned the slightest bit pink. Jan's heart soared. This girl was falling for the creator of this puzzle, whoever he was, and it made her heart glad. Sometimes lightning did strike. But judging by the way Elaine was shifting from one foot to the other, she wasn't as convinced.

"And you still have no clue who he is?" Bristol asked.

"No," Katelyn said, but her voice still held the slightest tinge of happiness.

"Nothing but dead ends," Jan said, shaking her head.

"Hmm." Bristol was looking toward the door. She tapped her fingers on the counter, and then stood up. She walked around the counter and stood in front of the glass door, peering out. "The crossword was taped here?" she asked, indicating the door.

"Yep. Just about where the name of the store is," Katelyn said. Bristol nodded, and then opened the door and looked outside. She looked up and down Main Street before coming back inside.

"You don't have security cameras at Tea for Two, do you?" she asked.

"No," Jan said, suddenly understanding where she was going with this. "Do you have them here?"

"No, unfortunately." She shook her head. "But I'm pretty sure the library does."

"Really?" Elaine's face lit up as she, too, understood what Bristol was thinking.

"There was a stretch a few years back where some of the buildings along Main Street were vandalized, and the library was hit quite a few times."

"Vandalized?" Elaine looked as confused as Jan felt. She'd heard of vandalism in Augusta, but Jan couldn't imagine that happening in a place like Lancaster.

"Just some words and pictures spray-painted on the outside of buildings. It was probably some kids being dumb, though I don't think the police ever caught them." She shook her head. "I don't think your place got hit, because it's set back a little from the road, but many of the other buildings along here did. They spray-painted an ugly word on the front of the bookstore. It was annoying to have to paint over it. But the library, being stone, was harder to clean up, and they got hit three or four times, I believe."

"Wow." Jan tried to wrap her mind around this. "I've never heard about this."

Bristol shrugged. "There's no reason you would have. It stopped right after the library made it known that they'd installed security cameras. I guess the kids wised up, knowing they would get caught if they tried it again."

"Do you think the library's cameras might have caught whoever left the puzzle?" Jan asked. She tried to judge how much of the street the library's cameras could have captured. The stone building was directly across the street from their own house, but the bookstore was only a little to the left. Depending on where the cameras were positioned and what angles they took in, it was possible.

"Of course we'd have to verify that the camera are still operational at this point. But it's worth asking Priscilla about."

Jan looked at Elaine, who was looking back at her.

"Shall we head across the street?" Elaine asked, eyebrows raised.

Jan laughed. "Like I could stop you even if I wanted to."

CHAPTER TWENTY-THREE

A few minutes later, Elaine and Jan were huddled over a computer in a small room in the basement of the library. Priscilla Gates had been surprised by their request to view the footage, but had gladly arranged for them to see it. She was about to lead story time in the children's section, so she hadn't been able to show them the footage herself, but she'd pulled Chris Cosgrove away from reshelving books in the reference area to help them. Chris was a junior in high school who volunteered at the library several hours a week, and though Jan had good things to say about him, Elaine had never interacted with him.

Chris had nodded at Priscilla's request, then gestured for the cousins to follow him and led them down the stairs.

As they walked down the stairs, Elaine tried to push a thought out of her mind, but it kept coming back in. Was it odd, she couldn't help but wonder, that no one else had ever found any of the crossword puzzles? Elaine didn't want to think too much about it—surely she couldn't really be suggesting—but it was starting to seem a bit odd. Was there any possibility that Katelyn was...?

"So you're hoping to get footage of the front of the Bookworm?" Chris asked. Elaine snapped back to reality. Chris had stopped at the bottom of the steps and was looking at them both expectantly. Elaine tried to focus on what Chris had said.

"That's right," Jan said, smiling up at him.

"To catch whoever left a crossword puzzle there?"

The smile on his face was kind, but his eyes made it clear he thought their mission was amusing. And, okay, maybe it wasn't catching a murderer or something similarly dramatic. But hopefully they would be able to solve this puzzle. Elaine nodded at him.

"Okay. I'm not sure if the cameras would capture that or not, but we can check." Long and lanky, he was wearing khakis and a fleece vest over a worn T-shirt, and his sneakers squeaked as he walked across the slick floor.

"How is the football season going, Chris?" Jan asked as they walked.

"It's okay. We won our first game last week, so we'll see how the season goes." He shrugged. The cousins followed him past the bathroom and the microfiche room to a small office at the end.

"Chris is the quarterback of the high school football team," Jan explained to Elaine.

"It's fun," he said. He pushed open the door.

"And he's got a 4.0 GPA."

Elaine thought Jan looked as proud as if he were her own grandson. "That's wonderful," she said, unsure how else she was supposed to respond.

"I like school." He shrugged, like none of this was any big deal, and flicked on a light switch. The lights slowly blinked on, buzzing and humming.

The walls were a dirty mustard color and the room was stiflingly hot, no doubt due to the hot water pipes that snaked up the wall, but there was a small table surrounded by a few chairs in the middle, and against one wall was a desk with what looked like some fancy computer equipment. He pulled two chairs from the middle of the room, placed them around the desk chair that was already there, and then he gestured for them to sit down. Chris jiggled the mouse to wake the desktop computer and typed something on the keyboard. Suddenly, the screen blinked to life.

"Okay, so what time do you think the crossword was delivered?" Chris asked.

"We don't really know. It was some time before 9:00 a.m. today," Jan said.

"But it could have been any time after the bookshop closed last night," Elaine said.

This news didn't seem to faze him. He simply nodded and used the mouse to navigate to a program on the desktop and double-clicked.

"So there are two cameras outside the library," he said as a program opened up. "One is at the back, and the other at the front." Chris typed something more into the keyboard.

Two video feeds popped up on the screen. One showed the rear exit of the library, as well as a collection of garbage cans, and, beyond that, woods. The other camera must be perched under the eave at the front left corner of the building. From its vantage point, you could see the entire front of the building, as well as most of the street, and...

"Oh, look, there's our house!" Jan said. The house was set far enough back from the road that you couldn't see the front door, so all you could make out was half the roof of the porch and a portion of the second story. "You could keep an eye on when we come and go if you wanted to!"

Jan seemed delighted by the realization, though it struck Elaine as a bit invasive. But no matter. It might be good security for them at some point. Her eyes traveled to the other side of the screen, where the footage cut off just before the Bookworm came into view.

"Well, that's too bad," Elaine said. She had known it was a long shot, but still, she had been hoping...

"Hang on," Chris said, shaking his head. "Don't give up yet. We won't be able to see someone actually go up to the door of the bookstore and tape it up, but we might be able to learn something." He clicked on the square in the top corner of the footage of the back camera, and the window went down to a small square. He enlarged the view of the front camera.

"You want to go start when the bookstore closed last night. So let's say sixish?"

"Yes, that sounds right," Elaine said, and Jan nodded. "I think that's when they close."

"Got it." Chris used a scroll bar at the button on the page to back up the footage they were seeing. The images on the screen got dark as he skimmed back through the night and stopped at footage that the numbers on the screen told him was taken just before 6 p.m. the day before. The frozen image had caught a woman and her child, his arms loaded down with books, headed toward the parking area at the side of the library, and a dark car driving down Main Street. The lights were on at Tea for Two, but the sky was still light. The image was grainy and difficult to make out, but you could certainly see what was going on.

"Let's start from here," he said, and both Jan and Elaine nodded. He pushed play, and the woman and her toddler walked on toward their car. The figures moved at what Elaine guessed was double time, and the cars on the street drove by faster than they normally would. Elaine tried to keep her eyes focused on the far left corner of the screen, where any action at the Bookworm would be most likely to show up. The numbers registered 6:07 when she saw the blue SUV she recognized as belonging to Bristol Payson come from the left of the screen and pass by the camera. So that's when Bristol had closed up the bookstore, then. Whoever had left the crossword had done it between then and the morning.

There was a period when traffic along Main Street increased—Lancaster's own version of rush hour—and a flurry of people could be seen walking down the sidewalks of the little downtown. Elaine recognized a few people, but as far as she could tell, none approached the bookstore. The last few stragglers emptied out of the library, but by 6:30 p.m. Priscilla could be seen taking the trash out at the back and locking the front door. By 7:00 p.m., the library and the road were mostly quiet. At 7:45 p.m., a man approached the library door, and, finding in it locked, dumped two hardcover books into the book drop. Exciting stuff.

Elaine thought back. She and Jan had been cleaning up din-ner around this time last night, and then Jan had gone upstairs and talked with Bob the phone for a while, and she'd tried to relax with a book before they'd both given up and headed early to bed. And sure enough, just after 8:00 p.m., more lights turned on in the upstairs of their home. By 9:30 p.m., all the lights in the house were shut off.

The video feed now showed long stretches of nothing, interspersed by brief appearances of a car or, more rarely, a pedestrian. "I'll speed this up a little," Chris said. Even at a faster speed, the long hours of the night unfurled slowly, with no incident. There were long stretches where nothing at all changed on the screen. At around 3:00 a.m., a cat started nos-ing around the library's garbage bins, and that was the most exciting thing to happen in hours.

Finally, around 6 a.m., the picture started to lighten just a bit. A light turned on in Tea for Two. Did Jan really get up this early all the time? Elaine hated the idea. Slowly, the picture bright-ened as dawn broke, and more cars started across the screen. A few people, dressed for the cool weather, hurried down the sidewalks, though it was tough make out their identities.

"Can you stop it?" she asked, pointing at the screen. Chris stopped the film, and the frame froze on the screen. The image was of a person—probably a woman—walking away from the bookstore side of the screen toward their house. "Could it be this person?"

Chris zoomed in on the figure on the screen. It was hard to tell, but it seemed to be a woman hurrying down the sidewalk. Just because she was out at this hour didn't mean she was up to no good, Elaine reminded herself, and she was probably hurrying because it was chilly out, not because she was running away from something she'd done.

"Check out that scarf," Chris said, pointing to the edge of the fabric that was knotted around her neck. Elaine saw what he was pointing at. There was some kind of symbol worked into the yarn, but she couldn't make out what it was.

"What is that?" Jan asked, leaning in to get a batter look.

"That's a Steelers scarf," Chris said, and Elaine realized what he meant. This was the logo for the Pittsburgh Steelers, the NFL team. And while there might be several Steelers fans in town, she only knew one who might be walking down the sidewalk on the far side, by the bookstore, at 6:30 a.m.

"That's Kate Pierce," Jan said, figuring it out at the same time. Elaine nodded. Kate Pierce ran Kate's Diner, just a few doors down from their tearoom, and she lived just a few blocks away, so she often walked to work.

"So it's probably not her that left the puzzle," Elaine confirmed, and indicated for Chris to start the film again. He did, and they stopped the film a few times as cars or pedestrian went by. Then, just after 7:30 a.m., Elaine saw a person she recognized going past on the far sidewalk. He was bundled up, so it was hard to tell who it was, but the Brittany spaniel and the German shorthaired pointer on leashes gave him away as Alan Oakley. Alan was on the board of selectmen and a member of Lancaster Community Church and was a familiar face in town, as were his two dogs, whom he doted on.

"Is that something in his hand?" Jan asked, leaning in toward the screen again.

Chris stopped the video and zoomed in. Jan's eyes widened as she saw what Elaine did—it looked like a piece of paper, clutched in his glove. From what Elaine could tell, it was a regular-size sheet of printer paper, just like the paper of the crossword.

"It doesn't mean anything, necessarily," Elaine said, though she noted the time on the screen: 7:32:15. He disappeared from the screen off to the right, in the direction of the bookstore. "How do we know what he did with it?"

"Just keep watching. Maybe there's something else," Jan said. Chris nodded and started the video again. Elaine practically held her breath as they watched. A minute passed, and then another fifteen seconds, thirty, forty-five—and then, there they were again.

The dogs appeared on the screen first, followed a moment later by Alan. This time he was facing toward the camera as he walked, and there was no doubt that it was him. She noticed his dark wool coat, his scarf, his heavy-framed glasses.

There was one other thing Elaine noticed.

There paper he'd had in his hand less than two minutes before, as he approached the bookshop, was gone.

CHAPTER TWENTY-FOUR

Alan Oakley?" Jan sat back in her chair and shook her head. It didn't make any sense. Alan had to be in his seventies. And he was married! Could he really be the secret admirer who had been leaving crossword puzzles for Katelyn?

"The video doesn't prove it was him," Elaine said, but her voice was uncertain.

"Where else could he have gone in that amount of time?" Jan asked. On the far side of the Bookworm was the Pine Tree Grill, and that wasn't open at this hour. Beyond that was the marina. Could he have managed to cross the street and gone to Oldies But Goodies, or Sugar Plum? But again, those businesses wouldn't be open at that hour either. And why would he have crossed back to the far side of the street, with his dogs in tow, if he'd gone to visit something on that side?

The only logical conclusion was that Alan Oakley had left the crossword for Katelyn.

The only problem was, there was nothing logical about that.

IT HAD ONLY taken Jan a few minutes to find the username Oakley on MakeYourPuzzle.com. And once she'd found that, it only took a quick search to uncover the fact that this user had created exactly three puzzles—the exact three that had been left for Katelyn.

Katelyn had been as shocked by the revelation as Elaine and Jan were, and she couldn't come up with any explanation as to why he would be have left her the crosswords either. And yet none of them could come up with any other logical solution for what they'd seen on the video. If Jan wasn't wrong, Katelyn had seemed rather deflated by the idea. After all, if Alan was behind the puzzles, something was very wrong with the secret admirer theory.

There was only one thing to do, Elaine had declared. Elaine was ready to hop in her car to go confront Alan directly, but Jan had convinced her that they should make one stop first. So less than a half hour after they'd discovered Alan's image on that video, they pulled up in front of the Whisper Art Gallery once again.

This time, when they walked inside, the counter was empty, but Jan could see Rachel working in the back office through the partially open door. Jan, channeling the confidence she always envied in Elaine, walked right around the counter and stood in the doorway. Elaine followed a step behind her, and out of the corner of her eye, Jan could see her grinning.

Rachel looked up from a computer screen and her eyes widened when she saw who was standing there. Rachel had shoulder-length brown hair and wore a plain navy-blue sweater and jeans. Her sister Elsa's presence was so striking, it was almost hard to believe they had the same parents.

"Hi, Rachel," Jan said. Elaine gave a small wave.

"Hello," Rachel said, sitting up a bit straighter in her chair.

"I don't know if you got our message, but we were hoping to talk to you," Elaine said, "about some flowers."

Rachel didn't say anything for a minute. She pressed her lips together and looked from Jan to Elaine and back to Jan.

"Did you buy the stargazers for Alan Oakley?" Jan asked.

At that, something in Rachel's face changed. She looked down at her desk, and then she nodded.

"I don't really know what all this is about," she said slowly. "All I know is that he asked me to get some lilies for his wife, and asked me not to tell anyone, so I tried to honor that." Her voice was even, and something in her manner made it seem like she was telling the truth.

"How did he ask you for them?"

Rachel shook her head. "I'm friends with the Oakleys. I teach Sunday school with Maureen, and she needed me to lead this week, so I stopped by Monday evening to pick up the leader kit so I could prepare. While I was there, Alan asked if I could do him a favor and run out and pick up a bouquet for him. Maureen was under the weather and he didn't want to leave her alone, but it was their anniversary."

"And he hadn't thought to get flowers for his wife before that point?" Elaine asked, tilting her head.

"I didn't really question it," Rachel said, "though now that you point it out, it does seem kind of strange. But at the time, I just thought, *What a sweet but clueless guy,* and I was glad to help him out."

"Did he ask you to get lilies specifically?" Jan asked.

Rachel nodded. "He told me stargazers were Maureen's favorite." She shifted in her seat. "He gave me twenty bucks and asked me to bring them by, and so I did. I thought I was doing something nice to help him out." Her computer dinged, and she tapped a key and looked back at them. "Judging by the fact that you two are looking into this, am I right in assuming that the flowers didn't end up going to his wife?"

"That's correct," Elaine said. "They were given to Katelyn Grande."

"Katelyn Grande?" Rachel looked as confused as Jan felt. "Why would he be giving flowers to Katelyn?"

"That's what we're trying to figure out."

Rachel shook her head. "I don't know what's going on. I'm sorry. Obviously if I'd known he was buying flowers for some other woman, I wouldn't have helped him. I probably should have realized something strange was going on when he asked me not to tell anyone. But who really thinks of stuff like that? I just took him at his word."

To Jan, the whole thing seemed strange, but she did believe that Rachel was telling the truth.

"Thank you for your help," Jan said and turned to go.

"I hope I didn't cause too many problems," Rachel said sheepishly.

"We appreciate your being honest," Elaine said before she too turned and they both headed out the door.

When they were back in the car, Jan said, "I think I believe her."

"I think I do too," Elaine said. "Which means we now have one very big task ahead of us."

"What's that?" Jan asked.

"Trying to convince Alan Oakley to tell us why he's been leaving secret messages for Katelyn Grande."

CHAPTER TWENTY-FIVE

They pulled up in front of the Oakleys' home a few minutes
later. It was a cute cottage in a neighborhood of modest
older homes a little way from the main commercial area in
Lancaster. The house was painted a light gray, and blue shut-
ters and window boxes overflowing with asters and chrysanthemums brightened it up, as did pots of mums by the door.
A towering maple tree stood in the middle of the lawn, and its
leaves had turned a glorious deep amber color. There was a car
in the driveway. Jan looked at Elaine, who nodded, and they
both got out and walked to the front door.

Jan pressed the doorbell, and a moment later, the door
opened. Maureen Oakley smiled when she saw them standing there.

"Jan. Elaine. What a lovely surprise," she said. She sounded
genuinely surprised and delighted to see them. "Please come
on in."

She stepped back and gestured for them to come inside.
The walked into the entry hall and Jan noticed a gorgeous
Chippendale sideboard beneath a beveled mirror in an ornate

mahogany frame. Maureen walked with a slight limp, thanks to a bout with polio when she was a child, but she wore tailored navy wool pants and a pink sweater set, and she gave off an air of elegance.

She led them down the hall, past a beautifully updated kitchen, into a generously sized living room with large windows. Jan saw that it overlooked a rose garden, the bushes heavy with the last blooms of the season, and a lovely stand of fir trees. Maureen gestured toward an overstuffed striped couch, and Jan and Elaine both took a seat. She sank into the cushions.

"You have a lovely home," Elaine said, and Jan nodded, taking in the matched set of armchairs, the good-quality Turkish rug in reds and blues, and the steamer trunk that served as a coffee table. It was graceful and inviting.

"Can I get you some oatmeal raisin cookies? Fresh out of the oven," Maureen said. So that was why the place smelled so good. Jan was about to decline, since she'd already sampled more than her fair share of the blueberry scones this morning, but Elaine said smoothly, "That sounds wonderful."

Maureen seemed delighted by the answer. "I'll be right back," she said, and turned back toward the kitchen.

"Always accept the cookies before you ask something difficult," Elaine said, nodding as if she was doling out sage advice. Jan puzzled through it, but failed to see the logic in it. But at least she had an excuse to try the cookies.

"So you didn't just send her away so you could dust for fingerprints?" Jan asked.

"What for? We already know it was Alan," Elaine said, as if everything about her fingerprint search had been perfectly logical all along. Jan was about to point out how nonsensical it all was, but just then, Maureen came back into the room carrying a plate of cookies and a handful of linen napkins. She set them down on the steamer trunk, and Jan saw that it was from a lovely bone china set decorated with pink flowers, and the napkins were embroidered with the initial *O*.

"Thank you. I'm so glad you stopped by. To what do I owe this surprise?"

Jan panicked. She hadn't really thought through what they would say when they got here. How would they politely ask if her husband was interested in a younger woman? Could they inquire in a nice way whether she knew he'd given flowers to and been penning puzzles for Katelyn, claiming they were from a secret admirer? Her mouth went dry.

Luckily, while Jan was sitting there like a dope trying to come up with a plan, Elaine jumped in.

"Well, for one thing, I wanted to see how your daughter is doing since we spoke about her last time you were in the tearoom," Elaine said smoothly. She picked up one of the cookies and set it gently on a napkin. "I've been so worried. Did the test results come back?"

Jan looked at Elaine, trying to keep up. She'd been worried? About Maureen's daughter? What was wrong with Maureen's daughter? Jan had a vague idea that she lived in Augusta and had children a little older than Jan's own grandchildren. Maureen was a frequent visitor to the tearoom, but Jan didn't know any of this.

"Oh yes, thank goodness, everything was fine. They tested the lump, and it was benign. We were so relieved to hear it,"

Maureen said. "Breast cancer doesn't run in our family, but you never know these days, with all the chemicals they put into everything. Anyway, she's doing fine, and you're so sweet to ask."

"Oh, I'm so glad to hear it," Elaine said, and Jan nodded. "That's a relief."

"It really is," Maureen said. She looked at them expectantly. Jan looked at Elaine, hoping she would know what to say.

Elaine looked unfazed. She took a bite of the cookie. "This is wonderful."

"Thank you," Maureen said, and Jan had to admit, she did seem pleased to hear it.

"The other reason we stopped by was because we wanted to ask sort of a strange question," Elaine said, taking another bite of the cookie. "We wanted to ask about Alan."

"Oh dear. What's he been up to this time?" Maureen laughed.

"Has he seemed to have been acting strangely at all?" Elaine asked.

"Not any stranger than usual," Maureen said, smiling. "Although, now that you mention it, I've been trying to get him to agree to spend the winter in Florida for close to two decades, and he's finally starting to talk about possibly looking into it, so that is strange," Maureen said. "My husband doesn't usually change his mind about things like that. Or anything, really."

She looked so earnest and carefree that Jan believed that she genuinely didn't know why they had come. If Alan was up to something strange, it seemed his wife didn't know anything about it.

"Do you know anything about some crossword puzzles he's made recently?" Elaine asked.

"Oh yeah, he's been playing around on this puzzle Web site." Maureen shrugged. "It's a bit strange, because he has never really been into puzzles until now, but when my husband dives into a new hobby, he goes all in. I've got a room of bowling trophies and a garage full of carpentry tools to prove it," she said. "Why?"

"Well," Elaine started, and then hesitated. "Do you know Katelyn Grande?"

"No." The word came out haltingly, suspicious. "Why?"

Elaine took another bite of the cookie, no doubt trying to give herself time to think. Jan jumped in.

"She's received a few crossword puzzles in the past week, each of them apparently created for her, and we've been trying to track down who made them," Jan said.

"Huh." Maureen seemed to think this through. "And you think Alan was behind them?"

"Well, we saw video footage of him leaving a puzzle for her on the door of the Bookworm this morning where she works," Elaine said. "And the puzzles seem to have been made on a puzzle Web site using his login."

"Well." Some of the warmth had gone out of Maureen's voice. "Why would he do that?"

"That's what we're trying to figure out," Jan said. She looked to Elaine. Should they bring up the flowers?

"Well, I don't know what to tell you." Maureen said. "I know he's been using that puzzle site, but I didn't realize why. And I don't know who this Katelyn is, so I can't tell you why he's been leaving puzzles for her."

"Do you think we could ask him about it?" Elaine asked. "It would mean so much to Katelyn to be able to get some answers about this."

"Well, he's out playing golf and he didn't take his cell phone, so I don't think we'll be able to get ahold of him just now," Maureen said. "But I'll definitely ask him when he gets home. You can believe me about that." She hesitated. "He hasn't done anything illegal, has he?"

"Oh no," Elaine said. "We're just trying to figure out what's going on. Would you ask him to get in touch with one of us?"

"Of course," Maureen said, biting her lip. "I would love to know what's going on too. I'll have him contact you right away."

"Thank you so much," Elaine said, and pushed herself up off the couch.

"Just one more question," Jan said. "It wasn't your anniversary this week, was it?"

"No," Maureen again hesitated. "Our anniversary is in August. Why?"

"Just wondering," Jan said, because she couldn't think of how else to answer without bringing up the lilies directly.

"I really must get the recipe for those cookies," Elaine said quickly. "They are wonderful."

Jan stood up as well, and after they said an awkward good-bye, they headed back toward their car.

"Did she seem a little odd to you, toward the end there?" Elaine asked they drove back to the house.

"Well, sure," Jan said. "We basically just told her that her husband is interested in another woman. It's understandable that she'd be a little off after that."

"Now, we don't know that Alan is interested in Katelyn," Elaine said.

Jan shook her head. "You keep saying the puzzles aren't from a secret admirer, but what other explanation is there?"

"For a while I thought they might be some sort of identity theft scam," Elaine said. "But knowing Alan is behind them, that pretty much rules that out." She thought for a few moments. "But with that possibility gone, I honestly have no idea."

CHAPTER TWENTY-SIX

They got back to the house just in time for Elaine to head out to Augusta to take her mom out for lunch. The whole way there, Elaine turned the morning's events over in her mind, but she couldn't get rid of the sense that something was off. They had pretty close to conclusive proof that Alan Oakley had been the one behind the puzzles, but something about that answer didn't sit right with her. Leaving aside the fact that he was far too old for Katelyn and was married, and even leaving room for the possibility that it might not be a secret admirer situation, something about it didn't make sense.

Elaine tried to put the crossword puzzles aside as she drove up to the Millpond Senior Community. It was a nice place, with differing levels of care for people in different stages. Her mother, Virginia, was in good health, and she lived in a small, well-kept bungalow on a street of small homes. The community maintained the buildings and the landscaping, and a nurse was on call twenty-four hours a day, which gave Elaine peace of mind. Living here allowed her mother a certain amount of independence, but she was surrounded by help if she needed it. Elaine parked in front of her mother's house and stepped up the path toward the door and rang the bell.

"Hello, honey. Come on in." Her mother smiled and moved out of the way, gesturing for Elaine to step inside. She wore a black knee-length skirt and stockings with a peacock-colored silk blouse, and a ruby brooch pinned to a handsome scarf around her neck. She was well dressed, as always, but she looked a bit thinner to Elaine; thinner and also frailer. But she knew better than to ask about it; her mother didn't like being interrogated—that was what she called it—about her health.

Elaine stepped inside the small house and followed her mother down the short entry hall. Hardwood floors ran the length of the home, with an open kitchen and dining area to the right and two small bedrooms and a bathroom to the left.

"Oh, hello."

Elaine was surprised to see a man sitting in her mother's kitchen. He had a full head of white hair and a handsome face, with ruddy pink cheeks. His long fingers were curled around a mug of coffee. Judging by the lines on his face and the spots on his hands, he was probably at least ten years older than her mother, but he wasn't bad-looking, his wide smile revealing rows of straight white teeth.

"Elaine, this is Richard," her mother said. "He just moved in to the main building." She gestured out toward the large building at the center of the complex, where there were wings of apartments and assisted living units. "This is my daughter, Elaine."

Elaine set her purse down on the counter and turned to the man and gave a too-bright smile. "Hello, Richard. It's nice to meet you." Elaine knew her mother enjoyed the attention of many of the men in the community, so she shouldn't have been so surprised to find this man here.

"It's nice to meet you as well. Your mother has been very kind to me. It's nice to have a friendly face around here."

"I'm sure." Elaine forced a smile, trying to read the situation. Was this more than a typical welcome-to-the-neighborhood greeting? She leaned against the counter and surveyed the room.

"Richard grew up in Lancaster," Virginia said, smiling at Elaine.

"Well, just until I was ten," he said, carrying his coffee cup over to the sink. "Then my dad got a job out in New Hampshire, and I spent most of my life out that way. But I always loved Lancaster. I have very fond memories of that town."

"Did my mother tell you that I recently moved there?" Elaine asked.

"She did," Richard said, nodding. "And how do you like it there?"

"I love it. There's something special about living in a small town," Elaine said. "My cousin and I opened up a tearoom, and that's been very fun."

"Oh, that sounds wonderful," he said. "Whereabouts?"

"Do you know the big white house on Main Street, just across from the library?"

"Oh, sure." He nodded. "The Gardner house?"

"Exactly. That's the family who owned it for years."

"Mike Gardner. I'd forgotten about him. We used to go swimming in the lake behind the house. He had the best dock for diving off of in the summers."

Elaine did some quick math and thought back through what she knew of the Gardner family. "Was Mike related to Paul Gardner?" She knew Paul had inherited the house from his parents, Harold and Beatrice.

"I think that must have been his father." He shrugged. "I have to admit I don't exactly remember too much about his parents except that his father was a stern man. But times were tough, and everyone was pretty worried about money in those days, so I imagine that might explain that." He set his cup down gently on the counter.

"Did you spend much time inside the house?" Elaine really wanted to know whether he had ever seen the ring or knew how it ended up in their wall, or whether he'd ever seen the family crest they'd found on the flue cover, but those seemed pretty unlikely. Still, it never hurt to find out more about the family that had owned the house for generations.

"Oh, probably. But I couldn't tell you a thing about it now. We just liked to run around outdoors. Mostly we hung out around the docks anyway, fishing and jumping into the water and looking for frogs. You know how ten-year-old boys are."

Elaine nodded. She did indeed. But she was grasping at straws here, trying to latch on to anything that might help explain how that ring had ended up in their wall.

"Does the phrase 'For Love and Blood' mean anything to you?" she asked.

"Elaine, there's no need to grill the poor man," her mother said. For a moment, Elaine smarted. Her mother could still make her feel like a child with just a few words.

"It's all right," Richard said. "Of course she'd be curious about her own house." He smiled and looked up at Elaine. "And you know, I feel like I have heard that somewhere. I can't place it, but yes, now that you mention it, that is definitely something I've heard." He was quiet a moment, and then he shook his head. "I know it will come to me, but now, it's gone."

He turned to Elaine's mother. "I should get going. Thank you for the coffee, Virginia. I hope we can do it again."

Elaine hoped he wouldn't get his hopes up. "It was nice to meet you," she said, stepping forward.

"It was very nice indeed to meet you as well. Good luck with the tearoom. It's a gorgeous old house, and I'm glad someone is going to take care of it."

He put on his hat and his tweed coat, and then he shuffled out the door.

"So," Elaine said, turning to her mother, "new friend?"

"Oh, hush." Virginia took one last slug of coffee and set her own coffee cup in the sink. "You know I just like to make people feel welcome. His wife recently passed away. It's hard to start over at a new place."

Elaine smiled but didn't say anything.

"Don't just stand there smirking." Her mother walked to the coat closet and pulled her coat off a hanger. "Are you quite ready to go?"

"Of course," Elaine said.

As her mother put on fresh lipstick and ran a brush through her hair, Elaine shook her head. She thought about what she'd said to Avery, about loving people enough to give them space to live their own lives. She felt a deep, abiding love for her mother, and she was grateful that her mother had a social life that kept her busy. She just hoped she wasn't breaking too many hearts in the process.

CHAPTER TWENTY-SEVEN

That evening, after Elaine had dropped her mother off at her bungalow and driven back to the tearoom, she found Katelyn and Jan huddled around the kitchen table, working on the last crossword.

"How did it go?" Jan asked, looking up as she stepped inside.

"It was fine. You know." She hung up her coat on a hook by the door. "Dining with my mother is always an interesting experience."

Katelyn tilted her head, questioning.

"Your mother is lovely," Jan said, shaking her head.

Elaine hung her jacket on a hook by the door. She knew it was true that her mother was a lovely person, and she was lucky to have her nearby and in good health. She decided to change the subject.

"How's it going here? Any luck with the puzzle?"

"We've got a lot of it solved," Jan said. "We can't figure out a few of the clues, but we got the gist of it."

"But it's not getting us any closer to figuring out why Alan Oakley made it," Katelyn said.

Elaine lifted the teakettle from the stove and pulled off the lid.

"I guess the secret admirer idea isn't as convincing now that we know who it's from," Jan said uncertainly.

"I suppose not," Katelyn said. Elaine held the kettle under the sink and let water fill it. "But now I'm even more confused about what this is all about. I mean, the secret admirer thing, improbable as it was, at least made some sense. Now, I don't even know what to think."

"And what about the lilies he left you? Leaving flowers for a girl is a clear indicator of romantic feelings," Jan said. "Isn't it?"

Elaine set the kettle on to boil and pulled down a basket of tea bags. "Would either of you like tea?"

Both women indicated that they did, but their focus stayed on the crossword in front of them.

"What we need to do is figure out a way to talk to Alan," Jan said. She tapped the end of her pencil on the table.

Elaine turned on the flame under the kettle, pulled down three mugs, and took the basket of teas over to the table and sat down. She let her eyes drift over to the crossword in front of Jan.

"I tried calling him a couple times while I was at work, but the phone just rang and rang," Katelyn said.

"And I went by the house again this afternoon. His car was in the driveway, but no one answered the door," Jan said.

"You did?" Elaine looked at Jan.

"I did." Jan looked over the selection of teas and reached for a ginger peach blend. She pushed the basket toward Katelyn, who took a peppermint tea. "I know I should have waited for you, but I was antsy, and I figured facing one of us might be less intimidating than both of us." She unwrapped the tea bag and smiled apologetically at Elaine. "We served on that adult education committee at church together in the summer, and I thought maybe I could get him to talk if it was just me."

"No, it's quite all right with me if you want to sleuth on your own," Elaine said. She picked a lemon mint blend and set it into her mug. "It's great, in fact."

"But nothing came out of it. Like I said, I'm almost certain he was home, but he didn't come to the door."

"His wife must have tipped him off," Katelyn said.

Jan nodded. "I think it's safe to say he's avoiding us."

Elaine was listening, but she was also distracted by something she had spotted on the crossword puzzle in front of her.

"But why is he avoiding us?" Katelyn asked. "I keep coming back to that. What kind of game is he playing? Why is he messing with me like this?"

Elaine reached over and slid the paper closer to her. They had decided earlier that this puzzle had a literary theme, and that seemed to make sense, judging by the boxes they had filled in. *Faulkner* was 17 down; 13 across was *Huck* as in Huck Finn.

"What possible goal could he have for making the puzzles?" Jan asked. "Maybe that's it. Maybe we just need to make a list of possible reasons, and something will make sense."

Elaine was listening, but she was also focused on the puzzle. *Tara*, like the name of the plantation in *Gone with the Wind*, was 4 down. And Elaine had to chuckle when she saw that the clue for 23 down was *Psalm* and the answer was *shepherd,* a clear reference to the Twenty-Third Psalm. Elaine had always thought the Bible contained some of the best poetry out there. But it was 14 across that had caught her eye. The clue was *de Bergerac.* The squares for the answer were empty.

"Maybe the puzzles weren't intended especially for me," Katelyn said.

"But the first one had your first and last name in it," Jan said.

Elaine counted out the spaces for the answer. Six letters. And the third letter was an *r.*

"And the second one was left inside my car," Katelyn added. "It's hard to see how that could have been meant for anyone else."

"Maybe he makes puzzles for lots of people, and we've just never known about it," Katelyn said.

"Maybe he's unhappy in his marriage and has a roving eye," Jan said.

"That's a horrible thought." Katelyn shook her head. "For so many reasons. I think it's more likely he's playing some elaborate joke."

Elaine thought back to a play she'd read in college. It was about a man with a big nose who wrote letters, she vaguely recalled. But that wasn't it. There was more to it...

"Maybe he's a bored man who needs something more to do with his spare time," Jan said.

"None of this makes sense," Katelyn said.

Elaine thought for a moment, and then it came back to her.

"Maybe he's writing the puzzles on behalf of someone else," she said.

Both Katelyn and Jan turned to her. The kettle started to whistle, but they all ignored it for a moment.

"Maybe he's writing the puzzles because there's someone else who *is* interested in you," Elaine said, looking at Katelyn, "but that someone doesn't know how to tell you. So Alan is doing it in his place." Elaine picked up the pen and carefully filled in the answer for 14 across: *Cyrano.*

"Wait a minute."

Katelyn saw it now, Elaine could tell.

"Cyrano de Bergerac." She shook her head. "I can't believe I didn't see that. Do you think...?"

"Wasn't he that guy who wrote letters for someone else?" Jan asked, and as she said the words, Elaine could see they made sense to her as well.

Elaine hopped up and turned off the stove, and she poured hot water into the three mugs.

"Cyrano de Bergerac was the main character in a French play," Elaine said. "He wrote letters to Roxane on behalf of Christian. Roxane fell in love with his words, but since she thought they came from Christian, she married him, when it was really Cyrano whose soul she loved."

"That's kind of a downer message, actually," Katelyn said.

"True. But I think the point here is that Alan Oakley may very well indeed be the one making the puzzles," Elaine said.

Jan nodded. "He could be making them, but that doesn't mean that he's your secret admirer. He could be making and leaving them on behalf of someone else."

Katelyn nodded, thinking it through.

Elaine watched steam rise up off the surface of her tea. It twisted and twirled, carrying the faintest hint of mint upward.

It did seem possible. Actually, it seemed the most plausible of any of the possibilities they had floated so far this evening.

But if it was true, that left one question Elaine didn't have the slightest clue how to answer.

Before she could voice her question, though, Katelyn asked it herself: "But who?"

CHAPTER TWENTY-EIGHT

Jan was feeling confident as she and Elaine sat down in the pew Sunday morning. She'd spotted Alan as soon as they walked into the church, seated on the far side of the church, right up near the front—his usual pew. Jan looked at Elaine, and, without a word, they both headed away from their normal seats on the left side toward Alan. As they approached, the first notes of "Great Is Thy Faithfulness" began to flow from the pipe organ. Elaine paused, and Jan gestured for her to sit down. Not only would it seem rude to try to talk to him now, the loud music pouring out of the recently refurbished organ would make it nearly impossible to hear. They would need to wait to confront him. They sat down as close to Alan as they could get, two rows behind.

"We'll get him after the service," Jan whispered, and Elaine nodded. They stood, along with the rest of the congregation, at Pastor Michael Ryder's invitation, turned to the page in the hymnal listed on the board at the front of the church, and began to sing.

Jan loved this hymn, and usually just being inside the old-fashioned church building soothed her soul. She loved the simple meetinghouse, with its solid wooden pews and its clean white walls and the steeple that rose high above town. Today, though, she kept her eyes on Alan Oakley. His white hair was carefully combed over the bald spot on his head, and he wore a dark-blue suit over a pressed white shirt.

Just as they began the second verse, Maureen came in through the side door, her purse tucked under her arm. She looked around the sanctuary and her eyes locked on to Jan's, and Jan could have sworn that she froze for a second before she went on and sat down next to her husband. Jan watched as Maureen leaned in and whispered something into Alan's ear, and he nodded, holding the hymnbook in front of him.

The congregation sat as the final notes of the song faded away, and Pastor Mike stepped up to the lectern and welcomed everyone. Jan tried to listen, but her mind was focused elsewhere. When they confronted Alan, they needed to find out why he had been avoiding them and who he was writing the puzzles for. Was it someone in this room? Jan looked around, taking in the sea of faces around her. Now that they knew Alan had made and delivered the puzzles, she supposed all the suspects whose fingerprints hadn't matched were back on the list. That meant Tag King, Frank Conrad, and Dutch Bigelow, at the very least. River White was probably still cleared, because he'd given the flowers he bought to his new fiancée and was unlikely to be interested in Katelyn. Bill Markham had been innocent, she was sure of it. But who was it?

Jan also ran through the list of ways Alan Oakley was involved in the community in her mind to try to come up with who he might be trying to help out.

He was on the board of selectmen, so she ran through the list of members of the town's governing board in her mind. Could Alan be writing puzzles for Eldon Carter? But he was married, so that seemed unlikely. Anita Picard of the I Scream Ice Cream stand was also on the board, but that didn't make any sense. Julie Yeaton was on the board and loved the tearoom, but Jan still believed that the puzzles were from a secret admirer, no matter what Elaine thought. Was one of the members connected to someone for whom Alan was writing the puzzles? Jan couldn't see it.

Okay then, maybe it was a dog owner in town. Alan loved his dogs. Or maybe it was someone Alan knew from church. The only problem with that, Jan realized, looking around the packed sanctuary, was that there were probably a good hundred people here this morning, and more who were involved in the weekly programs and ministries. How would she ever figure out who...

Wait a minute...What in the world...? Just as it seemed Pastor Mike was about to wrap up his sermon, Alan and Maureen Oakley slid out of the pew and stepped into the aisle. They moved, as quickly and quietly as they could, toward the back door of the church. As they passed, Maureen gave them a quick glance, and then looked away, while Alan kept his eyes trained on the back of the church the whole time. Were they really leaving? How could they...? But she watched as Maureen clutched her purse and her Bible in one hand, and both held their jackets over their arms as they pushed open the heavy wooden door and vanished outside.

Had they just given them the slip? Jan tried to figure out what to do. Should she go after them? Would that be rude? Or understandable? Jan felt frozen in place, trying to figure out what to do, and after what felt like an hour of back-and-forth but was probably only a few seconds, she decided to go for it.

But just as she started to rise, Pastor Mike announced, "Let us pray."

Jan sank back into the pew and glanced back at Elaine, who shook her head gently. They would get them another time, then.

Well, one thing was certain. Alan and Maureen were avoiding them.

After church ended, they went right back to Alan and Maureen's house, but their car wasn't in the driveway. Jan followed Elaine up the path to the front door, and she knocked, a loud, solid knock. They waited, but there was no answer.

"Do you think they're in there?" Elaine asked,

Jan wasn't sure. She leaned in and put her ear on the door. "It's pretty quiet," she said uncertainly.

Elaine reached out and put her hand on the door handle.

"What are you doing?" Jan asked. "We can't just go in!"

"I'm not going in," Elaine said, using her free hand to gesture for Jan to keep her voice down. "I'm just checking to see if it's locked." She pushed down the flap on the handle and pushed, but the door held. "Let's go see if there are any lights on the side of the house."

"How are you going to..."

But her cousin was already off the porch and was heading around the side of the house. Just as she rounded the corner, though, someone stepped out of the house next door.

"Are you looking for Maureen and Alan?" she asked cheerfully. It was a cool, windy day, and the woman wore a fleece and rubber boots over her jeans. She was probably in her forties, and she had a pair of gardening shears in one hand and a watering can in the other. "I think they're gone. They were headed to Augusta to stay with their daughter."

"Augusta?" Jan felt the air whoosh out of her lungs. The state capital was only a short drive away, but if they were going to stay with their daughter, who knew how long that would last. "For how long?"

"I'm not sure," the woman said. She shook her head and a gust of wind blew a strand of hair into her face. "She told me they were leaving earlier this morning than they would like so they could get up there in time for their granddaughter's dance recital, but I'm not sure how long they were planning to be away. At least a few days, I think. She asked me to check on their plants on Wednesday, if that helps."

"Wednesday?" Jan felt silly repeating everything this woman had just said, but she didn't know how else to respond. They wouldn't be back for at least three days. How could they find out about the puzzles if they couldn't talk to them?

"Thank you for your help," Elaine said cheerfully, but Jan could read her cousin well enough to see that she felt the same disappointment. The woman waved and headed around to the side of her house and knelt down in front of the first plant in the row of rosebushes.

Jan knew they could and would try to get ahold of the Oakleys by phone before then, but she was doubtful they would answer, based on what she'd seen so far. It seemed they wouldn't get answers from Alan until Wednesday, at the very earliest.

"Do we drive to Augusta?" Jan asked, only half-joking.

"I wish." Elaine shook her head. "We'll have to keep sleuthing from here, I guess." She pushed her hair back as the breeze blew. "But for now, we'd better get back. We've got a tea party to host."

Jan nodded and started to follow her cousin back toward the car. But halfway across the lawn, something caught her eye. Movement in the front window of the house directly across the street. She could have sworn she saw a face looking out at them. Jan looked again, and she saw that the face was gone, and the curtain was moving just a bit on the far side of the glass as if it had suddenly snapped back into place.

Had someone been watching them?

CHAPTER TWENTY-NINE

A very arrived at the tearoom a little before 2:00 p.m., when her guests were scheduled to come. Paula walked her into the house and watched as she surveyed the dining room, which Elaine and Jan had filled with flowers from Blooms and set with plates and cups from Avery's favorite Limoges Plaisance pattern. Avery then went into the kitchen, where Jan was working on the special chocolate chip scones Avery had requested.

"Thank you for doing this," Paula said, smiling at Elaine. "She has been really down recently. I think the transition to middle school has been harder for her than any of us were expecting."

"It's not an easy time in life," Elaine said, straightening a fork that had gone askew. "I think most kids go through some sort of adjustment. It takes a while to find yourself in a new place and figure out who your friends are."

"I know. It's just hard to watch your kid go through it." Paula nodded. "But she's been really excited about this. I think she's hoping that it will smooth things out with Alicia."

"Well, I hope it goes well," Elaine said. She knew there were a thousand ways everything could go badly. For example, what if the others didn't show up or thought they were too cool for tea, or were mean to her, or...

But there was no sense in imagining all the bad outcomes. Better to focus on the ways this could help Avery.

"Okay, I need to go. I've got a bunch of errands to run. But I'll be back in two hours. Call or text if you need anything," Paula said. Elaine nodded. Mothers these days always seemed to be dashing from one thing to the next, with no time to enjoy anything. But no matter. She waved good-bye and headed toward the kitchen. As she stepped into the hallway, she saw a girl, lanky and lean, being ushered down the hallway by Archie. She wore a knee-length skirt and a nice purple blouse, and she looked around, wide-eyed, at the tearoom.

"You must be here for Avery's tea party," Elaine said, and the girl nodded, her stick-straight brown hair hitting her shoulders. "Come on back this way. And welcome to Tea for Two."

The girl followed Elaine down the hall slowly, nervously. "I'm Elaine. I'm Avery's aunt. Well, not really aunt, I guess. I think it's something more like second cousin, but I can't keep track of these things. How do you know Avery?"

The girl looked up at her, wide-eyed. "Orchestra."

"What do you play?"

"Flute."

Well, this girl wasn't winning any prizes for eloquence, but Elaine got the sense she was simply overwhelmed. Elaine tried to remember that she'd probably never seen anything like the tearoom before, and since she seemed not to know Avery that well, she probably wasn't totally sure what she was walking into.

"Hi, Jen," Avery said shyly as the girl walked into the room. She gave a small wave and held her elbows.

"Hey." Jen looked around, taking in the floral wallpaper, the long cherry table and chairs, and brass sconces that brightened up the room. The table was set with full place settings at each seat, and she gawked at the number of spoons and plates. "This is cool."

After a few minutes of awkward conversation, more of the girls showed up, and soon the dining room was full of preteen girls in their Sunday best, talking and laughing. Elaine let Avery take the lead as host, and she was pleased to see the girl greet each guest and welcome her. Elaine had printed out a menu to set at each place setting, and the girls *oohed* and *aahed* over the list of pastries and the five types of tea they got to choose from.

Elaine tried to stay out of the way as much as possible, and Jan stayed busy for the most part in the kitchen while the girls gathered. Once the girls had all arrived, Archie went into the room and explained the tradition of afternoon tea among upper-class Brits, and the girls were enthralled, no doubt by his accent as much as what he was saying.

Elaine hovered in the doorway to the kitchen, watching the group interact. There was one girl with smooth, dark-brown hair, and the other girls looked toward her a lot, as if seeking her affirmation when they said or did anything. She seemed to relish the attention, and a few times Elaine saw her make a pointed comment at one of the other girls. Elaine remembered her name was Bella. So she was the queen bee. And she knew the power she wielded, Elaine realized. She was no doubt the one who decided who was in and who was out. Avery seemed to hover at the fringes, a bit uncomfortable, but certainly part of the group today.

"Which one is Alicia?" she asked Jan. Jan looked up from the tray of cookies she was arranging at the counter. She wiped her hands on her apron and walked around the island toward the door.

"The blonde," she said, indicating a girl in a stylish black-and-white dress. Elaine nodded. She seemed to be on the edge of the group as well, and Elaine had noticed that she'd been especially warm to Avery when she'd arrived. Elaine saw how Alicia tried especially hard to make Bella happy. Alicia, after all, was new to the group, and still not quite a core member, Elaine could see. But she also noticed Alicia make an effort to make sure Avery was included when Bella had suggested fake British names for each of the girls. Bella had declared herself to be Elizabeth Windsor, while others received names like Violet and Edith and Mary. Avery was given the name Rosamund. It seemed to Elaine like the girls had watched a wee bit too much *Downton Abbey,* but they seemed to be having a good time, so she didn't interfere.

After Archie had finished his spiel, Elaine brought in the trays of tea sandwiches and scones and pots of clotted cream and jam, and Jan set down a teapot by each girl's place setting.

"*Ooh,* how *chah-ming,*" Alicia said in a bad British accent, and all the girls dissolved into giggles. Soon, the room was full of laughter and phrases uttered in various accents that Elaine assumed were meant to be British. Most of the girls had never used a tea strainer before, but they figured it out, Elaine noted. And these girls used way more sugar and cream than the typical customer, but they seemed to be enjoying both the tea and the food. They each held their little pinkies out as they drank.

"I think it's going well," Jan said, coming up next to where Elaine was standing in the doorway to the kitchen.

"I think so too," Elaine said. They were all laughing about something a girl with red curls had said, Avery right along with them. Whatever tension had filled the room at first seemed to have dissolved. "They seem to actually really be enjoying this."

"Of course they are. Everyone loves tea," Jan said.

True, everyone loved tea. But tea didn't magically make girl drama vanish, Elaine knew. Girls this age could be cruel, and no amount of sweet pastries could soothe the hurt of a friend who had moved on. Still, it sure seemed to be helping. The girls were all now laughing over a joke Avery had made about clotted cream.

Elaine knew a tea party couldn't fix everything. But she was hopeful, watching the girls interact, that Avery wouldn't feel excluded after this. Elaine didn't know if she would end up being good friends with these girls. She wasn't sure she wanted her to be—that Bella seemed like a piece of work. But they were having a good time together today, and she knew that had to help.

Elaine was about to turn back to help clean up in the kitchen when she saw Bella reach under the table and pull something out of her purse. It was her cell phone, and . . . what in the world? It was some sort of stick. She unfolded it and fitted her phone on to the end of it.

"What is that?" she whispered to Jan.

"Selfie stick." Jan shrugged. "For taking pictures of yourself. Where have you been?"

Elaine shook her head and watched as Bella held the phone out in front of her and the girls all leaned in close together.

"Say cream cheese," Alicia said, and the girls all laughed and posed for the camera.

Selfie sticks. Huh. What would they think of next? Elaine had to smile. She may not understand why kids these days felt the need to document and share every moment of their lives on social media, but she did understand that these girls were enjoying this afternoon, and that Avery was a part of it. Elaine wasn't sure how things would go Monday when they were all back at school. Maybe they would all go back to leaving Avery out. Maybe. But judging by what she was seeing here, she doubted it.

"I think she's going to be just fine," Jan said.

As Elaine watched them all gather together for another shot, and saw Alicia put her arm around Avery's shoulder, Elaine had to admit she agreed.

CHAPTER THIRTY

Monday morning, Jan and Elaine were at the door of the bookstore a few minutes before it opened. Elaine pressed her face against the glass door, trying to peek inside.

Bristol's car was parked in the lot behind the store, and the lights were on, but the door was locked. Katelyn's car wasn't here so she probably wasn't here yet, unfortunately, but maybe Bristol would...

Just then Bristol walked to the front of the store, her arms laden with a stack of picture books, and saw Elaine's face pressed against the glass. She laughed. She came to the front door and unlocked it and ushered the cousins inside.

"Just can't wait to get your hands on some good books, huh?" Bristol laughed.

"Exactly." Elaine flashed a smile.

"Oh, this place smells heavenly," Jan said, taking a long sniff. It really did smell wonderful, Elaine had to agree. Coffee was brewing at the beverage station at the back, and mingled together with the clean scent of books and paper was some warm woody scent that made you think of autumn.

Elaine looked around the shop. Soft classical music was playing. The books were lined up neatly on the shelves, and an elegant display on the counter showcased some new children's books. Bristol had changed out the books at the front table, and now a display of fall books was front and center. Halloween was only a month away! It was hard to believe how quickly time passed these days.

"So what can I help you with today?" Bristol asked, setting the books down on the front table. Right. She was no doubt wondering why they had been so impatient to get here this morning.

"We were hoping to talk to Katelyn," Jan said. "She's not here by any chance, is she?"

"I'm afraid not," Bristol said. "She called a little earlier to let me know she'd be late today. Her father had some sort of medical problem and she needed to get him in to the doctor first thing this morning. She'll be in as soon as she can." Bristol arranged the books into a neat stack. "Still working on those puzzles for her?" Bristol asked.

"Yes, unfortunately," Elaine answered. "Though your tip about the library's security cameras was really helpful."

"She told me it revealed Alan Oakley was behind the puzzles," Bristol said, shaking her head. "Have you made sense of that yet?"

"No, but we do think he's writing the puzzles on behalf of someone else," Jan said. "A Cyrano de Bergerac situation, at least sort of."

"Ah." Bristol thought for a moment and nodded. "Now that makes a little more sense. But who's Alan writing them for?" She straightened the other stacks of books on the front tables.

"That's the million-dollar question," Elaine said. "Last night we came up with a list of everyone we could think of who might have some connection to Alan, and we were hoping to run it by Katelyn to see if any of the names sparked any sort of recognition."

"Who did you come up with?"

Jan pulled the list out of her purse, and as Bristol made her way around the counter and opened the cash register, Jan started listing names. Elaine tried to listen and watch Bristol's reaction to the names, but something snagged at the back of her mind. She closed her eyes for a moment, trying to focus. What was it?

Then she realized that it was the music. The song playing out over the store's loudspeakers was familiar. Where had she heard this piece before?

She listened, eyes closed, for a moment. She hadn't heard the music quite like this, but the melody was hauntingly familiar, as though she'd heard it many times before. And then, slowly, like pieces of a puzzle coming together, it came to her.

This was the piece Avery had been practicing for her cello challenge. It was the piece she'd been determined to nail so that she earned first chair.

"What is this music?"

Both Jan and Bristol were looking at her like she was nuts. She realized one of them must have been talking, and she'd completely interrupted. But she needed to know.

"Do you know what this song is?" she asked again. "I think it could be important."

"I can check," Bristol said. "It's from a classical mix that Katelyn put together. Hang on." She moved from behind the counter and crossed the main space toward a small back room at the rear of the store. She hovered in the doorway, and Elaine could tell that she was looking down at an iPod that sat on a dock.

"It's from Beethoven's Sixth Symphony," she called. "Also called the *Pastoral* Symphony."

Elaine thought back to that first puzzle. The word *pastoral* had been in that puzzle, she was sure of it.

"Do you have the copy of the first crossword puzzle?" she asked, turning to Jan.

Jan was still looking at her like she was unstable, but she nodded, and she slowly reached into her purse and pulled out the manila folder she'd been using to carry the puzzles around.

"It's right here." Jan found the puzzle and laid it on the counter. Bristol had returned to the front of the shop, carrying the iPod, and looked down at the puzzle, along with Jan and Elaine.

Sure enough, there it was, at 38 across. Elaine didn't know a ton about music, but she knew this was not one of the famous pieces of music that everyone knows, like Beethoven's Ninth or Vivaldi's *Four Seasons*. This was a piece that only someone pretty familiar with classical music would think of. Elaine scanned the rest of the puzzle. There were several other composers named. "Do you have any Haydn in that playlist?"

Bristol touched the screen and scrolled through the list of tracks in the playlist. She held out the iPod to show her that, sure enough, Haydn was included.

"How about Debussy?" she asked.

"Yep, it's here." Bristol looked down at the puzzle. "And so is Tchaikovsky's *Romeo and Juliet*."

"So. The question now is, who of our suspects is familiar enough with the store's playlist that they would know all this?" Jan said.

Elaine shook her head. "And who would know enough about music to know what these pieces are?"

But even as she asked the question, the answer was obvious.

Frank Conrad was a music teacher. He was Avery's music teacher, the one who had assigned the *Pastoral* Symphony to his middle school orchestra. Several of the other suspects had listened to classical music, but none of them had had made any reference to this specific and somewhat lesser-known symphony. But she was certain that Frank knew this piece of music. And he no doubt knew the other pieces as well. His fingerprints hadn't shown up on the puzzles...but then, they wouldn't, would they? He'd never touched them. And he'd flat-out denied writing the puzzles...but then, he hadn't written them after all. He'd gotten Alan to write them for him!

"Do you have a phone book here?" she asked.

Once again, both Jan and Bristol looked at her in confusion, but this time Bristol complied without question.

"Right here," she said, pulling a local white pages from a low row of bookshelves behind the counter.

"Is there an address listed for Frank Conrad?" she asked.

"Frank Conrad?" The name obviously was familiar to Bristol, judging by the light that clicked on in her eyes. It only took Bristol a few moments to flip to the right page and find the listing for *C*'s. "There's no listing for him at all," she said.

Well, that wasn't all that unusual, Elaine realized. So many people these days only used cell phones and didn't have landlines at all. But how could she find out if her hunch was correct?

"If you're looking for his address, I bet we have that here," Bristol said. She set the phone book down and turned to the computer on the counter. She logged in and then moved the mouse and clicked to open a program. "We have a customer loyalty program," she said. "Frank Conrad comes here enough that I'd be surprised if he wasn't enrolled. And you have to fill out a form with some basic information, like address and phone number, to join." She clicked around for a moment and then nodded. "Yep. Here is it. 132 Tennis Avenue. Just a little ways from here, right?"

That was it. That was on the same street as Alan. This had to be the house across the street from Alan's. The one where someone had clearly been watching them the other day. Jan was already typing the address into the mapping program on her phone.

Bristol was still looking at the computer screen. "This is interesting. Frank mostly buys books that have to do with music somehow, but for the past six months or so, he's also been buying Katelyn's pick of the month. And"—she leaned in and squinted at the screen—"he mostly comes in during Katelyn's shifts."

The connections were too clear to be a coincidence.

Elaine turned and looked at Jan. "It looks like we have our man."

CHAPTER THIRTY-ONE

They waited until that afternoon to talk to Frank. Instead of driving to Augusta and trying to corner him in his classroom again, Jan and Elaine waited until late afternoon, when they guessed he would be home from work, to drive by his house. And sure enough, there was a car in the driveway when they pulled up.

They parked on the street and walked up the path toward the door. Jan looked back over her shoulder and noticed that Alan's house was still, the driveway empty. He and Maureen must not be back from Augusta yet.

Frank's house was small, but carefully maintained. The lawn was neatly mowed, though there were no window boxes or other colorful flourishes. The paint was a utilitarian light beige. His car was a compact two-door, and as they walked past it up the driveway, Jan could see that the backseat was full of music books and instrument cases. There were blinds but no curtains in the windows. It was clear to her a man lived here alone.

"What are we going to say?" Jan whispered as they stood on the porch.

"I don't know," Elaine said. "But I'll figure something out."

Jan reached out and pressed the doorbell. She heard it ring inside the house, and then she heard footsteps. Someone was on the other side of the door, no doubt looking out the peephole. Jan tried her best to look friendly and nonthreatening.

After what felt like an eternity, but was probably only a few seconds, the door swung open. Frank Conrad stood in the doorway, wearing a button-down shirt partway tucked into his jeans and a dark-green sweater vest. Jan noticed there was a small hole in the toe of one of his gray socks.

"I knew you'd make your way here soon enough," he said, a shy smile on his face. "Please come in. I'll explain."

He had that same awkwardness that Jan had noticed before, but there was also something gentle and genuine about him. Jan stepped inside after Elaine, and he led them past a kitchen in desperate need of a remodel and past a table piled with student papers. He'd been in the middle of grading homework, Jan realized. He led them into a living room done with a beige carpet and matching brown leather couch and chairs. The only thing on the walls was a flat-screen television. He gestured for them to take a seat on the couch, and he lowered himself into an armchair.

"So. The crossword puzzles are from you?" Elaine asked.

Well. She wasn't beating around the bush, then.

Frank nodded.

"Why the mystery?" Elaine asked directly once again.

Frank sighed and seemed to struggle with how to answer.

"It wasn't supposed to be a mystery," he said. Jan noticed that he was fidgety, like he wasn't sure what to do with his hands. They both waited for him to go on. "I guess you've figured out that the puzzles were made for Katelyn Grande," he said, and they both nodded and waited for him to go on.

"I've . . ." He cleared his throat, and his cheeks turned pink. "I guess I've had a crush on her for a while. She was always so nice when I went into the Bookworm, and she's so pretty, and"—he blushed an even deeper shade of red as he admitted this—"I found myself going there more than I really needed to when I knew she'd be working. But I never knew what to say."

"You were shy around her?" Jan asked as gently as she could.

He nodded, his fingers clutched together. "I haven't dated a lot. And she's—she's so smart, and she always knows the right books to recommend, and she makes those crossword puzzles, and—I don't know." He shrugged. "I'm just a middle school music teacher. What would she possibly see in me? It seemed pretty impossible."

Jan felt her heart warming to him. From what she could tell, there was a lot to see in him. He was awkward, but he was sweet, and he was kind. And he genuinely seemed to care about Katelyn. Most single women she knew would give anything to find a man who adored them the way this man seemed to care about Katelyn. One glance at Elaine showed that she was feeling about the same way.

"So how did you come up with the idea of crossword puzzles?" Jan asked.

"Well, I'm friendly with my neighbors. I lived in this house when I was a preschooler, before my family moved to South Africa. My parents moved back here when they retired, and Alan and my father used to go fishing together sometimes. I inherited the house when my parents passed away, so I've known the Oakleys for decades. I feed their dogs while they're out of town, and they bring in my mail. That sort of thing." He shrugged. Jan waited, anxious to see where this was headed. "Well, one day late in the summer, I was out mowing my lawn and Alan went by walking with his dogs, and we got to talking. At first we were just talking about neighborhood stuff, but then Alan looked over at my house and asked..." He stopped and shook his head. "Well, you know Alan, right?"

Both Jan and Elaine nodded.

"He sometimes just says whatever he thinks. So this day, he asked why I wasn't married. I told him I hadn't found the right girl yet, and he pressed me for what I was looking for in a girl, asking more and more, you know, I guess trying to find someone for me. Finally, he got me to admit that I had my eye on Katelyn. And he wanted to know why I didn't just ask her out. Well, eventually, he got to the point where he understood I didn't really know how, and he came up with this."

"Secret messages in anonymous crossword puzzles?"

He shook his head. "It wasn't supposed to be secret or anonymous. The first puzzle had my name in it."

Jan looked at Elaine. "It did?"

He sighed. "There was a reference to a Polish writer. I told Alan it was too obscure." Jan remembered the clue, and that they hadn't found the answer that fit. They both looked at him, waiting for him to go on. "It's Joseph Conrad."

"Conrad is Polish?" Elaine asked. Jan knew of his most famous book, *Heart of Darkness*, about a voyage up the Congo River, but she hadn't read it, and, well, neither the name nor the plot indicated that he was Polish.

"Pen name," Frank said, shrugging. "Like I said, I told Alan that one was too difficult. In any case, even if she didn't get that clue, I had hoped she would think of me."

"She did," Elaine said gently. "You were one of the names that came up early in our investigation. That's why we came to visit you. We just weren't sure."

Jan knew Elaine was being kind by not pointing out that it wasn't Katelyn who had first surfaced his name. But even if Katelyn had been lukewarm about him at the beginning, Jan felt confident she'd been swayed by the romantic notion of the puzzles, and would at least give him a shot. She had a feeling it would go quite well, actually.

"My first name was in the puzzle too," he said, shrugging. "Frank." Jan remembered now that that it had been in the puzzle, as the answer to the clue *forthright*. How had they missed that? "And there were other clues about me too."

"Like what?" Elaine asked. They hadn't solved all of them. Had they missed these?

"Seven-letter word for *pedagogue*, for one," Frank said.

"Oh my goodness. Teacher. A pedagogue is a teacher." Elaine slapped her forehead. "I can't believe we missed that one."

"So, yeah. I thought Katelyn would figure out who it was from. But even if she missed all that, I thought Avery would have told you it was from me."

"Avery?" Jan looked at Frank. "My granddaughter Avery?"

"Yes. She didn't tell you, I gathered pretty quickly."

"Avery knew the puzzles were from you?" Jan was still trying to wrap her head around this. How was her granddaughter involved?

"She's the one who got the first puzzle to Katelyn," he said. "When Alan heard about the crossword event at your tearoom, he thought I should go. But I had to lead practice for the marching band. They're competing in a tournament in a few weeks," he explained. "So I couldn't go to it. But Alan asked around, and he was pretty sure Katelyn would be there, and decided it would be the perfect opportunity to give her the puzzle. And Avery had mentioned she would be there that day, so I asked her if she would mind making sure Katelyn got it."

"Avery did that?" Jan asked weakly.

Her granddaughter had spent so much time at the tearoom in the past week. How did she not mention that she knew the solution to the mystery they were chasing?

"Why didn't she tell us?" Elaine wondered.

He shrugged. "I don't know. I wondered that as well."

"So you didn't ask her to keep it a secret?"

He shook his head. "It didn't occur to me that I'd have to."

They would need to ask her about that. For now, though, she had more questions for Frank.

"So after the first puzzle, when it was clear Katelyn didn't figure out who it was from, why didn't you just tell her? Why the second puzzle?"

He didn't answer for a moment, and then he sighed. "That was Alan's idea again. Maybe I should have stopped it. I just didn't know what else to do. He seemed to think another puzzle would make Katelyn happy. He's been married forever and he and Maureen seem really happy, so I figured he knew what he was talking about. And I didn't have a better idea, so I told him to go ahead with it."

Jan could see how it had unfolded now. Alan had been driving this thing all along. Alan, bored, no doubt thrilled for the opportunity to be involved in something secret and exciting, had come up with the puzzles to help Frank's romance with Katelyn, forgetting that beneath the excitement for him, a real person's feelings were at stake. Two people's feelings.

"Why make the puzzle anonymous that time? And leave it like he did in her car, with a bunch of flowers?"

"Once it became clear that she didn't know the first puzzle was from me, he convinced me it would be more romantic to let her figure it out. To let her 'be wooed by the idea of romance,' is how he put it."

"In other words, to keep it a secret."

He nodded.

"And the third time?"

"I hesitated more that time. I thought, if she hadn't figured it out by then, she either wasn't going to, or else she had figured out they were from me and wasn't interested. But Alan promised that he knew what he was doing, so I told him he could do one more."

Jan had to admit, Alan actually hadn't been too far off in the end. As convoluted as his logic had been, it had worked out not too differently than Alan had thought. Katelyn had fallen for the idea of romance, and was, Jan thought, probably far more likely to give Frank a shot now than she would have before the puzzles started arriving.

"He must have spent an extraordinary amount of time making the puzzles," Elaine said. "They were not professional quality, but they were well done."

"I think he really enjoyed it," Frank said. "He really got into this whole thing."

Jan could see how it had all happened now. How Alan had gotten excited about the idea, had created the puzzles, had convinced Frank to go along with it. But one thing still didn't make sense to Jan.

"We tried to get ahold of you a week ago, and you didn't call us back. And when I came in to your classroom and asked about them, you pretended you didn't know anything about it. Why didn't you admit it was you behind the puzzles when we came to talk to you?"

"Like I said, it was Alan's idea to keep it a secret after the first one went unsolved. He promised me it would be better to string her along for a while. So I told him I wouldn't tell anyone. And he promised he wouldn't tell anyone either." That explained the escape act Alan had given them, then. "When you showed up at my classroom, I panicked. I wanted to tell you it had been me, but I had promised him, and . . . I don't know. I guess I was embarrassed. It had all become something of a game to Alan, I think, but to me, it was still just my pathetic attempt to get the attention of a pretty girl, and it wasn't working. Who wants to admit that?"

Jan could hear the pain in his voice. Not just pain over a few crosswords not going as planned, but what she suspected was years of relationships not working out the way he'd hoped. She guessed she could understand his hesitation and his desire to keep his crush quiet.

"But you knew we were looking for who sent the crosswords to Katelyn," Elaine said. "You knew she was interested in finding out who was behind them."

He shrugged. "I didn't know if she was pleased or not. I just decided to trust Alan, and he said to keep it quiet. And now..."

He let his voice trail off.

"And now?" Jan prompted gently.

"And now, you'll tell her it was just me. I'm sure after all this, she probably thinks I'm nuts, and there's no way she'll go out with me."

Jan thought back to the excitement she'd seen in Katelyn's face when she thought of a secret admirer. She thought of how moony, in her father's words, she'd become, imagining someone out there had a crush on her.

"On the contrary," she said. "My impression is that she's a bit swept off her feet by how romantic this whole thing is. After all, someone has gone to very elaborate lengths because he cares about her. I think most women would be flattered, but I believe Katelyn is actually very impressed by how smart and cultured the puzzles are and is falling for the person who wrote the puzzles."

"But I didn't even write the puzzles," Frank said. "Alan did."

Right. There was that. Now that Jan thought about it, it hadn't worked out so well for Cyrano de Bergerac either. Roxane had gone and married the man she thought had written her the letters, not the actual tortured soul behind the words who loved her.

"But it's not really the puzzles themselves she's excited about," Elaine said quickly. "It's the feelings behind the puzzles that's made her so happy. It's that someone cared enough to do all this for her. From what I've seen so far, I think she will be thrilled when she finds out you were behind them."

Jan agreed. But they had to do this right. She thought for a minute. The puzzles so far had been like something out of one of the romantic movies Katelyn loved. That, Jan was sure, was part of what was so appealing to Katelyn about all this. Jan thought about the romantic comedies she'd seen. As Katelyn had pointed out, they usually included some big, dramatic romantic gesture that brought the two together—the raised boom box in *Say Anything* or the sprint past security at Heathrow in *Love Actually*. Katelyn had admitted she would like something like that herself. Something like being serenaded...

"I think there's a good chance Katelyn will be thrilled when she finds out you're behind the puzzles," Jan said carefully. "Especially if we do this the right way."

"What do you mean?" Frank asked.

Jan thought for a minute more, and then said, "I have an idea."

CHAPTER THIRTY-TWO

That evening, Elaine was on the couch in the sitting room, flipping through the book of family crests again, searching for a picture of a shield—an escutcheon—that featured an anchor and a tree trunk. She was glad to finally know what the symbols were most likely meant to represent, but it wasn't getting her any closer to finding the name of the family.

Jan came into the room carrying two steaming mugs of chamomile tea.

"Bless you," Elaine said, setting aside the book as she reached out to take the tea. Small wisps of steam rose up off the surface.

"Still at it, huh?" Jan sat down on the couch next to Elaine and set her tea down on a side table.

"Still at it, and becoming more and more convinced I'm never going to figure out what family this crest belongs to."

"And you're sure it's a family crest?"

"I'm not really sure of anything at this point. But Archie seemed to think it was likely." She'd filled Jan in on her conversation with Archie and how he'd helped her figure out the meaning of the symbolism in the crest. "And what else could it be?"

Jan shrugged. "Colleges often have logos that look like that, with a shield in the middle."

"I guess that's true." Elaine wouldn't even know where to start looking into college crests. There had to be thousands of them just here in the States. How would she even start to look through all the possibilities? The very idea made her head hurt.

"May I?" Jan gestured at the book.

"Of course." Elaine took a long, deep sip of the tea and felt it wash through her. It had been a busy day, and they had already started to put the plan Jan had come up with at Frank Conrad's house into action. Elaine hoped the surprise they had in store for Katelyn would be enough to convince her to give the humble music teacher a chance.

"Did you know there's an index of symbols at the back of this book?" Jan asked.

"What?" Elaine turned and saw that Jan was flipping through an index at the back of the book. "I hadn't noticed. What does it do?"

"You can look up a specific symbol, and it will list all the crests in the book that include that symbol," Jan said.

Elaine felt like smacking her forehead. "Are you serious?"

"That's what it looks like to me. Here, let's look up one of the symbols. What were they?"

"An anchor and a tree trunk."

"Okay, let's look up all the crests that include anchors." She flipped the page and ran her finger along a column of text.

"There are probably four dozen names that use that symbol."

"Let's cross-reference it with the tree trunk."

Jan was already flipping to another section of the index.

"About fifty or so of those."

"Are any of the names the same?"

"Give me a second. I'm checking."

A minute later, she flipped to a page toward the end of the section of pictures.

"Is this your crest?" She held the book out to Elaine and pointed at a picture in the lower right-hand corner. It was a blue-and-yellow shield that looked remarkably like the one scratched on to the flue cover.

"I think it might be," Elaine said. She got up and retrieved the flue cover, and then held it near the book. They both looked from one to the other several times.

"I think it is it," Jan said.

Elaine nodded. It had to be. The etching was crude, but it was a match—or as close as they could probably come given what they had to work with.

Under the shield in the picture in the book, there was a thin scroll with the words "For Love and Blood" written inside it.

"This is the family motto!" Elaine couldn't believe it. They'd really found it.

Jan ran her finger under the letters of the name under the shield. *Wood*.

"This is the crest of the Wood family," Elaine said. She was still having a hard time processing this. The flue cover really had contained a family crest, and now they'd determined which family it belonged to.

"This is amazing," Jan said.

Elaine had to agree. It really was amazing. They were that much closer to finding out the truth about the sapphire ring.

"There's just one problem," Elaine said reluctantly.

Jan smiled knowingly.

"Who in the world are the Wood family, and what do they have to do with how that ring ended up in our wall?" Elaine asked, shaking her head.

"Exactly," Jan said.

Still, though there were many questions left unanswered, they were getting closer to finding out what had really happened.

"This is good though," Jan said. "This is a huge step."

Elaine knew her cousin was right, as she so often was. But they still had so many questions—yet those could wait for another night. Tonight, she'd simply bask in the knowledge that, day by day, they were getting closer to solving this mystery.

CHAPTER THIRTY-THREE

Tuesday afternoon, Elaine was surprised to hear a familiar voice in the tearoom around midafternoon. She had just brought a tray of half-eaten scones back to the kitchen and was dumping the leftovers in the trash. She looked over at Jan, who was spooning out leaves of chamomile tea into a tea ball and setting it inside one of their charmingly mismatched teapots.

"Did you know Avery was coming over today?" she asked.

"No, I didn't," Jan said, her face brightening. "But that sounds like her, doesn't it?"

Elaine nodded. Avery was chatting with Archie in the west parlor. Elaine set the empty tray on the counter and stuck her head out into the room. Avery saw her and smiled, and a moment later she said good-bye to Archie and bounded over to the kitchen.

"Guess what!" she said. She set her cello down on the floor by the door and slid her backpack off her shoulders. Her eyes were bright, her smile wide. She was excited about something.

"What?" Jan picked up a potholder and used it to heft the steaming tea kettle off the stove.

"I made first cello!"

Oh, that's right. Elaine had been so wrapped up with planning the surprise gesture for Katelyn that she'd forgotten about Avery's orchestra challenge.

"That's wonderful!" Elaine said.

"I'm so proud of you," Jan added. She gestured for Avery to come in for a hug. Avery obliged and walked toward her grandmother with her arms outstretched. "You worked so hard at it, and it paid off."

Elaine had a fleeting moment of wondering whether Frank Conrad had given Avery the chair as a way to thank Jan and Elaine for helping him, but quickly decided that wasn't likely. Avery really had worked hard on that piece, practicing until she could play it flawlessly. Elaine had heard a definite improvement in the way she played it over the weekend as opposed to just a few days ago.

"And even better than that, Alicia said congratulations," Avery said, beaming. "And it seemed like she meant it. And even Bella was nice about it, even though she only got third chair. She even invited me to sit with them at lunch sometimes."

"That's wonderful," Jan said. "The tea party must have helped after all."

"Are you going to?" Elaine added. "Sit with them?" She thought about the girls Avery had been sitting with at lunch that time they'd peeked into the cafeteria. They had seemed like sweet girls, definitely more in line with what Elaine wanted for friends for Avery than smooth-talking Bella and her herd of followers. Would Avery leave them behind now that she had an in with the popular crowd? Elaine had wanted to stop the teasing and get the girls to see that Avery was worth getting to know, but had they done too much?

"Nah," Avery said. "Maybe once or twice, but honestly, they mostly talk about reality shows and things I don't care about. I like sitting with Yasmina and Diane." She shrugged. "But it's nice to be asked, you know?"

Elaine nodded. She did know. And she knew what it meant to have Alicia know that she could be friends with Avery and also with Bella and her crowd, if she wanted to.

"And Alicia?" Elaine said gently. "How are you feeling about her?"

Avery didn't answer for a minute. She toyed with the strap of her backpack. "I guess we're probably not going to be best friends like we used to be," she said. "And I'm sad about that." She seemed to think for another minute, and neither Jan nor Elaine moved. Soft conversation and the sound of spoons hitting porcelain teacups was the only noise. "But it doesn't mean we can't be friends at all," she finally said. "It'll just be different."

Elaine nodded, thinking about the ways her friendships had grown and matured through the years. She hadn't remained friends with the woman from the army base. But she had grown closer to other women. That was the nature of friendship, she thought. Sometimes relationships changed. And it could be difficult to say good-bye to someone who had moved on.

She looked over at her cousin Jan. But sometimes you grew closer to people you never expected to.

Then she thought about that phone call from Nathan she had yet to return. And, she realized, sometimes, you just weren't sure which was the right direction for a friendship to go.

"I'm glad for you," Elaine said.

"Me too," Jan added. "And on a very different note, I also have a question for you."

Avery looked up at her grandmother, eyes questioning.

"Why didn't you tell us about the crossword puzzle Mr. Conrad gave you to pass on to Katelyn?"

"Huh?" For a moment genuine confusion clouded her eyes. But then recognition seemed to dawn, slowly. "Oh, right. I forgot about that."

"You knew that we have been trying to figure out where the puzzle came from, right?" Elaine said gently. "Why didn't you just tell us?"

Avery cocked her head. "You've been doing what?"

Elaine was confused. She looked at Jan and saw consternation in her face.

"For the past week and a half, we've spent basically all our time trying to figure out where the crosswords Katelyn Grande has been getting have come from," Jan said. "But we found out that you knew all along. Why didn't you tell us?"

Avery looked confused. "When were you looking into that?"

Elaine tried to read the girl. Was it possible that she really didn't know what they had been so focused on the past ten days? It didn't seem possible, and yet… Avery seemed to be genuinely confused. Elaine knew that preteens could be myopic, and she supposed they hadn't really talked with Avery directly about it, but could she really have been so wrapped up in her own problems that she'd honestly had no idea what Jan and Elaine had been up to?

"You did bring a crossword puzzle from Mr. Conrad to the puzzle event, right?" Jan said. There was a note of frustration in her voice.

Avery nodded.

"And you made sure Katelyn got it?"

"I put it on the top of the stack of puzzles that guy had put down." She shrugged. "But then I forgot about it."

"You forgot about it?" Elaine could see Jan was a perplexed as she was. "You mean, you just didn't think to check in at all to see if Katelyn had gotten the puzzle, or what came afterward? You never checked in with Mr. Conrad to see how things were going?"

Avery looked like a deer in the headlights.

"No," she finally said. "Now that you say it all like that it sounds kind of strange, I guess, but I really didn't. I pretty much forgot about it after I set the puzzle down."

Neither Jan nor Elaine said anything for a moment.

The thing was, Elaine believed her. It was exactly the kind of thing an eleven-year-old girl would do.

Avery shook her head. "I'm sorry." And she did sound contrite.

"It's all right," Elaine said. There was no need to shame the poor girl. Kids at this age... well, they believed the world revolved around them. And given all the drama that had been going on in Avery's own life, she could well imagine how the girl might have done what her teacher had asked and then moved right on to her own problems again. It was self-centered, but it was their job to instruct her to be otherwise. "It sure would have saved us some trouble, but it will all turn out all right in the end."

It sure would have saved them trouble if Avery had simply told them what she knew, but now that Elaine thought about it, she wasn't sure it would have been better. The fact that it had taken them a while, and several puzzles, to get to the answer, had given Katelyn time to, well, become interested in meeting her secret admirer. Maybe it had worked out for the best this way after all. Things usually did.

Avery gave Elaine a tentative smile, and Elaine moved toward her and wrapped her in a hug. It felt good, and Elaine was hit with a pang of longing to hug her own grandchildren. She missed them, missed being able to hold them like this. But failing that, she was grateful for the chance to get to know Avery better. Elaine liked having a special connection to the girl.

"It's not a big deal." Jan gave a smile. "But you can definitely make it up to us."

Avery gave her a wary look.

Ah yes. Elaine saw now what Jan was doing, and she realized once again how clever her cousin was.

"With what?" Avery said, uncertain.

"We need your help with something," Elaine said. "With a surprise for Katelyn."

As they filled her in on what they had in mind, a smile spread across Avery's face.

Yes, Elaine thought. This should work out perfectly.

CHAPTER THIRTY-FOUR

J an and Elaine had to wait until Friday to put their plan into motion. It had been tough to keep things quiet in that time, and they had had to dodge Katelyn's questions about their progress on the puzzles for a few days now. They hadn't wanted her to know that they'd discovered who was behind the puzzles, because that would have ruined the surprise of what they had planned, so they had had to stay away from her as much as possible, since they were both terrible liars.

Jan had spent the morning anxiously checking and rechecking her notes, but by the time noon rolled around, she felt confident that they were as ready as they were ever going to be. She couldn't predict how the next few hours would go, or what would happen when Katelyn discovered it had been Frank Conrad behind the puzzles all along, but Jan hoped that her hunch was correct, that Katelyn would be thrilled. He seemed like a good man, and he cared enough about her to arrange a grand gesture like nothing Jan had ever seen.

Finally, a little past noon, Jan picked up the crossword puzzle they'd spent the last few days making online, looked at Elaine, and nodded.

"You ready for this?" Elaine asked, taking her coat off the hook by the door.

"I think so." Jan tucked the puzzle into her purse. "Let's just pray this goes well."

"I've been doing that all morning," Elaine said, winking.

They walked over to the Bookworm together, and as Elaine pushed open the door, Jan checked to make sure everyone was where they were supposed to be. Good. Bristol was there at the counter, and Katelyn was toward the back of the shop, unpacking a box of books. Thank goodness. If something had prevented her from coming in today, the whole plan would have gone up in smoke.

"Right on time." Bristol said quietly as Jan closed the door.

"You're still okay with this?" Jan asked.

"The shop is quiet. I'll manage just fine on my own." She winked at Jan. "You just have to promise to keep me posted on how it goes."

Then Bristol turned toward the back of the shop. "Katelyn? Jan and Elaine are here to see you."

Katelyn nodded and set down the box of books and made her way to the front of the store.

"Something strange happened this morning," Elaine said to Katelyn. "There's a crossword puzzle."

Jan started to pull the puzzle out of her purse, and Katelyn gasped. "Where did you find this one?"

"It was at the tea room," Elaine said carefully. They'd agonized over this part. They hadn't wanted to lie to her, even if they both believed it would have been justified. So Elaine preferred to keep things vague.

"Oh my goodness," Katelyn said. "Did you see Alan leave it? Did you talk to him? Where did he leave it?"

"Let's try to solve it and see what it says," Elaine said.

Katelyn must have been too excited to realize that Elaine was avoiding answering her questions. Either that or she realized something was up and figured it was best to comply. In any case, she reached for the pencil that Bristol held out for her, and she looked down at the puzzle.

Katelyn looked up pretty quickly, her brow wrinkled.

"This one's different," she said.

"Just try to solve it," Jan said, holding back a smile.

This puzzle was indeed simpler than the others had been. There were just ten clues, five down and five across, and the grid was much less defined. They had worried about that for a bit, then decided that it didn't matter. They didn't need Katelyn to believe this was the same as the other puzzles as much as they needed her to solve it quickly and take the next step.

Jan watched as Katelyn filled in the answers to the clues, one by one.

Secret, she wrote in the boxes for 1 down.

Admirer was the answer for 2 across.

Revealed, she wrote in 3 down.

She looked up at them, and they nodded and indicated for her to go on. Slowly, she filled in the rest of the boxes.

Perhaps

Love

Truman

Middle

School

Music

Room

Please

"What in the world?" she looked up at Jan, and then looked toward Elaine.

Jan shrugged. "I guess you'd better follow the directions."

Katelyn then turned to Bristol, who laughed and told her, "Go. I can handle things here."

"Is this for real?" Katelyn asked.

"I guess you'll have to go to find out." Jan could only imagine Katelyn must be confused, overwhelmed...but judging by the sparkle in her eyes, Jan thought she must be just a little bit pleased as well. Jan didn't know if she'd guessed yet who would be waiting for her in the middle school music room, but she hoped she would be pleased.

"I guess I'll take my break now," Katelyn said.

"I think that's a very good idea." Bristol gestured for her to get going.

"I can drive you," Elaine said, and Bristol nodded her agreement. If she thought it was strange that Jan and Elaine were clearly planning on coming along, she didn't say so. This was helpful, because Jan and Elaine needed to be there to give the signals to make things go according to plan.

"I guess I'll grab my jacket," Katelyn said. She was moving slowly, still bewildered.

"We'll be right here," Jan said, laughing.

As Katelyn walked toward the back of the store, Elaine leaned in to Jan. "Do you think she knows?"

Jan shrugged. "Can't tell. But she is coming along, so I guess that's a good sign."

"You guys have to call me as soon as this is over," Bristol said.

"Of course," Jan promised, and a moment later, Katelyn reappeared in her blue wool coat, her purse tucked under her arm.

"Shall we?" Elaine asked with a smile, and pushed open the glass door of the shop.

Jan sent a quick text to Frank, letting him know they were on their way. Then she called and spoke to Sally, the receptionist, to tell her they were on their way so she could buzz them in.

On the ride to Augusta to get to the middle school, Katelyn peppered them with questions from the backseat.

"Do you guys know what this is about?"

Jan smiled and nodded.

"Is this from the same person who sent the other ones? Not Alan, but whoever was behind them?"

Jan nodded again. She could tell Elaine was trying hard to focus on the road in front of her and not give away anything, like they'd agreed. They both wanted to try to keep what was about to happen a surprise.

"Can you tell me who it is?" Katelyn asked.

Jan shook her head. "All we can say is that it is someone who cares about you a lot."

She asked questions the whole ride, but Jan thought they did an admirable job of avoiding most of them. Still, it was something of a relief when she climbed out of the car in the school parking lot.

Jan sent another quick text to update Frank. They'd arranged one final signal, a text Jan would send as they walked down the hallway toward the music room. "Shall we?"

Katelyn took a deep breath, let it out slowly, and nodded. Elaine laughed. "You're not going to face an executioner here."

"I know. I'm happy. It's just..."

Jan thought she understood what she was going to say. It felt like there was a lot riding on this. After all this buildup, if it turned out Katelyn was unimpressed, all her hopes—not just of the secret admirer, but of finding someone to settle down with—felt like they would be in jeopardy.

"Just enjoy the moment," Jan whispered. "It's not the rest of your life. It's just someone who cares enough about you to find a creative way to tell you."

Katelyn nodded, took another breath, and then nodded.

"Okay. Let's go see what this is about."

They crossed the parking lot quickly and stepped inside the building.

"Where's the music room?" she asked.

Jan pointed down the hallway. The school was quiet, and their footsteps were the only sound for a moment. Then they turned the last corner, and Jan quickly sent one last text. Katelyn looked back at Jan and Elaine, both of who nodded, and then she turned and started down the hallway. When they were a few feet away, Jan first heard it: a violin, playing low, languorous notes. Then, a cello joined in. Katelyn's eyes widened.

Jan whispered a prayer that this would go well.

"What do I do?" she asked.

"Go on in." Jan nodded toward the door.

Katelyn put an uncertain hand on the door handle, and then she pulled, and stepped into the room. When Jan followed a moment later, she saw what Katelyn saw: the full middle school orchestra and band, facing her, playing what Jan now recognized as Beethoven's Sixth. The song Avery had been practicing for weeks.

Frank Conrad stood in front of the class, his back to them, conducting. On the whiteboard behind the class, someone had written, *Katelyn, will you go to dinner with me?*

Jan and Elaine tried to fade into the background and let Katelyn take it all in. Katelyn hovered in the doorway, and Jan couldn't tell from her face what she was thinking. Was she pleased? Disappointed? Jan thought it was clear now that it was Frank Conrad who was asking her out, but was she still confused? Jan couldn't tell.

Avery, seated at the far end of the row in the first seat, looked up from her music briefly and smiled at them, and then turned back to the pages on her music stand.

As the music continued, Katelyn took a few more steps into the room, and a slow smile washed over her features. Jan felt her shoulders unhitch slightly. Katelyn had wanted a serenade. Jan tried to relax and enjoy the music, but she was too on edge, waiting to see what would happen.

After what felt like an eternity, the last notes of the short section of the piece died out, but Jan didn't move, waiting to see what would happen next.

Slowly, Frank turned around. He was wearing a suit and tie. Jan felt a surge of affection for this man. He was trying so hard. She hoped Katelyn could see that, though she knew that that didn't mean Katelyn would feel the same way he did. The human heart was a tricky thing. But looking at Frank now, vulnerable, his heart exposed—in front of a class of middle schoolers, no less—looking at Katelyn like she was the most beautiful woman he'd ever seen, she sure hoped Katelyn was feeling some of the emotion he was.

Katelyn smiled and shuffled nervously. "Hi, Frank," she said. "You did all this?"

He nodded. His cheeks were pink, and his movements were awkward. He was so nervous.

The whole class was silent, watching what would happen. Thirty pairs of eyes were fastened on Katelyn.

"I think you're really wonderful, but I didn't know how to tell you....I wanted to..." He was speaking too quickly, his words coming out in one big rush. Jan silently begged him to slow down, to not let the emotion of the moment ruin what he was trying to do. "The puzzles were my way of trying to tell you how I feel. But that didn't work, so I thought, maybe..." He coughed and looked down at the ground, then back up at her. "Well, I'm better at music than at talking, so I hoped this might say what I feel better than I could. I thought maybe if I...but I didn't know..."

"Yes."

The one simple word silenced him.

"Yes?" he repeated uncertainly.

"Yes, I'll go to dinner with you," Katelyn said.

Frank stood still at the front of the room, looking at her like he wasn't sure he was hearing her right.

"You—you will?"

And then Katelyn laughed, and the tension seemed to dissipate from the room.

"She said she will, Mr. C," called a girl that Jan recognized from the tea party as Bella.

"I will." Katelyn's face broke out into a wide smile.

One of the boys in the back row set his tuba on his lap and started a slow clap. The other kids in the orchestra quickly joined in, and soon the whole class was cheering for their teacher. Several of the boys were blowing horns, and a couple of the girls were giggling, but everyone seemed to be genuinely happy for them. Jan caught Avery's eye, and she smiled and clapped her hands together.

Jan watched, a wave of emotion rolling through her. It was completely cheesy. And there was no way to say whether the date would develop into a relationship. Only God knew if these two people would end up together. But seeing this all right now, watching how these two both looked so hopeful, so excited, Jan had high hopes.

Katelyn turned back to Jan and Elaine and said, "I'll find a ride home."

Well, Jan thought. That was indeed a good sign.

"Another mystery solved," Elaine whispered, linking her arm through Jan's.

"True enough." She watched as Katelyn took a tentative step toward Frank.

"And I am not too proud to admit that you were right," Elaine said. "It was a message from a secret admirer all along."

"Of course it was," Jan said. "But I'm glad you didn't just go along with what I thought was right. It's good when you question me. That's why we make a good team."

"We do make a good team, don't we?" Elaine asked, smiling.

A year ago, Jan could never have imagined standing here with her cousin, running a tea shop and solving mysteries together. It was funny to see the way God had drawn them together, how He had given them gifts and talents and opportunities that worked so well together.

"Well, shall we get back to the tearoom?" Elaine asked.

"I guess we should," Jan said reluctantly. Still she lingered, enjoying these sweet moments. Jan had never been more grateful for the ways God was working in their lives. For the ways He had led Jan and Elaine to each other, and the ways He was bringing others into their lives as well. She thought about Bob, and Rose and Archie, and the guests and friends who came through their doors every day.

Yes, God had blessed them. Jan thanked God, and then, with one last glance back at the happy couple, she and Elaine turned to go.

They all had so much to be thankful for, and Jan couldn't wait to see what happen next.

ABOUT THE AUTHOR

Elizabeth Adams lives in New York City with her husband and two young daughters. When she's not writing, she spends time cleaning up after two devious cats and trying to find time to read mysteries.

AVERY'S FAVORITE CHOCOLATE CHIP SCONES

2 cups unbleached all-purpose flour

⅓ cup plus 2 tablespoons sugar

1 teaspoon baking powder

½ teaspoon baking soda

½ teaspoon salt

6 tablespoons (¾ stick) chilled unsalted butter, diced

1 teaspoon (packed) grated lemon peel

1 cup semisweet chocolate chips

¾ cup chilled buttermilk

1 large egg yolk

1 teaspoon vanilla extract

Milk (approximately ¼ cup or enough for glaze)

Preheat oven to four hundred degrees. Butter and flour baking sheet or line with parchment.

Sift flour, one-third cup sugar, baking powder, baking soda, and salt into large bowl. Add butter and lemon peel. Then work butter and lemon peel in using your fingers or a fork until mixture forms uneven crumbs. Mix in chocolate chips.

Whisk together buttermilk, egg yolk, and vanilla in small bowl. Add buttermilk mixture to dry ingredients and mix until they come together as a moist dough. Gather dough into ball. Press dough out on lightly floured surface to eight-inch round. Cut into six even wedges. Transfer wedges to prepared baking sheet, spacing one inch apart.

Brush scones lightly with milk; sprinkle with remaining two tablespoons sugar. Bake until scones are crusty on top and tester inserted into center comes out clean, about twenty minutes. Serve warm.

Read on for an exciting sneak peek
into the next volume of Tearoom Mysteries!

Burning Secrets

by Rebecca Adams

Jan Blake opened her warm oven, smiling as she inhaled the aroma of cinnamon, nutmeg, and banana.

She'd worked all week perfecting the recipe for her mini banana loaves, and even she had to admit she'd succeeded. The secret was the buttery streusel topping. Jan's mouth watered at the memory of the many tastings it had taken to perfect the recipe.

"Something smells delicious." Jan's cousin, Elaine Cook, appeared in the doorway of the kitchen, already dressed in her emerald-green Victorian gown.

Jan closed the oven door and added two more minutes to the timer. "Really? Oh, I hope so. I want everything to be just right."

The women of Lancaster Community Church had decided to host an event at Tea for Two and the cousins had worked hard to ensure everything went according to plan. Jan hoped they could provide a truly memorable event for such an influential group within their community. It could mean a good deal of future business for their tearoom. Many of these women were visiting the tearoom for the first time, and Jan wasn't about to waste their chance to make a good first impression.

"It will," Elaine said. "But you should go get dressed. We only have a few minutes before they arrive."

Jan glanced at the clock above the sink. Three o'clock had snuck up on her. Too much last-minute tinkering with her recipe. "Can you take these out of the oven for me when the timer goes off?" Jan asked Elaine as she removed her apron and hung it on the hook next to the door.

"Of course," Elaine said. "Now go."

Upstairs, Jan pulled her burgundy Victorian gown from the bedroom closet. It had recently been returned from the dry cleaners and had that crisp, clean smell to it. She dressed quickly, and glanced at herself in the mirror above her dresser to be sure she hadn't missed a button. One look at her reflection and she had to laugh at the thin dusting of flour on her nose.

An occupational hazard, she supposed.

As she wiped the powder away, something outside her window caught her eye. In the distance, black smoke billowed from a building near the lake.

What on earth?

It looked like more than your standard leaf-burning fire— the smoke was thicker, blacker.

Jan watched for a few moments trying to determine where the fire was coming from, to no avail. At this distance, it was hard to say. She imagined it wouldn't take long to find out. In Lancaster, word spread quickly.

It was time to open the tearoom. She took one last look at the smoke, silently prayed that no one was injured, and then walked down the winding staircase and into the entry hall, where she saw Rose Young, one of their employees, greeting the church women with her usual charming smile.

Jan glanced briefly into the east parlor off to her right as she stood facing the door. She took a moment to admire the Victorian-style curtains hanging from the windows, which were the loveliest complement to the lace tablecloths on every table in the tearoom.

A collection of mix-and-match tea settings graced each table. While they'd initially settled on a variety of mismatched teacups, saucers, and teapots for financial reasons, it had turned out to be one of Jan's favorite happy accidents. They'd found that unique cups and saucers at each place setting sparked interesting conversations as their guests dreamed up stories about the history of the pieces.

In fact, every time they purchased another teacup or teapot from a flea market or estate sale, Jan let her own imagination roam free, inventing a provenance for each. How exciting to think their little tearoom was filled with history.

"Jan, everything looks lovely," one of the women said, pulling Jan from her daydream. Jan thanked her and began to usher the women to their tables. As she did, Maureen Oakley appeared at her side. A friend and regular at Tea for Two, Maureen had been kind enough to organize this little gathering with the help of Sarah Ryder, the pastor's wife. The women of Lancaster Community Church had certainly welcomed the cousins and their little business with open arms, and Jan was grateful. Entertaining friends with a special high tea hardly felt like work at all.

"Thank you so much for having us today, Jan," Maureen said with a smile. "It's a wonderful way to introduce some of our younger women to this delightful tradition you all are carrying on."

"Thank *you*, Maureen," Jan said. "We're thrilled to share our tearoom..." Jan stopped before finishing her sentence. Something wasn't right.

"Jan? Are you okay?" Maureen laid a gentle hand on Jan's arm. "You look a little pale."

She gasped. "My banana bread!" Jan would know the smell of overcooked baked goods anywhere. She rushed to the kitchen and found her cousin standing beside the oven holding a pan of burned mini loaves.

"I didn't hear the timer," Elaine said, her face full of apologies.

"Oh no." Jan wanted to cry at the charred streusel topping.

Elaine frowned. "I was distracted, Jan. I'm so sorry."

"Don't worry," Jan said. "We'll whip something else up. No use crying over burned banana bread." She smiled. "Now, you go entertain our guests. I'll need about twenty minutes. Do you think they'd like to hear a story about one of our more exotic teas?" Jan asked.

Elaine smiled. "Good thinking." She disappeared into the parlor and moments later Jan heard music—one of her favorite Mozart piano concertos. Jan looked at the burned loaves.

"I can do this." Jan gave herself a little pep talk, but she couldn't ignore the way her heart raced as she ran through a list of ingredients in the refrigerator. She had leftover finger sandwiches and the chilled dough for her miniature maple croissants. Those could work with the other items on her menu. She could still save this tea. She'd simply have to keep her wits about her.

Jan moved around her kitchen with ease, her baking station set up for convenient access to the ingredients she used most often. With everything at her fingertips, Jan found it easy to create the pastries and desserts their customers raved about. She worked at the island in the center of the large kitchen, assembling her croissants. They were a sure crowd-pleaser and something she could finish quickly and from memory. She was humming along to the concerto as she worked, lost in her own world, when the back door opened. She hadn't even realized it was unlocked.

Jan stopped stirring and turned toward the door just in time to see Macy Atherton slip in.

"Goodness, Macy. You gave me a scare!"

"*Shh!*" Macy hissed as she entered the kitchen. "Are they already here?"

Jan cracked an egg into a glass bowl to make an egg wash. "The women from the church? Yes. Why aren't you out there with them? You could've used the front door, you know. It's much nicer out that way."

Macy paced in a circle around the kitchen, making it difficult for Jan to stay focused on her recipe. Jan glanced up at her and noticed her brow was even more furrowed than usual.

"Macy? Is everything okay?" Jan set her whisk down. When Macy didn't respond immediately, Jan grew concerned. It wasn't like Macy to be quiet for too many minutes in a row.

Macy turned toward Jan. "Why does it smell in here? Did you burn something?" Macy sniffed loudly. "It smells like something burned."

"Just a little burnt bread," Jan said as she fished a brush out of the drawer and began applying the egg wash to her croissants. "Feel free to join the other women in the parlor, Macy. I think they're enjoying a presentation on the exotic teas of India at the moment."

Macy shook her head and sat on a stool across from her. "I need your help, Jan."

Jan's eyes darted to the other woman. Several years her junior, Macy Atherton had been a constant supporter of the tearoom since they opened, but her show of support had often been encased in criticism, making her one of those personalities that challenged Jan's goodwill. She'd always tried to see the good in people, and she supposed if Macy needed her help she would find a way to give it.

Jan still remembered the first time Macy visited Tea for Two. Elaine had interacted with her, but she told Jan later Macy had complained about her scones being too dry. Jan was thankful her cousin had been on high alert and sent Macy out with a small bag of ginger cookies on the house. Despite her initial complaint, Macy had sent her daughter-in-law to the tearoom with a rave review.

As owner of Green Glade Cottages, Macy had sent many of her guests their way ever since. Proof that you should never judge a book by its cover.

"Believe me, if I could go to anyone else, I would," Macy said, nearly scoffing. "You aren't exactly my first choice for a private investigator."

Jan inserted two sheets of croissants in the oven and then closed the door and turned to Macy. "I suppose that's good, since I'm not a private investigator."

Macy frowned. "What do you call it then?"

"I'm the co-owner of this tearoom, and I bake some pretty delicious desserts, if I do say so myself." Jan waggled her eyebrows for effect.

"Don't be coy, Jan," Macy said. "I know all about you and your cousin and your side business getting to the bottom of things that need gotten to."

Had they really developed such a reputation around town? Something about the idea excited her. She'd never have thought of herself as a master sleuth, but she and Elaine did seem to have a knack for putting puzzles together. Jan *had* always loved a good puzzle.

"Well there's no 'side business,' but we have found ourselves in the middle of a few mysteries lately. How do you think we can help you?"

"Someone started a fire in one of my cottages this morning," Macy said, unmistakable fear on her face.

Jan stilled. So that's where the smoke had originated. How awful. "Is everyone okay? Are *you* okay? And why are you here—shouldn't you be with the police or the fire marshal or somebody?"

Macy began pacing again. "I'm fine. Everyone is fine. It was a relatively small fire—I mean, thank goodness, it's been put out—and the building is still intact. That's not the problem."

It sure sounded like a problem to Jan. "Then what is?"

Before Macy could answer, Elaine appeared in the doorway. Behind her was Arnie Sheffield, one of the Kennebec County sheriff's deputies. Elaine's eyes darted back and forth between Jan and Macy, confusion spreading across her face.

Macy turned away.

"There you are, Mrs. Atherton." Deputy Sheffield's voice cut through the muffled melody of the distant concerto playing in the other room. He held his campaign hat with both hands in front of his chest, revealing his neatly trimmed, wavy brown hair. The man was likely just thirty years old, and yet he clearly commanded authority in this room. "We have some talking to do."

FROM THE
GUIDEPOSTS ARCHIVES

This story, by Laura Davis of Soddy-Daisy, Tennessee,
originally appeared in *Mysterious Ways*.

It doesn't get any better than this," my friend Richie always said. And I mean always. He said it every day, to everyone he knew. He believed it too. I never saw a person get more joy out of life. My husband worked with him at a Chattanooga engineering firm, and we'd quickly become part of his social circle. People gravitated to Richie. It was easy to see why. His sense of fun ran the gamut from riding his motorcycle to tromping with pals through the woods to parties on his porch. Sooner or later you could count on him to say those magic words: "It doesn't get any better than this."

Then, three years ago, Richie was diagnosed with lung cancer. He'd been a heavy smoker most of his life. He'd quit four years earlier, but not soon enough.

Richie went through chemotherapy and radiation, dropped weight, lost his hair. But on days when he was feeling up to it, he loved sitting down to a hearty meal. He'd raise his glass and make a toast: "It doesn't get any better than this."

The company offered Richie early retirement. He didn't want that. He loved being around people too much. He worked until he no longer could, till about a month and a half before he died, at age sixty-two.

At his funeral, it was tough to keep sad thoughts at bay. There, printed on the church program, was his favorite phrase, but we wouldn't hear him say it anymore. For Richie, the days didn't keep getting better, did they?

After the service one of Richie's coworkers came up waving the *Chattanooga Times Free Press.* I figured he wanted to show us Richie's obituary. Instead he opened it to the crossword puzzle. "Look," he said, pointing to the clue for 61 across. "It doesn't get any better than this."

I scanned the puzzle until I found the answer. It might as well have been filled in by Richie himself.

61 across: IM IN HEAVEN.

A NOTE FROM THE EDITORS

We hope you enjoyed Tearoom Mysteries, published by the Books and Inspirational Media Division of Guideposts, a nonprofit organization that touches millions of lives every day through products and services that inspire, encourage, help you grow in your faith, and celebrate God's love.

Thank you for making a difference with your purchase of this book, which helps fund our many outreach programs to military personnel, prisons, hospitals, nursing homes, and educational institutions.

We also create many useful and uplifting online resources. Visit Guideposts.org to read true stories of hope and inspiration, access OurPrayer network, sign up for free newsletters, download free e-books, join our Facebook community, and follow our stimulating blogs.

To learn about other Guideposts publications, including the best-selling devotional *Daily Guideposts*, go to Guideposts.org/Shop, call (800) 932-2145, or write to Guideposts, PO Box 5815, Harlan, Iowa 51593.

Sign up for the
Guideposts Fiction Newsletter
and stay up-to-date on the fiction you love!

You'll get sneak peeks of new releases, recommendations from other Guideposts readers, and special offers just for you . . .

And it's FREE!

Just go to Guideposts.org/Newsletters today to sign up.

Guideposts   **Visit Guideposts.org/Shop or call (800) 932-2145**

nd more inspiring fiction in these best-loved Guideposts series!

Sugarcreek Amish Mysteries
Be intrigued by the suspense and joyful "aha" moments in these delightful stories. Each book in the series brings together two women of vastly different backgrounds and traditions, who realize there's much more to the "simple life" than meets the eye.

Miracles of Marble Cove
Follow four women who are drawn together to face life's challenges, support one another in faith, and experience God's amazing grace as they encounter mysterious events in the small town of Marble Cove.

Secrets of Mary's Bookshop
Delve into a cozy mystery where Mary, the owner of Mary's Mystery Bookshop, finds herself using sleuthing skills that she didn't realize she had. There are quirky characters and lots of unexpected twists and turns.

Patchwork Mysteries
Discover that life's little mysteries often have a common thread in a series where every novel contains an intriguing mystery centered around a quilt located in a beautiful New England town.

Mysteries of Silver Peak
Escape to the historic mining town of Silver Peak, Colorado, and discover how one woman's love of antiques helps her solve mysteries buried deep in the town's checkered past.

To learn more about these books, visit Guideposts.org/Shop